ACCLAIM FOR CAR

FLIGHT RISK

"Cara Putman's new novel, *Flight Risk*, is more than an unputdownable legal thriller. This rich, multilayered story features real characters finding their way through a morass of problems that add to the depth of this compelling story. *Flight Risk* is Putman at the top of her game. Highly recommended!"

—COLLEEN COBLE, *USA TODAY*
BESTSELLING AUTHOR OF THE LAVENDER
TIDE SERIES AND *STRANDS OF TRUTH*

"Cara Putman skillfully weaves a current-day story of intrigue and suspense in *Flight Risk*—sure to be a hit with her tribe of followers."

—CRESTON MAPES, BESTSELLING AUTHOR

"Only Cara Putman can create a legal thriller that keeps me up all night. *Flight Risk* is her best yet!"

—DIANN MILLS, BESTSELLING
AUTHOR OF *FATAL STRIKE*

"Putman does it again! *Flight Risk* is a gripping page turner with three-dimensional characters and real drama."

—RICK ACKER, BESTSELLING
AUTHOR OF *GUILTY BLOOD* AND
WHEN THE DEVIL WHISTLES

"Cara Putman does it again. A plane crash, murders, a traumatized teen, and a crack lawyer who will do whatever it takes to protect her family and her clients. Throw in a little romance and *Flight Risk* is a brilliantly woven story that takes the reader on a breath-stealing ride. I highly recommend this book."

—LYNETTE EASON, AWARD-WINNING,
BESTSELLING AUTHOR OF THE
BLUE JUSTICE SERIES

"I thought I'd sit down and get a feel for Cara Putman's newest novel, *Flight Risk*. Oh. My. Word! The story snatched me up on the first page and raced me breathlessly though the pages. This is a don't-start-before-you-go-to-bed suspense story. Cara has penned her best novel yet."

—CARRIE STUART PARKS,
AWARD-WINNING AUTHOR OF
FORMULA OF DECEPTION AND
PORTRAIT OF VENGEANCE

"In her legal thriller, *Flight Risk*, Putman weaves a story that proves what you read in the news isn't always what it appears to be. Separating truth from what is perceived to be true takes her characters on a journey with twists and turns that will keep the reader turning the pages, anxious to see how it all fits together."

—MARTHA ROGERS, BESTSELLING
AUTHOR OF *BECOMING LUCY* AND
CHRISTMAS AT HOLLY HILL IN THE
WINDS ACROSS THE PRAIRIE SERIES

DELAYED JUSTICE

"Putman skillfully illustrates the individual pain and heartache behind stories of abuse in this captivating third Hidden Justice novel . . . [and] threads a believable layer of faith into the characters' development and offers spiritual asides that enhance rather than crowd the narrative. This character-driven inspirational thriller is an honest look into the hard work of addressing past harms."

—PUBLISHERS WEEKLY

"*Delayed Justice* will hold you to the end . . . A very timely story!"

—SUSAN PAGE DAVIS, AUTHOR OF
THE MAINE JUSTICE SERIES

"*Delayed Justice* is a timely and compelling legal thriller that will have you turning the pages in search for justice. Putman packs an emotional punch and tackles tough issues head-on while demonstrating God's redeeming love."

—RACHEL DYLAN, BESTSELLING
AUTHOR OF *DEADLY PROOF*

IMPERFECT JUSTICE

"This is the way legal thrillers are meant to be—compelling, intelligent, and deeply satisfying."

—RANDY SINGER, AUTHOR
OF *RULE OF LAW*

". . . a frightening yet compulsive reading experience."

—*LIBRARY JOURNAL* STARRED REVIEW

"The second book in Putman's Hidden Justice series is intricately plotted and thoroughly engrossing . . . This page-turner is smart, thoughtful, and appealing to readers who enjoy legal thrillers and solid mysteries."

—*RT BOOK REVIEWS*, 4 STARS

"The hopeful ending will satisfy fans of romantic suspense."

—*PUBLISHERS WEEKLY*

"*Imperfect Justice* is solidly written with great tension and a feminine-yet-tough heroine."

—*CBA MARKET*

"A legal thriller that takes on a burning social issue and the role of faith and strength in meeting that challenge. Like all good storytellers, Cara Putman makes you care. She is at the top of her game with *Imperfect Justice*."

—JAMES SCOTT BELL, BESTSELLING
AUTHOR OF *ROMEO'S RULES*

"*Imperfect Justice* tackles a gritty subject, and Cara Putman writes with finesse and delicate sensitivity. This legal thriller had me turning pages long after even lawyers have retired for the night, and the fine threads of romance and faith brought hope where often there is none. With a superior story of law and crime, the verdict is in: *Imperfect Justice* will stick with you long after you've devoured the last gripping page."

—JAIME JO WRIGHT, AUTHOR OF
THE HOUSE ON FOSTER HILL

BEYOND JUSTICE

"With its menacing mood, crisp dialog, and quick pace, Putman's action-packed legal thriller highlights a complex political scene. Starring a determined female attorney who will stop at nothing to resolve her case, this title will please fans of Joel C. Rosenberg and John Grisham."

—LIBRARY JOURNAL

"Putman's new legal thriller is exciting from start to finish. The author builds suspense throughout, and, just like real life, it's not easy to distinguish the good people from the bad. This story is well thought-out and incredibly detailed. The author's expertise shines through and adds a tremendous amount of credibility to the story. Danger, adventure, and intrigue pour from every chapter."

—RT BOOK REVIEWS, 4 STARS

". . . a relatable and fascinating story . . . Remarkably akin to today's news headlines . . . a legal thriller that is intricately written to keep readers on edge."

—CHRISTIAN MARKET

"Cara Putman's legal background has definitely been put to good use in this nail-biter of a romantic suspense/legal thriller. The tension is gripping and the suspense rarely lets up. The story should come with a warning label: Expect high blood pressure and no sleep if you start this book. You won't be able to put this one down until the very end."

—LYNETTE EASON, BESTSELLING,
AWARD-WINNING AUTHOR OF THE
ELITE GUARDIANS SERIES

"Cara Putman's expert legal mind shines in *Beyond Justice* as she weaves a gripping, suspenseful tale of intrigue that takes on one of the hardest issues of our time. Hayden McCarthy is one feisty heroine who doesn't let anything get between her and the truth—no matter the cost—even if it's her own life. John Grisham should watch his back!"

—JORDYN REDWOOD, AUTHOR
OF THE BLOODLINE TRILOGY
AND *FRACTURED MEMORY*

FLIGHT
RISK

OTHER BOOKS BY CARA PUTMAN

FLIGHT RISK

CARA PUTMAN

THOMAS NELSON
Since 1798

Flight Risk

Published in Nashville, Tennessee, by Thomas Nelson. Thomas Nelson is a registered trademark of HarperCollins Christian Publishing, Inc.

Thomas Nelson titles may be purchased in bulk for educational, business, fund-raising, or sales promotional use. For information, please e-mail SpecialMarkets@ ThomasNelson.com.

Publisher's Note: This novel is a work of fiction. Names, characters, places, and incidents are either products of the author's imagination or used fictitiously. All characters are fictional, and any similarity to people living or dead is purely coincidental.

Library of Congress Cataloging-in-Publication Data

Names: Putman, Cara C., author.
Title: Flight risk / Cara Putman.
Description: Nashville : Thomas Nelson, [2020] | Summary: "ECPA bestseller Cara Putman returns with a fast-paced romantic suspense that is ripped from the headlines"-- Provided by publisher.
Identifiers: LCCN 2019043824 | ISBN 9780785233275 (trade paperback) | ISBN 9780785233213 (epub) | ISBN 9780785233329 (downloadable audio)
Subjects: GSAFD: Romantic suspense fiction. | Christian fiction.
Classification: LCC PS3616.U85 F58 2020 | DDC 813/.6--dc23
LC record available at https://lccn.loc.gov/2019043824

Printed in the United States of America

20 21 22 23 24   LSC   10 9 8 7 6 5 4 3 2 1

I wrote this book during a season filled with good . . . and really hard. God reminded me that even while I felt isolated, I wasn't alone. Thank you isn't big enough to express my deep gratitude to Beth Vogt. Beth, your daily reminders of God's truth and the calls where you validated what I was feeling while walking me to truth were truly sanity savers. I am more grateful than words can say for you.

Ashley Clark, Casey Apodaca, and Pepper Basham, you were the heart sisters I needed at the time my world rocked again. Thank you for being a safe place to be real, to be honest, and to question. Your wisdom, grace, and truth were gifts. So very grateful for you three.

And to Eric. Those two years were good . . . and so very hard. I'm grateful for where we are today. I have always loved you and always will. I can't wait to see where God takes us next.

CHAPTER
ONE

"Savannah, call for you on line one. Says he's a reporter. Never heard of him."

The receptionist's voice interrupted Savannah Daniels midsentence, and she gave Emilie Wesley, one of her associates at her small law firm, an apologetic smile. "Take a message, Bella. Emilie and I are still working on the Mnemosyne mediation." She clicked off the intercom, then turned back to Emilie. "Where were we?" She shivered and reached beneath her desk to turn on the small heater that sat at her feet. It would be April before she felt warm again.

Emilie tapped her notepad. "You were explaining what the company is creating."

"That's right." Savannah glanced over Emilie's head as she organized her thoughts about the complex technology. After years of working alone, she was learning a special synergy happened when two or more legal minds tackled a problem from multiple angles. "So the company's wunderkind created software that is like a satellite backup to the black box on planes. Instead of being a physical box that records the data, Mnemosyne's system automatically syncs the data back to its servers via satellite technology."

"It works?" Emilie stopped taking notes, her brows knit together. An attorney who also worked as a reporter for an online newspaper, Emilie had a quick mind that easily processed details.

Savannah nodded, thinking where to take this next. "Early tests indicate it does." The mediation would start in a couple of days, and she needed Emilie's help to get the preparatory brief finished. Mediation had to work, because her clients needed the case to settle before they ran out of money to keep the company functioning.

Breaking the complex down into something simple was one of Savannah's superpowers. She'd need every bit for this case.

Emilie made a note, then tapped her pen against the paper. "And the plaintiff claims Mnemosyne has infringed on their tech."

"That's right. I haven't seen anything to back that up, but they are fighting hard."

"Savannah?" Bella's voice crackled over the intercom again. "The reporter insists he needs to talk now."

Savannah glanced at Emilie, who had already stood. "We can finish later. I've got enough to get the next level of argument outlined."

"Thanks." Savannah grabbed the receiver and punched the light. "This is Savannah Daniels."

"Good morning, ma'am." The male voice was deep, the kind that resonated across a line and made Savannah smile. "This is Jett Glover with the *Washington Source*, and I wondered if I could have a minute of your time."

Jett Glover? As she searched her memory for reporters she'd talked to in the past, her brain twinged as if the name should be familiar, but she came up as blank as a first-year law student. "Should I know you?"

His chuckle was wry. "That, as they say, is a problem." The hint of self-deprecation drew her in even as she reminded herself to be guarded. He could be a private investigator or attorney masquerading as a reporter before suing one of her clients. "I'm writing an article that includes your ex-husband, Dustin Tate."

Savannah stiffened and pushed back in her chair. Their divorce had been finalized a lifetime ago. For fifteen years she had avoided thinking about him any more than necessary. Why would a reporter contact her about him now? Reporters were even worse than opposing counsel, and she felt her guard build. "Why?"

"An interview would make it easier to explain."

"I'm sorry, but I don't take random media interviews."

"I think you'll want to this time." There was an arrogant certainty in his voice that made her dislike him. No way would she let him into her space.

"While I appreciate your call, my workload makes it impossible. Have a nice day."

She hung up and leaned back as she pinched the bridge of her nose. The last distraction she needed was trying to imagine why her ex was the subject of any reporter's focus. As far as she was concerned, their lives had diverged when he left her two months before she graduated from law school.

Focus.

She glanced at the open brief on her monitor. The mediator, William Garbot, was expecting it before five. While Emilie was a masterful writer, Savannah needed more time to fill her in on the nuances of the Mnemosyne case. It was complicated with counterclaims and preliminary injunctions that prevented her client from continuing the tests required to get the technology approved by the Federal Aviation Administration and to market. Garbot liked having time to read the briefs and check the law before the mediation started. Going through the legal issues with Emilie had given Savannah a couple of new thoughts. She would need her clients to review the brief to confirm she'd simplified the science correctly.

Her calendar said it would be a quiet day in the office. A day she'd blocked out strategically to write the brief and catch up on the work that had stalled while she wrestled the Hollingsworth case to settlement and quickly resolved an emergency for Juice Store, a new client. She'd work on something else while giving Emilie an hour to massage the brief.

A rap at her door pulled her attention back to the moment. "Yes?"

"You have an appointment."

Savannah opened her eyes and squinted against the overhead brightness at Bella. "You know as well as I do there's nothing on my calendar."

The trusty receptionist arched a brow at her. "Really?"

"I meticulously add things to the firm's calendar."

Bella didn't even bother to hide her eye roll. "Girl, I have worked for you for ten years. I know that this new leaf will last approximately two more weeks before it blows away." She hooked a thumb over her shoulder. "Besides, this guy is someone you want to meet."

"Fine. Who is it?"

"Jett Glover." Bella handed over a business card. "Said you might want this."

"I just told him no."

"Yep."

"And now he's here?"

"Yep."

Savannah let that sink in a moment as she studied the slip of card stock. "And you think I should meet with him?"

"Yep."

Savannah cracked a smile. "I see you're a woman of many words this morning. Fine. I'll come grab him in a minute."

Bella nodded, none of her perfectly coifed silver-blonde hair moving, but there was a gleam in her eyes that made Savannah wonder what she was really up to. What had the man said to get past Savannah's first line of defense?

After making him wait another five minutes, Savannah stood,

squared her shoulders, and straightened the skirt of her black suit, then gave her jacket a quick tug. This would have to be sufficient battle armor. Anything that had the fingerprints of her ex wouldn't be great. If a reporter was involved, the truth was probably worse than the typical yuck. As she strode into the lobby, she lifted her chin and extended her hand to the man who stood looking at the framed photos of Old Town Alexandria's landmarks.

"You must be Jett Glover, the man who ignores clear statements."

He turned and grinned, then took her hand. The instant their hands connected, she wanted to yank hers back, but that would acknowledge the immediate, electric effect he had on her. As her gaze collided with the man's blue eyes, she felt her breath hesitate. Heat flushed her face in a flash.

———

His task was simple: learn the name of the fourth man who traveled with Dustin Tate. Jett's editor would run the article this week with or without the name, but Jett wouldn't be satisfied.

So here he was, claiming an appointment when the call didn't work.

He hadn't anticipated the sparks flying from the woman's eyes.

Savannah Daniels, he'd learned when looking into her, was something of an icon among local attorneys, who respected her small firm and regarded her as someone who spoke the truth and meant what she said. She taught the occasional class at her alma mater and focused her energy on fighting for underdogs.

He noted the surge of annoyance that flashed up her face and had the urge to explain he wasn't usually so devious. But he guessed she didn't like to be bothered with minutiae.

He could press that to his advantage.

"Thanks for seeing me."

"I didn't invite you."

"Reporters don't always wait for invitations." He gave her his best Clark Gable grin, the one that usually left women swooning at his feet. She barely batted an eyelash. *Alrighty then.* "As I mentioned, I'm with the *Washington Source*." She turned and walked back down a hallway behind the receptionist's desk. He pocketed the business cards he'd grabbed from the holder on the desk while he'd waited, then followed Savannah down the hall, trying to ignore the deliberate pace she set that displayed her feminine curves. Not what he needed to notice right now. "This week we're running an article that your husband is featured in."

"Ex." The word was a staccato exclamation as she turned into an office.

"Noted. Ex." He followed her into the nice-sized room. The art on the wall was what he noticed first. Splashes of color against a pale field of yellow. The piece hanging behind her desk looked like a Jackson Pollock wannabe in primary colors, revealing a suppressed anger. He would have guessed she'd prefer something more pastoral or Impressionist, with a peaceful vibe.

He pulled out notes he didn't need while she stalked behind a large desk. She didn't know how many years he'd invested in writing about the truth. How he was always just one bad article away from looking for another job. This article could be Pulitzer worthy whether she gave a statement or not, but he wanted the whole truth. "Did you know Dustin Tate was a private pilot for wealthy bad boys who have more time and money than good taste? He may have done more than fly them."

Her nostrils flared as she coolly studied him.

"Did he like to live the high life when you were married?"

"On what we made?" She stared at him like he was mad. "Even if he did, why would that be relevant today?"

"Maybe we could sit."

She crossed her arms, leaving the heavy desk as a barrier between them, and he had to admire her unwavering focus. Fine, he'd take the lead. He was more comfortable there anyway. He sank onto the edge of a leather chair in front of her desk. Then he leaned back and crossed an ankle over his other knee, carefully arranging the crease of his pants.

"There's a lot you don't know about your ex-husband."

"That's a given in the fact he's my ex. Look, we divorced fifteen years ago. I stay out of his current life as much as possible." But her gaze darted away, suggesting she protested too much. Interesting.

He kept his gaze laser focused, and she finally eased to the edge of a chair across the desk from him. He'd claim that as a victory. "I've investigated a group of four men who make trips to Thailand and other countries in Asia about once a quarter. Your ex is one of them, the pilot for each flight. Seems to participate in their in-country activities too."

She shrugged, an elegant motion. "I don't see why that's newsworthy."

"These trips victimize young girls."

The only indication his words registered? The faintest flicker at the corner of her eyes as she glanced at a photo that sat on the edge of her desk, one of a girl with long blonde hair and a bright smile, maybe high school aged. She caught him looking at the photo and stiffened.

The photo had to be Savannah's niece since the woman had no children. Jett pressed forward. "Do you worry about his daughter?"

She went completely still, as if she'd been transformed to stone. "This meeting is over."

"You care about your niece." That would break through her icy reserve. It did. Just not in the way he anticipated.

In one movement she stood and then left her office. The door barely clicked shut behind her.

A moment later, while he was still trying to figure out what had happened, the receptionist reappeared. "If you'll follow me."

While the accent was Southern, the tone was steel. As if she knew he'd gone too far.

CHAPTER
TWO

The *Washington Source* offices were humming when Jett returned.

He sank to his desk and typed up his notes. There weren't many. And he still had a hole in his investigation.

The elusive fourth person of the traveling team.

His research was solid. There were four hotel rooms. Four on the flights. Four of everything except names.

There had to be a way to uncover that detail. Once he did he'd be ready to finish the story and hit submit. Then the editors and fact-checkers could work their magic. With his box of files, meticulously labeled and filled with receipts and source notes, the fact-checkers would have an easy job. Just the way he liked it.

Get the research done and get it right. Then write the story.

"Glover." His name squealed from the intercom on his phone.

He snatched up the handset before his editor's growl proceeded further. "Yes, sir?"

"In my office." The call ended.

Jett sighed and grabbed his cell phone, tablet, and stylus, all the better to capture any more demands Ted Lance had for him. After weaving through the bevy of cubicles, he reached the man's corner office and marched through the open door.

Ted sat behind his massive desk, feet kicked on top of it, hands linked behind his head as he looked out the windows. That was the stance the man took when he was wrestling a problem, and Jett didn't like that he'd been called in for that. Such meetings usually led to Ted pressuring his journalists.

The space was large with a sitting area around a round table that could seat six. A bank of windows illuminated the space with natural light that was overshadowed by Ted's frown.

"We've got a hole on the front page Wednesday. Your exposé on the Donnelly trips will run below the fold unless something better comes in."

Jett's back stiffened and he clenched the tablet in front of him. "It'll be ready, but I still haven't ID'd the fourth member of the team."

Ted turned to look at him, left eyebrow reaching his silvery hairline. "You saying the research isn't solid?"

"Of course not. It's my best work so far, and you know I've turned in a string of great investigative reports since you brought me over five years ago."

The man waved his words away. "All that matters today is whether that article is ready for the fact-checkers."

Jett clenched his jaw and tried to inhale, but it was like breathing through a straw, the kind used to stir coffee. "I need to find the missing member."

"You're out of time." Ted pulled his feet off the desk and then bounced forward in his chair, leaning his elbows on the desk. "If you wait until everything is perfect, you'll get scooped. How long have I paid you to work on this article?"

"Only three months."

"It's a miracle you haven't been beat to press." The man's frown deepened as he stared at Jett. "Is that what this is about? The article doesn't have a legal leg to stand on? You've been leading me on? Getting the paper to pay for trips to Thailand?"

"No." Jett barely kept from yelling the word. "This is a good article and you know it. The content is excellent. But I am missing one piece."

The man fisted his hands on top of the desk. "Get the article with your supporting research to the fact-checkers before you leave today. Otherwise, you're done on this story. Do it, and I'll give you two weeks to write a follow-up with information on your mystery person."

That was the best offer he'd get, so Jett nodded and then turned to leave.

"I need an answer."

"Yes. You'll have the finished article tonight."

"By five."

"Yes."

He returned to his desk and immediately pulled up the article for one more review.

That evening after putting the article to bed, Jett sat in his rented house, laptop open on his lap, the screen a blur of pixels. The home was spare yet filled with an eclectic mix of furniture and doilies he never would have selected. Maybe that's why he spent so much time in the shed out back. He should go to bed. Get some sleep after a crazy long day in anticipation of the article dropping and Ted pressing him hard, but his body refused. It was wired from all the coffee and Pepsi he'd consumed during the unending hours, and now the caffeine refused to release its hold.

The article was good.

As good and detailed as he could make it.

A rich professional baseball player. A hero to children all over the region and country.

A man who isn't what he seems.

When someone travels outside the country, it's to experience new places, flavors, and cultures. But when Logan Donnelly
leaves the country, it's to exploit the defenseless. It's not enough
that he does it. He takes others with him to engage in activities
that are illegal here . . . and there. But as a wealthy American, he
is above the law in Thailand.

Jett sighed as he reread the opening lines, words that were emblazoned on his mind. Ted had insisted he lay it on thicker than Jett
preferred.

He set the computer to the side and grabbed a well-worn sweatshirt emblazoned with Duke's Blue Devil mascot, a leftover from his
undergrad days. It might be old, but it was comfortable and a warm
layer as the temperatures dipped below average for early December.
He pulled it on and headed to the oversized shed in the backyard. The
neighbor's house was swathed in Christmas lights. The glow reinforced
that the calendar said he should put up Christmas decorations, but it
wasn't really his house or his style. Not when there was no one to enjoy
them with.

He unlocked the shed's door and then flipped on the light, revealing his work area. He stepped over to the side and turned on the floor
heater, then flipped on a radio. Country music from the nineties filled
the space, with occasional Christmas honky-tonk thrown into the mix.

The grit of sawdust covered the concrete floor beneath his shoes
and the aromas of the various woods he worked with filled his senses.
He considered the boards he'd laid out on the worktable, then ran a
thumb along the rough edge of a walnut plank, noting the swirls and
whorls. It would make a beautiful dining room table for the right home
if he could get the pieces to come together in the mosaic he pictured in
his mind. His caress slowed as he sensed a catch in the grain. Looked
like he'd missed a spot when planing it.

Someday he'd transform this into a piece of furniture his dad might have admired, even if the man had forfeited the right to see it.

Jett picked up the plane his grandfather had used, hefting its weight in his hand. As he held the muscle-powered tool, he knew a power plane could accomplish the task much faster, but he liked the connection between his body and the slab, the whisper of the blade as it feathered down the surface. It was something he'd watched his father and grandfather practice, and when he spent time in this place, he felt a connection with them. It was ethereal, but it was there, and on nights like tonight it didn't matter if he ever finished the table. All he wanted was a connection to something bigger than himself.

Otherwise he felt untethered.

He could never explain that reality to his mother without hurting her, so he stayed silent. But he also knew it was one reason he remained alone.

Pieces of the man he was couldn't, wouldn't, deal with the tragedy of his youth. He slid the plane along the surface of the walnut plank in a steady stroke. He blew and watched the fresh sawdust rise into the air. It was an action his dad had made at the end of each stroke.

Jett found peace in the long, even movements. A steadiness filled him as he repeated the motion time and again.

Tonight it didn't calm his thoughts.

CHAPTER

THREE

WEDNESDAY, DECEMBER 9

The article was horrifying.

Worse than anything her imagination had conjured over the thirty-six hours between that reporter's intrusion and Bella sliding the folded paper onto Savannah's desk.

The plane lands at Suvarnabhumi Airport outside Bangkok. It rolls to a stop outside a small, private terminal. It's not the first time the plane has carried these passengers to Thailand. The mechanic greets the travelers by the fake names on their passports. Men known in the States as Logan Donnelly. Dustin Tate. Evan Spencer. An additional companion. The four are met by a driver who also knows them from repeated trips. He understands exactly where to take them. As the group climbs into the taxi, the mechanic moves to the plane. It will be serviced efficiently and thoroughly. The moment the men signal they are ready to leave, the plane will be prepared for immediate departure.

With more than eight million residents, Bangkok is known for its dense neighborhoods, crowded canals, and bustling streets lined with ornate shrines and glittering storefronts. Throughout the city, traditional teak buildings clash with modern high-rises.

These men have arrived to visit Bangkok's darker side, and to exploit the people forced to work in the shadows of the sex industry.

Nausea roiled as Savannah tried to absorb the horrid words.

If even half of the article was true . . . Savannah swallowed against the rising bile.

She didn't want to believe the men traveled for pleasure trips, the clandestine opportunity to do what was illegal here. Yet as she continued to read, the words were stark, black and white, no shades of gray. They shimmered with truth, but was it fool's gold?

She tried to pray, but nothing came except the next sip of oxygen. She'd been married to one of the band. Even if it had been a lifetime ago and few would remember, she couldn't simply ignore it. The light of her life was Dustin's daughter. She forced another breath. She hadn't told the reporter the full truth because she would do anything to protect her niece.

Savannah grabbed her keys and purse before heading to her car.

She needed to get to Addy Jo before someone else did.

Addy was caught between a pain-addled mom who self-medicated with alcohol and a dad with a complicated past. He'd married one sister, then fathered a child with the other.

The teenager was proof good could come from the worst situations humans created. The girl was a shining light in Savannah's world. A spot of hope and joy in what should have been an unrelenting mess of human brokenness and sin.

That precious young woman was about to learn that her father was front-page news.

Every professional baseball player has one goal at the beginning of the season: make it to the World Series. If his team doesn't make it, October is traditionally the time of year when Major League Baseball players work on skills or kick back after another intense season.

That's not what Logan Donnelly was doing two years ago, nor in the off-seasons since.

There's a synergy and symbiotic relationship between the ballplayer and his fans. The player gives his all on the field, in Logan's case, pitching. Little boys wear his jersey, pride sparking in their eyes. Women wonder how to catch his attention. And grown men bet on whether he will beat the other team, one at-bat at a time.

Jett's inbox was filling with emails from colleagues congratulating him for the award-winning exposé. Well, they didn't say the award-winning part yet, but they would.

He'd spent several days in Thailand retracing Logan Donnelly's steps, a process that left Jett with the knowledge it would take another year of showers to finally feel clean. He'd known human trafficking and the sex trade existed, but he'd never walked the streets and seen the women and children for sale.

Some sins soap didn't touch.

This investigation had overflowed with evidence of how depraved a man could be.

His next piece needed a subject that would restore his faith in mankind, if that was even possible. That wasn't exactly the point of investigative journalism though.

The honest part of him admitted he was jaded. Really jaded.

Ted Lance walked by Jett's desk and hooked a finger. "My office."

The gruff bark required an immediate response.

He hadn't talked to Ted since the story dropped, so he hoped this would be a good meeting. Not the you're-about-to-be-fired kind.

The editor had been with the *Source* since its inception as an upstart challenger to the venerable *Washington Post*. Hard to believe it wasn't that long ago that the *Post* had been the challenger to the *New York Times*, and now that role had landed squarely on the scrappy *Source*. The proliferation of free information and fake news on the internet was threatening to kill the advertising streams that sustained the paper. The *Source* needed a Pulitzer or similar recognition almost as much as he did.

As he grabbed his tablet and stylus, Jett anticipated the speech he'd get inside Ted's office. *You've got two weeks. Press your advantage and do it on a shoestring budget. Get the story right, but get it faster than the competition.*

Ted leaned a hip against his battered armada of a desk as he waited for Jett. His shirtsleeves were rolled up, and all he needed was a cigar snapped between his jaws to complete the image of a hardened editor who cared only about the story. He opened the lid of a wooden box and offered its contents to Jett. "Take one."

Jett stared at the Cuban cigars, feeling the weight of the offer. Other reporters got one when a story hit well. But not him. Not until now. He shoved his hands in his pockets. "Thanks, sir, but I'm not much of a smoker." Like ever.

Ted shook his head with a short chortle, then pulled out a cigar and tucked it into Jett's shirt pocket. "Have one anyway. You can enjoy it on the way to the airport."

"Airport?"

"I want you in Boston."

"Why?" He'd spent two days last month poking around Beantown talking to people who knew Donnelly.

"You've got two weeks for your follow-up on the mystery traveler. And a birdie told me that Donnelly might get traded back home to one of Boston's teams. He's quickly becoming too hot to handle here, thanks to your piece. Chase that story down." He pulled an envelope from a drawer. "Here's your flight itinerary, rental car, hotel."

"Who am I supposed to talk to there that I can't from here? Calls should work."

"Not this time. We need you there to discern what's true and what's rumor. Frankly, if Donnelly's too hot to handle here, he should be too hot there. You're the reporter. Figure it out. Just make it worth our while."

"Sure." What else could he say? He opened the envelope to see he had two hours to get to the airport. Good thing he kept an overnight bag in his car. He'd plan his attack in the air.

———

Before she pulled her car out of its slot, Savannah shot her niece a text. On my way to get you. Still at school?

It was that time of day when Addy would step onto a bus for the trip back home.

Why?

Thought we'd grab burgers at Five Guys. That should get Addy's attention.

Okay. Next came a shrug emoji. I can wait fifteen minutes.

Savannah could make it if all the lights aligned perfectly. See you soon.

The sky was the heavy gray that suggested a flurry of snowflakes was possible, but she needed it to hold off. At least until after evening rush hour. There was no way she'd make it if even a flake started drifting through the sky.

She exhaled, then adjusted the rearview mirror and noticed each line etched next to her eyes. Today she felt every one of her thirty-nine years and unfulfilled dreams.

Her Mazda SUV wanted to fly, but she eased along King Street to Bailey's Crossroads.

She wanted to fly too but was far from it.

She'd imagined life married to her college sweetheart, but that had vanished into mist when her college-love-turned-husband detoured to another path and abandoned her. If the article was true, maybe that was for the best, but could she have misread him so much?

Her career launched at a large firm where she made more in a year than her parents had in five. Then she hung out her shingle and still wondered some months if there'd be enough left to pay her personal bills. And now she'd taken on the responsibility of additional attorneys. It had felt so right as she brought them on one at a time. Now? The pressure was enough to crush her.

Then there were the two point four adorable mini-mes that were supposed to fill the middle seat of her swagger wagon and make her life complete. Instead, she went home each day to her rescue kitten, a cute tuxedo cat she had named Rhett, before she realized he was a she. Another example of her slightly out-of-step life. Friday she'd celebrate turning forty with her girlfriends and was no closer to children than she had been at twenty.

The Jeep in front of her slammed on its brakes. She crushed her own and skidded to the side to avoid hitting it, glancing in her rearview mirror, tensing until the van behind her stopped.

She relaxed and her shoulders dropped.

She'd been living life with her shoulders touching her ears. Knots tightening her back until it felt locked down. Her friends could run and push themselves with cardio. Her body could barely handle daily walks and stretching.

When had she become an elderly woman in a youngish body?

She glanced in the rearview mirror again as traffic inched forward.

Father, I need to get to Addy before she hears about her dad from someone else. Teens could be cruel or thoughtless. *Can you help me out of this funk? Before I reach Addy?*

Traffic took off and in minutes she was through Bailey's Crossroads and at Justice High School. The greasy Five Guys combo sounded perfect at the end of a long day, but not until she made sure Addy was good.

When Savannah pulled into the high school's drive, she spotted a small cluster of students lingering around some of the metal benches with curved arms along the path to the main doors. She eased her car along the curb and waited a moment, searching the gathered teens for Addy's small frame.

At one bench several young men in the jock category, tall and muscular, joked and elbowed each other, proudly wearing letter jackets. They watched three girls approach another who waited on a bench alone. The girls needed more clothes to survive the beginnings of winter's cold without getting sick. Savannah squinted to see better through the sunlight.

Addy Jo's long, blonde curls appeared gilded in the light. She was reading a textbook and didn't look up as the gaggle of young women strutted toward her. There was something about the girls' demeanor that had Savannah turning off her car and then stepping from it. Was it the swagger in their steps? The arrogance on the face of the leader?

Whatever it was, Savannah pulled her purse onto her shoulder over her wool trench coat and hurried along the sidewalk.

"Addy?"

The girl didn't hear her as she glanced up at the others, earbuds dangling from her ears. A slight frown tipped her lips, and Savannah could imagine her distrust. She wasn't the popular, cheerleading type.

A girl with hair the orange of Anne of Green Gables looked like she'd stepped out of an American Eagle ad with her perfect if heavy makeup and precisely ripped jeans, layered top, and denim jacket. She elbowed her friend, a pretty Latina dressed in the same ripped style, and stopped in front of Addy. "So your dad likes girls."

CHAPTER
FOUR

Addy kept reading as if she hadn't heard, but Savannah noted the pink crawling up her neck.

Savannah's breath hitched and she wanted to run to Addy's defense, but she felt the stares of the boys and hesitated. She didn't second-guess anything in a courtroom, yet five teenage boys gave her pause? She saw baseball jerseys through their open jackets before she turned back toward Addy. The redhead's voice rose.

"He's all over the web."

The girl next to her chimed in. "Did you know? Of course you did."

Addy tried to stand, but one of the girls pushed her back down and leaned into her face. "Are you a pervert too?"

"What do you mean?" Addy winced as the back of her legs rammed into the metal bench.

"What do you mean?" The third girl mocked her with a whiny voice, and Savannah squared her jaw and marched forward in her best don't-mess-with-me style. "You'd have to be blind to not see the story. It's everywhere."

The ginger-haired girl snickered and pressed forward until she practically stood on top of Addy. "With a dad like that, no wonder you're such a loser."

"Addy." Savannah elbowed her way around the mean-girl posse. "Let's go."

When Addy turned her way, there were tears in the girl's blue eyes, but she didn't seem to see Savannah. Savannah leaned down and grabbed the teen's backpack, huffing at the weight. "Come on, kiddo."

"We weren't done." The ringleader tried to assert an authority she didn't have.

Savannah chuckled without glee. "You are done, or I'll report you for bullying." She edged Addy to her feet and then guided her through the kids. "Come on, Addy."

Her niece walked with Savannah but looked more like a lifeless mannequin than her vibrant normal self. Savannah helped her into the small SUV where she collapsed forward. Savannah walked around the car, climbed in, and waited. For what? A sign of life? Some sign the girl was made of titanium and the words had simply bounced off?

The lengthening silence made it clear those were fanciful dreams.

Savannah shifted to look at her niece. "Addy Jo, do you know what those girls were talking about?"

The girl sniffled and then nodded. "The article. Fifteen or twenty people emailed it to me."

"While you were in school?"

She nodded again. "Aunt Savannah, we're on laptops all day." She flopped against the seat. "Did he do those things?" Her words were a whisper Savannah almost missed, but they reverberated through her soul.

"I don't know." But she would find out. For Addy. Her world was already being wrecked by the insinuations, and only truth would restore it.

The ride was quiet and Addy didn't perk up when they pulled into the Five Guys location near Bailey's Crossroads. Savannah remembered when there'd been one location on King Street, but this one had the same great burgers and fries that would have her car smelling heavenly.

She kept an eye on Addy as she texted a warning to Stasi, her sister, that they were on the way to the apartment with food. After Stasi had been injured at work, Savannah had found and paid for their housing. It was a way to be present for her niece, though the young woman was a constant reminder of how terribly Savannah's dreams had derailed.

When they arrived, Stasi had set the table and was pouring glasses of sweet tea. Savannah's sister refused to remember that Savannah preferred unsweet, so Savannah would choke it down. It was worth it to have the time with Addy.

Stasi glanced at Addy, then stiffened. "What's wrong with you?"

"Nothing." Addy headed toward her room with her backpack. "I'm just great. Thanks." The door slammed behind her.

Stasi turned on Savannah, hands planted on her hips. "What did you do to her?"

Savannah set the bags on the table and then pinched the bridge of her nose. Dinner was a bad idea. She needed time and distance from her sister after a day filled with stark reminders of Stasi and Dustin's betrayal. "Some students were tormenting Addy when I arrived to pick her up."

"Why?"

"They wanted to make sure she knew her dad is a pervert."

"What?!" Stasi's nostrils flared and her eyes went wild.

"The *Washington Source* article about his activities in Thailand." Savannah started pulling burgers and fries from the bags and placing them on plates so she didn't have to look at her sister. "Have you seen it?"

"Yes, I've seen it. If you'd been on time that wouldn't have happened."

"On time? I arranged to get her fifteen minutes before I arrived." Of course Stasi would make it Savannah's fault. Life was always her fault as far as Stasi was concerned.

"You should have protected her."

"You're her mother!"

"Stop it!" The young teen had left her room and, in that moment, looked like her father. Her intensity overwhelmed the beauty she'd acquired from her mom. "Dad is here."

Her face crumpled, and Savannah stepped toward her, then hesitated as Addy's words sank in. Dustin? Here?

A knock at the door had Addy shuddering, then pressing past Savannah without a glance at her mother. She opened the door and stepped back. "Hi, Dad."

Dustin stood there, dark hair short on the sides and mussed on top like he'd run his hands through it numerous times. There was a haunted look in his eyes as his gaze swung between Savannah and Stasi, but then he looked at Addy and something melted. "How's my girl?"

"I'm scared, Daddy."

"He doesn't care about you, Addy." Stasi's words were laced with venom. "You should know that by now."

"Stasi . . ." Dustin dragged out her name as a warning as Addy started to shrink. Savannah resisted the urge to get involved, but Stasi stalked from the room before anything else could be said.

Dustin turned back to Addy and tipped his chin slightly so he was looking into her eyes. "I'm sorry you had to see the article. Let me take you to get ice cream and I'll tell you what I can. You can ask any questions you have, and I will answer them." There was a hesitancy to his words as if he wasn't sure Addy would let him.

Addy didn't race into his arms as she normally did. But after she considered his words, she stepped into his embrace, muffling her words. "I know you didn't do those things, Daddy." A moment later she was following him outside, smiling and seeming to be lit from the inside.

As Savannah watched them leave, she had to acknowledge that Addy was something Dustin had done very well. Addy knew he loved her, knew she was adored.

Still, as the burgers and fries went cold on the table, Savannah couldn't deny she hadn't been what Dustin needed in the aftermath of 9/11. How easily he had walked into Stasi's arms.

Some sins were hard to forgive no matter how willing she was to try.

CHAPTER
FIVE

Jett sat in the driver's seat of his rental car and stared at the Cape Cod bungalow's door. More doors had closed in his face since he'd returned to Boston than Jett wanted to count, though he should be used to it at this stage in his career. *No* was his least favorite word, but if he hung in there long enough he chanced pay dirt that made each ignored question, slammed door, or dropped call worthwhile.

He just needed one open door.

Ted Lance pinged him a couple of times a day. Why he was so vested in this article, Jett wasn't quite sure, unless there was something happening that played out at higher levels of the paper. But that didn't quite make sense.

A tap on the passenger window startled him. An older man with salt-and-pepper hair that gave him a distinguished air was leaning down. Jett rolled down the window a bit. "Can I help you, sir?"

"That's what I wanted to ask you. You've been sitting here staring at that house for fifteen minutes. You all right?"

"Just wondering if the occupants are home."

"We usually find that out by knocking on the door, son."

No one had called him son in a very long time. "I suppose you're right. I should go knock."

"Or you could step out of your car and ask your questions while I walk the dog."

Jett noted the dog seated next to the man. It had the look of an Australian shepherd with a bit of a brindle coat. The thought of stretching his legs while talking to the man sounded like a great idea. "It would be nice to get out of the car for a bit." Jett stepped from the car and stuck his hand out. "I'm Jett Glover."

"I know." The man took off, then glanced back. "You coming?"

Jett speed walked to catch up. "How did you know who I am?"

"I read."

"Sure, but you're from Boston. I've never written for a paper here." The walk had a faster clip than Jett had expected. The man took his walks seriously . . . or his dog did.

"Doesn't mean I don't read."

"What's your name?"

"Albert Donnelly. Logan's dad."

Jett took a closer look as it clicked into place. The men's profiles were the same and with the still-athletic build, it was easy to see where Logan's talent came from. "Did you play baseball?"

"In college. Then I coached off and on. The game's been good to our family."

"I can see that."

"Can I ask you a question?"

"Yes, sir." He supposed it was only fair to answer one or two before he asked them.

"What put you onto Logan?"

"For the article?"

"What else?" The man glanced at him with an expression that emphasized how dumb he thought the comment was.

"Got an anonymous call."

"Noticed you only mention Logan and Dustin. Evan escaped the brunt of your focus."

"He was pretty boring."

The man snorted. "He likes to look that way."

"I need to find the fourth member of their band."

The man nodded, then paused for his dog to sniff a mailbox. "For someone who published a long piece, there's a lot you haven't figured out."

"Then help me." Jett shoved his hands into his khaki pockets as he waited for the walk to resume. "I'm committed to the truth."

"It's not my story to tell." The man sighed. "I don't like what you've done, but it's up to Logan to decide to share his side of the story."

"Logan didn't say much." And that was the problem, especially when combined with the hostile interview with Dustin and a muddied conversation with Evan. The interviews hadn't produced much more than his independent investigation had. "If I'm missing something, tell me. I'll get the rest of the story."

The man was silent as they continued around the block. As they neared Jett's rental, the man paused and with a hand signal told his dog to sit. "The key to the story is the fourth person."

"Then get me that guy's contact info, and I'll do the rest."

"I don't have it. Even if I did, they have to come forward on their own."

Jett fished in his back pocket for his wallet and then pulled out a business card. "Give him this with a request to call." He paused, hand extended. "I want to hear what he has to say."

"Seems you should have done that before publishing the story." The man finally took the card and studied it as if memorizing the information.

"Can I get your number?"

"In case you want to take another walk?" A mischievous glint lit the man's eyes.

"Something like that." He never knew when he'd need to confirm some tidbit.

The man rattled off the number, then paused. "Be careful about your assumptions." He tipped an imaginary hat and then crossed the street and walked up to his door.

Jett took a couple of steps after the man. Paused in the middle of the street. "Can I ask one more question?"

"Sounds like you are."

"Is Logan being traded to come here? Play for a Boston team?"

The man turned toward him and studied him a minute. "You'll have to ask him about that." Then he continued across the street.

Jett considered following him but was confident he wouldn't get anything more. Instead he climbed into his car and made short work of jotting notes of all the man had said. It wasn't much, but it reinforced he had to find this fourth man.

He drove from the neighborhood and stopped when he found a coffee shop. After he ordered a tall black coffee, he found a table and pulled out his laptop. He added his handwritten notes to the database he'd created for this investigation. Then he spent a few minutes trying to find new connections as he drew a mind map. Evan Spencer and Logan Donnelly had played together in college, then gone to different major league feeder teams, with Evan disappearing after a couple of uninspired seasons. Yet the two had maintained a friendship that led as far as Thailand.

Logan's friendship with Dustin Tate started in college, where Dustin was the upperclassman. The point of connection seemed to be Logan's first-semester foray into the flight club, where Dustin was president. He'd abandoned it but had stayed friends with Dustin even when Dustin shipped overseas on deployment after deployment.

Jett rubbed his forehead as he stared at the chart, looking for some connection to the identity clouded in smoke and shadow. Logan was the connection between the others, so he had to be the connection here. While Mr. Donnelly didn't want to tell who that was, someone knew the fourth man.

Who would know the trio well enough to talk about the fourth?

His mind strayed to Savannah Daniels. While she'd argued she didn't know her ex well, she had frozen in a way that suggested they were still in touch, probably through his daughter. More important, she might have a good guess or intuition about the mystery person. He pulled her card from his billfold and smiled when he saw the cell phone number. When she didn't answer his call, he shot her a text, then followed it with an email.

The message was the same in both formats.

Did you see the article? He included a link in case she hadn't. Comments coming in. Outrage like expected. Anything to add? He refrained from adding *please*. He hit send and prayed she'd answer. Then he turned to the article and noticed it had over ten thousand shares. Interesting. Nothing he'd written before had ever approached that number.

It would be interesting to see what people said when they shared the article, so he popped over to Twitter.

After a few tries he entered a search that pulled up a list of tweets related to the story. As he scanned them it was clear readers were split:

InsiderWDCStyle: The Source gets it wrong. Again. Donnelly a hero to have in this town for all his philanthropic work. No one works harder for no reason than Donnelly. Shoddy journalism needs to be corralled by those who care. Where's congressional oversight when you need it?

The retweets and responses in agreement numbered too many to read. Fortunately, tweets like that were countered by other voices.

RightSideAllTheTime: Logan Donnelly another rich fraud. When will we learn . . . no one can be trusted. Those with the money do what they want while the rest of us follow the law.

Jett wanted to discount someone with a Twitter handle that cocky, but others agreed. Everyone had an opinion. It was good PR for his story. What he didn't see was another news service picking up and running his article. Instead they summarized with snippets. Then one thread caught his attention.

SoulFreedomThaiNow: @RightSideAllTheTime be careful to talk about people you don't know. There's always more to the story. Sometimes the truth has to be cloaked for the protection of others.

UndergroundVigil486: @SoulFreedomThaiNow

"Want the trueth? You can't

handle the trueth." Trueth is

hidden in front of us, but we refuse

to see the evil under our noses.

The handle struck him as odd. UndergroundVigil486? And what was the consistent misspelling about? Someone channeling their inner Shakespeare?

The next tweet from the paper reduced his 1,500-word story to 280 characters.

Flight manifest. Hotel receipts. Shaky video. All the proof to
show Logan Donnelly and team were on the ground harming
minors in Thailand. Proof looks robust and unassailable. Pitcher
not a darling anymore. Will team keep him? Time will tell.
@WashingtonSource4You

His phone buzzed, and he glanced at the screen. It was an unknown
number, yet it niggled at the corners of his mind. Maybe Savannah getting back to him? "Hello?"

"Is this Jett Glover?" The voice was maybe male but muffled and
nondescript.

"It is. What can I do for you?"

"You're off base on your article."

"Which one would that be?"

"The athletes are there to save the girls."

Jett hesitated just a second as he pulled his phone from his ear long
enough to turn on a recording app. "What do you mean?"

"You've got the story all wrong."

A slither of unease traveled through him. "You're misinformed."

"No, I'm not. I've been there."

Could this be the fourth man? "Do you have proof?"

"Of course."

"I'm in Boston. When can we meet?"

"This weekend." The man hesitated. "In DC. I'll contact you with
a time."

"I'd like to set that now, before either of us gets pulled into other
meetings." Jett scrambled to fill the gap before the man could hang up.
"My sources are solid, but I'm willing to listen if you can send me anything that raises a question." He'd invested weeks in researching the
story to get it right. He'd spoken to a dozen witnesses and corroborated
the flight manifests with taxi driver interviews and hotel receipts. "I'll

be back in town tomorrow." He'd change his flight to an earlier one as soon as he got off the call. "I can meet you anywhere."

"I'll get back to you about a time." The man's voice was unwavering.

The disconnect beep burned Jett's ear, and he quickly hit redial only to have the call go straight to a generic voice mail. All right. This was a call he couldn't miss. He'd make sure his phone stayed charged.

In a 24–7, all-the-news-all-the-time world, patience to let a story grow organically was nonexistent. To level up to the *New York Times* or *Wall Street Journal*, he'd need a Pulitzer or similar award. This story fit the bill for one of those awards, and readers were eating it up, but the call churned his gut. It wasn't simple to find his cell number. This caller was someone he'd met or was connected to him somehow.

And the call highlighted an unease he'd ignored in the face of Ted's demands to get the article out yesterday.

While the proof seemed unassailable, something made it difficult to reconcile the men's wild parties in Thailand with their straitlaced, stateside image.

He'd keep the meeting and would know soon enough if the source had anything of value. He could also request insights via his social media profiles. Readers liked to feel he was accessible and their input mattered. It was possible he'd find the person who could fill in the missing information about the fourth traveler. Lacking an ID for the fourth didn't change what the other three had done. He quickly typed a message in Twitter: Seeking fourth person who traveled to Thailand with Logan Donnelly. Comment here or DM me.

CHAPTER
SIX

FRIDAY, DECEMBER 11

Friday morning Savannah headed straight to the firm and her office. She needed to get her head down and work without distraction—either internal or from her team—before her clients arrived for mediation that would start after lunch.

This needed to go well or her client Mnemosyne, a software development company that planned to launch a primarily digital black-box alternative, risked running out of money.

She sank into her desk chair and blew out. The buttery yellow walls of her office didn't match the grège the pricey designer had used everywhere else. If she couldn't have a window, she could pretend the room was filled with a soft light. Paired with the cherry wood of her desk, credenza, and bookshelf, the color made for a space that had a hint of femininity. The bold art on the wall over the credenza behind her desk was a piece she had found at a local artist's shop tucked inside the Arsenal. Today it made Savannah think of a flurry of thoughts racing out of control into a collision, matching her own fractured thoughts. Maybe the designer had been right in advising against it all.

But right now she had to focus on the mediation and couldn't consider the times she should have taken someone's advice, whether it was the designer's opinion about a more muted shade or her mom insisting she shouldn't marry before finishing law school.

Each decision was water under the bridge, but on days like her fortieth birthday, it was hard to keep her stiff upper lip and press on.

She shook her head and pressed the depressing thought away as she pulled the file in front of her.

An hour later her phone buzzed and Bella's voice filtered through. "Clients are looking for parking and should be here any minute."

"Thank you." They were early but that was not surprising. "Let me know when they arrive."

Savannah stayed in her desk chair for a minute. It was an expensive number, an ergonomically appropriate chair she'd bought to celebrate a tough trial victory five years earlier. It served as a visual reminder that she was very good at winning for her clients. On days when self-doubt was her closest friend, she needed the tangible token. It was too easy to forget her accomplishments when each hearing felt like a slog to survive.

Mediation was only marginally easier, requiring similar work to an oral hearing. But when it worked, mediation could shortcut a trial, saving time and money, which is what her current clients needed.

Savannah's phone dinged.

Running late but be there soon.

Emilie. The woman had probably stayed up late working on an article for the paper or meeting with a domestic violence client in her downtime.

Emilie had joined the power team after unraveling a twisted case involving the death of one of her domestic-violence clients. Her big heart for marginalized people was a great balance to Hayden McCarthy, who'd come to the practice under Savannah's mentorship. Hayden recently had an impressive win against the government for the murder

of a juvenile in an immigrant detention facility. Her combination of litigation smarts and drive had increased their flow of cases. Savannah
hoped their friend Jaime Nichols would come aboard soon too. A
criminal-defense lawyer would round out her team perfectly.

She texted a reply to Emilie. No problem. We haven't started
final prep.

Savannah finished an email to update a client on an upcoming hearing date, then closed her eyes. If the clients weren't here, she'd take two
minutes, that's all she needed to clear her mind quickly.

A rap on her door roused her, and Bella stood in the doorway. This
morning she wore a dark suit with a ruby-toned blouse adding a pop of
color. Her silver hair was styled in waves around her face. The woman
projected the perfect competent first impression Savannah needed, in
addition to being a crack queen of all trades. There wasn't much she
couldn't do or hire out via her paper Rolodex of contacts.

"John and Rochelle are here, and they're nervous as a cat near a fox.
I've put them in the small conference room like we discussed."

"Thanks. Send Emilie that way when she arrives."

"Will do." Bella made a show of looking at her smartwatch. "Don't
forget your lunch appointment."

Savannah met her gaze and quirked an eyebrow. "Really? I know
it's my birthday."

"Of course you do, but let the girls have fun celebrating you."

"Absolutely." Between prep and mediation. "Time for the clients."
She'd seen how much kinetic energy John had on the best of days.
Savannah could imagine what he was like when nervous.

"Hayden needs to talk something over with you too." Bella stepped
back from the doorway as Savannah came through. "She'll walk with
you to lunch."

"Thanks, Bella."

Savannah paused outside the conference room. Rochelle Lingonier and John Martin were the impressive brains behind Mnemosyne. They'd named their nascent company after the Greek goddess of memory, because their code used satellites to stream live data to a series of mainframes. Their devices could replace the current black boxes, which Savannah had learned were actually orange.

The problem was that a competitor, Flight Technology Solutions, had sued Mnemosyne for patent infringement, alleging the tech actually belonged to FTS. The mediation marked seventeen months of wrangling and delays and an effort to avoid an expensive trial whose outcome was far from certain.

John stood as she entered.

"Is this it? Will we finally get to resume our tests?" John pushed his glasses up his nose. The injunction had halted the final tests to prove the efficacy of Mnemosyne's system to the Federal Aviation Administration. "Every week of delay means someone else could beat us to market."

Savannah could have predicted his words. "John, that's today's goal."

"We can't wait much longer." His gaze darted everywhere but avoided her eyes.

"You have got to relax and trust me. This is why you've hired me."

Rochelle eased back into her seat. About fifteen years older than John, she was the adult managing a brain who hadn't quite grown up. In different circumstances, Savannah would have called Rochelle to meet for coffee, because she sensed they could be friends. But for now, she needed to keep the lines drawn between client and attorney. "Exactly. We trust you to guide us through this storm. It's just taken longer than we'd hoped." The lines around her eyes were deeper than when they'd first met. "What do you need from us today?"

"Listen. Take notes on your impressions of FTS's arguments. You'll understand the technical claims better than I will."

John pulled out his phone and started clicking away.

"Does it matter if mediation works?" Rochelle's hands twisted together on top of the table.

"It should. Don't forget, you hired me because I think four steps ahead." At least four. Her phone pinged and she glanced at the screen. Emilie had just arrived. "We go in expecting today to be successful. If it isn't, I'll be ready with the next knockout option."

Emilie slipped into the room, her thin form clothed in an understated chic sheath that hinted at her old family money. John barely glanced up, though he usually took full advantage of enjoying Emilie's quiet beauty, something the woman tolerated but didn't encourage. Sometimes Savannah wanted to grab his phone and launch it far away.

"Everything okay, John?"

He paused, face blank, and then it flashed into focus. "Not until this is over."

Rochelle nodded, her short bob swaying. "It's in the back of my mind constantly. There's no escaping the reality that we could lose our tech with this lawsuit."

"Let's see what happens this afternoon. If anyone can mediate this, Mr. Garbot can." Savannah had seen great things happen when he managed disputes.

The questions continued and Savannah briefed the pair on what they could expect. Before she knew it, Hayden was knocking on the door.

"Ready for lunch?"

Savannah stood and glanced at John and Rochelle. "You are welcome to join us at Il Porto. It's great Italian with a nice atmosphere."

John shook his head. "We'll grab a quick bite at La Madeline and meet you here at one."

Rochelle slid on a lined denim jacket that had a fun ruffle along the bottom. Its style indicated she worked with a younger labor force. "Does that work for you?"

"Of course. Is there anything I can do to help John relax?"

"Not really. It's a hard place to be. This feels like our last chance."

"I understand. Legal wranglings are nerve-racking." Savannah turned to Hayden and Emilie. "I'll get my coat and meet you there."

Emilie nodded. "I'll go ahead and make sure our table and drinks are ready."

Hayden waited while Savannah grabbed her purse and her long navy trench coat for the quick walk. She stopped at the reception desk to update Bella. "We'll be back in an hour, but call or text if Mr. Garbot arrives earlier and indicates he's ready. We can be back in five minutes." Well, it would take a bit longer, but not much. The restaurant manager had the firm's credit card on file for those meals she had to leave on a moment's notice.

John held the door as the foursome exited the firm. Cold air rushed into the reception area, and Savannah shuddered.

"Feels like it's dropped twenty degrees since I arrived this morning." Savannah stepped outside and noted the inch of slushy snow that had fallen. Traffic inched down King Street toward Jeff Davis Highway, with pedestrians carefully picking their way down the sidewalks lining the historic streets.

John was quiet as he strolled onto the sidewalk with his hands shoved in his khakis pockets. His Eddie Bauer vest probably wasn't warm enough for the turn the weather had taken. He and Rochelle headed across the street toward La Madeline, while Hayden continued with Savannah down King Street.

Savannah took a minute to breathe in the cold air and try to clear her mind. She'd never tire of winding her way through crowds down the bustling street of town houses and storefronts, many of which were decorated for Christmas, lending a festive air to the street. Today the businesspeople and tourists were bundled up, but the excitement on their faces mirrored what she'd see in the spring or summer. An energy pulsed here, but one different from striding down K Street or along

Constitution Avenue in the District. While you could look across the Potomac at certain points and see the Capitol or the monuments, this area felt like a slice of history preserved for modern times. She'd never regretted making Old Town Alexandria her base.

She bobbled as her foot hit a compacted bit of slush and slipped, but she managed to stay upright as Hayden reached out a steadying hand. "Careful."

Savannah grinned at the picture. "How many times have I told you that?"

"Enough. Glad to return the favor." Hayden's words puffed out on a cloud.

Il Porto's white-painted brick building with burgundy shutters sat proudly on the corner of a busy intersection. Savannah waited for a car to pass, tires spitting out the dirty mix of snow, before crossing. Her shoulders relaxed as she opened the door and the rich aroma of fresh Italian food wafted toward her.

She'd barely stepped inside when she felt arms wrap around her and heard a squeal. She knew it was Caroline Bragg before the petite dynamo said a word.

"Happy birthday, friend." Caroline's words were as heavy with joy as they were with the South.

Savannah turned around and gave her younger friend a hug. "Thank you."

"Of course." A dimple at the side of Caroline's mouth popped out impishly.

"Happy birthday, boss." Jaime Nichols walked up with a mock frown. It was good to see a new freedom in the woman. It had come at a high and very public cost, but was worth every hard-fought moment.

"Does this mean you're joining the firm?"

"Not yet. I'm really not sure it will be right for me." Jaime shrugged but there was a light in her eyes. "No offense."

"None taken." Savannah bit back a smile at the hint of Eeyore that still poked out from Jaime's manner. One didn't change completely overnight, but Jaime was well on her way to owning her fresh start.

Emilie waited at their table. Someone had lit the candles even though during the day they were usually flameless. A couple antipasto boards rested atop the paper-covered white cloth. In her usual efficient manner, Emilie had already ordered a round of iced tea as well.

Something about the atmosphere of the restaurant, with its red-tile floor and heavy-beamed ceiling, made her feel like she'd stepped into old-world Italy. Relaxing had become a visceral and immediate response after so many good, fellowship-filled meals within its walls.

After a round of hugs, the gals settled at the table and placed crisp white linen napkins in their laps.

The waiter approached in his black pants and white shirt covered with a gold and black vest. The colors always reminded her of her under-grad alma mater's colors. Purdue wore the black and gold with a pride similar to the restaurant's staff.

"Look." Emilie had a crazy grin on her face as she tugged Hayden's left hand from the woman's lap.

Hayden blushed to her dark roots and tried to tug free. "Emilie."

"I can't believe you won't lead with your news." Emilie wrinkled her nose as she nudged Hayden's shoulder. "Looks like I'll need a new roommate in a few months."

"This isn't the time." Hayden tried to tug loose again, then contin-ued in a stage whisper. "We're here to celebrate Savannah."

Savannah caught a flash of light as Hayden's hand moved. "Hayden, does this mean Andrew finally proposed? I can't believe you didn't say anything on the walk over."

Caroline didn't wait for the answer but stood with a squeal, napkin flying from her lap, and scurried around the table for a hug. "Girl, it is about time."

Even Jaime smiled. "That's great news."

After they placed their orders, Savannah tried to stay fully present, but Hayden's wonderful news only highlighted her own aloneness. She wondered if pity was why Hayden hadn't wanted to tell her. The girls were passing her right by, but she had to be fine with it because there was little she could do to change her situation. Not when she couldn't make it past a first date. Guess that's what happened when one had a strong personality. Being her own boss at age forty certainly hadn't moderated that in her.

The scent of spicy tomatoes and other wonderful Italian aromas wafted toward them as their waiter and a second man approached the table loaded with trays of food.

The conversation flowed over the antipasti course and into the pasta della casa. Every bite of her manicotti alla fiorentina was wonderful, the ricotta and spinach blending perfectly. Just when she knew she couldn't take another bite and get anything done afterward, thanks to the food coma, a waiter came out with a slice of cheesecake. Her mouth watered as she took in the raspberries atop the homemade delight. She put a hand on her stomach and then smiled. "I hope you brought fresh forks for everyone."

The handsome waiter flashed a bright smile. "Whatever the birthday *donna* wishes is my command." He gave a slight bow and turned away. A moment later when he returned, a fist of forks at the ready, his demeanor had changed.

Emilie watched him a moment. "What's wrong, Antonio?"

"There has been a horrible accident. It is on the TV in the office."

"What kind of accident?" Savannah leaned toward him. "Does it involve someone you know?"

"No." The man shook his head, and not one of his dark hairs moved. Yet his eyes were weighted with sadness and the shadow of something more. "It is a plane. It looks bad."

"Oh no." The memory of a plane careening by as she looked out a courtroom window in downtown Washington, DC, years earlier flashed through her mind. Savannah fought a shudder as she withdrew a credit card from her phone case and placed it on the bill, only for Hayden to slide it back to her and replace it with her own.

"Thank you."

Please let this be a terrible accident and not the beginning of another 9/11.

Jaime's head was bowed over her phone as she clicked the screen. "Looks like an isolated crash."

All Savannah could think was that Jaime should add *so far* to her sentence. "That's what we all thought on 9/11 too."

Then a second plane careened into the Twin Towers. She saw the plane that hit the Pentagon, and a fourth plane crashed in Pennsylvania, killing one of her fellow law students. She cleared her throat and stood, motioning the gals to join her.

"Let's get back to work and see what we can learn."

As they left her favorite restaurant, her phone buzzed and she paused to pull it out of her pocket.

She glanced at the text message on the screen and her blood froze.

911. From Addy. Their emergency code.

TWO YEARS EARLIER

"Daddy, can I have the keys?" Gracie smiled at him, her teeth perfect after the years in braces. She seemed to smile all the time, as if inviting comments about her beauty, but he shrugged the thought to the side.

She was perfect. He would protect her to the end. That's what fathers did, at least the good ones. And that's what he was. A good father. He would never repeat the sins of his father.

"Daddy?" The quizzical wrinkle in her forehead telegraphed he'd drifted into his thoughts.

He chuckled as he pulled the keys from their hook by the door. "Where are you headed?"

"Meeting the girls at the Pink Penguin for froyo."

He glanced out the window, at the six inches of fresh snow that had fallen overnight. The roads were barely clear. Maybe he should keep her home where he knew she was safe. "Isn't it too cold for anything frozen?"

She rolled her blue eyes, so much like his wife's. "Dad, it's just an excuse to get together."

"I don't know if you're ready to drive on the snow."

"Mom had me out on it several times last year. I know what to do." She held her hand out and wiggled her fingers for the keys as she gave him her brightest smile. "Besides, it's only a mile from here. What can go wrong?"

He handed her the keys. Two hours later her words haunted him.

He might never know what had gone wrong, but when he took the call from Lauren, her best friend since kindergarten, asking where Grace was, he knew he'd always hate himself for letting her go.

What could go wrong?

His family was about to find out.

CHAPTER
SEVEN

Savannah hurried along the sidewalk as fast as the falling snow allowed, composing a text to Addy as she walked, keeping one eye on the ground and the other on her phone. No response. So she called. No answer. Savannah left a message telling her niece to contact her immediately.

Addy knew not to use that code unless she had an excellent reason that required instant intervention.

The rest of the walk to the office was hushed as she sidestepped the accumulating slush. She wondered how the weather would play with rescue efforts around the crash. Savannah's mind kept flashing to the September 11 attacks. Dustin lost a buddy who'd been assigned to the Pentagon, and his death had hit him hard. Dustin shipped out the next month, because life was too uncertain to stay. He left divorce papers behind.

It was his way of making sure she knew he wouldn't be back . . . without speaking a word.

She'd ignored the documents for the two years he was deployed in the hope that when he returned he would have changed his mind. He didn't, and when he came back, he pushed to get it finished.

With no-fault divorce in Virginia requiring a year apart, Uncle Sam had helped with that detail. Savannah had stared at the divorce pleadings and wondered if she could pull a *Sweet Home Alabama* and simply refuse to sign.

Then Stasi, her sister who lived on the edge, became pregnant with Addy a year after he returned. And Dustin was the dad.

The truth was a kick to Savannah's gut, and it stole her last hope of reconciliation. Dustin stayed long enough to see Addy born, then served on another tour, and when he returned, announced he liked being single and dragged her to the courthouse. Four years after her nightmare started, it ended without the miracle she'd longed for.

"You okay, Savannah?" Hayden's question startled Savannah from her thoughts.

"Yes, just thinking about 9/11." She forced a small smile in place as they reached the end of a block.

"I think we all are." Emilie slipped next to Savannah and locked arms with her. Her blue scarf made the color in her eyes pop. "There's no reason to think this is anything like that day."

"Absolutely." Savannah took comfort from being with her friends as they reached the firm.

When she entered the lobby, the first thing she noted was the warmth. Then she took in Bella's face, which looked pale as she sat at the reception desk and watched a local news channel on TV. A Western World Airways flight had crashed shortly after takeoff into the Fourteenth Street Bridge. Helicopter shots of the broken plane, half submerged in the Potomac, were obscured by swirling snow. Before Savannah could make sense of the images, Reginald Nash and his client, a representative for Flight Technology Solutions, walked in. Reggie wore his usual good-ol'-boys-club look as he sauntered into the lobby. From his heavy trench coat covering a seersucker suit, which looked woefully out of place in the cold, to the derby he set aside, he presented himself as the quintessential older man who didn't think women in the legal arena had anything to offer. She'd never understand why law had so many holdouts, but change came as long as she stared them down, one at a time. As the older generation retired, the younger men who replaced them were more open to women and the strengths they brought to negotiations and trial work. She didn't really care if they underestimated her, because she could use that and her intuition to her advantage.

Savannah checked the small conference room and noted John and Rochelle were back, half-eaten pastries and mugs of coffee in front of them. "We'll be ready to begin soon. We're just waiting for the mediator to arrive."

Rochelle looked up and nodded, then Savannah continued down the hall.

When she reached her office, she hung up her coat before collecting the three accordion folders that held the files she'd need for the next few hours. If they were successful, her clients would walk out free of the lawsuit. A trial would bankrupt them, a fact the other side understood very well. This complicated her strategy.

She braced herself to wage war against Reginald Nash.

She barely had time to reorient her thoughts with strategies before Bella stood in her doorway. "Did Mr. Garbot arrive?" Savannah asked.

"Yes." Bella had regained some of the color in her cheeks. "William is waiting in the large conference room. Nash and his client are cooling their heels in the reception area."

"Thanks. I'll collect John and Rochelle."

Bella left with a graceful spin, and Savannah moved to the small conference war room where John and Rochelle waited. Since the mediator would alternate between sides, John and Rochelle would use this space for working when the mediator wasn't with them.

Rochelle set her iPhone aside with a small smile. "We ready?"

"Just about. How soon can you restart the tests after the lawsuit ends?" Savannah already knew the answer, but needed them to remember. To let the information calm them and remind them of the strength of their position once the judge lifted the injunction prohibiting developing and selling the software.

Rochelle met John's gaze, and they engaged in nonverbal communication that was more effective than many people's words. Then she focused on Savannah. "Days. We just need thirty days of data to analyze in conjunction with the prior data. That should be sufficient to give us the statistical validity to convince the FAA and NTSB that we are a viable option and can sell the product to airlines." The National Transportation Safety Board wasn't eager to adopt new technologies, but this duo seemed on the right track.

"In the meantime, we're doing what we can." John rubbed his hands down his khakis and looked to the side. "We've continued the pressure and salt-water tests in the lab, the only ones allowed. It's not cheap, but we've got much more than is required to exceed the NTSB's requirements." John held his right thumb and forefinger about an inch apart. "We were this close. And then this lawsuit."

"They don't have a case, right?" Rochelle begged for reassurance.

"No. Not based on what we've seen from them so far." Savannah smiled, calm and in control. "Let's see how it goes." She looked from one to the other, pausing to connect with each. "This can work. But I need you to go in there and talk to the mediator. He's good, and you need to let him do his work. By the end of the day all of this could be over except the judge's signature on the settlement."

John studied her. "Words like *lawsuit* and *infringement* are terrifying."

"It's outside our comfort zones." Rochelle stifled a small shudder.

"But this is mine. Don't forget we countered their claim of patent infringement with one of our own. You had the technology and patent first. All we have to do is prove it. Then they disappear." She infused her words with every molecule of faith she could muster. "Let's go in there with confidence, heads high."

The two nodded, then followed her to the larger conference room with John on her left and Rochelle on her right.

———

An hour later she fought disappointment as the mediation looked like it would only be a tangent and not the solution she'd hoped. They'd made their opening statements with the mediator sitting at the head of the table between the parties. William Garbot had a distinguished look with his tailored suit and close-cropped salt-and-pepper hair. He listened intently and took notes, then Reggie took off his gloves and the initial round began to derail.

The more he talked, the more Savannah wanted to pull out her phone and check for updates on the crash, or do anything other than listen to his bluster.

"Savannah, don't you agree?" His nasally voice slipped past her distracted thoughts. He must have finally ended his diatribe about her odious clients and their stolen code.

She smiled at him. "I make it a practice to never agree with opposing counsel."

"Might not be the best idea." Reginald's smile was as fake as a three-dollar bill.

"I'll decide that." Her phone dinged, and she checked to make sure it wasn't Addy before silencing it.

"You seem distracted, Ms. Daniels." Reggie's patronizing tones about had Savannah climbing the walls.

"Not at all." She caught the nervous glance John and Rochelle exchanged. Time to get this moving. "Mr. Garbot, are you ready for us to separate?"

The mediator's expression was hooded, unlike his usually open, fatherly demeanor, though he continued to treat her with patience and respect. "I'd like to have a bit more background first." He pointed to Reginald and his client. "Y'all sued Mnemosyne for patent infringement, claiming you created the system first. Then"—he turned to Savannah—"your clients countersued, claiming the code was theirs first."

She leaned forward and smiled firmly. "Yes. As we outline in the memo we submitted, Mnemosyne's employees generated the unique code and the delivery system ahead of FTS. We have the patent to prove it."

Nash snorted. "That's what this lawsuit is supposed to determine. They stole our technology."

"No, they took it from us." Savannah glared at Nash, then forced herself to pause. "His client has submitted no evidence that reinforces their claim to have created the device or the supporting technology first. Mnemosyne, on the other hand, has both a patent to protect the idea and a copyright to protect the actual code."

She smiled brightly as confusion flashed in Reggie's eyes. She glanced at Rochelle and John and had no doubt the executive and dreamer would become incredibly successful and save lives. "My clients will never accept the terms you've outlined. They have worked too hard to build Mnemosyne to have your client steal its heart."

Rochelle nodded and John straightened as if Savannah's words instilled hope. She turned to the mediator. "If this is how the mediation will proceed, we can end it now. There's no need to waste your time, Mr. Garbot."

"Now wait a minute, Savannah." Reggie patted the air with his hands in a pacifying gesture that only increased her frustration. "We should at least see the process through."

"Why? So you can continue to gouge your client for fees?" She stood and collected her files into a neat pile. "You are welcome to stay, but I will not do the same to mine. They are hard-working individuals who expect me to protect their best interests." Interests that did not align with another wasted moment or word.

William Garbot gathered the papers in front of him as well. "I'll begin with Mr. Nash and his client." His tone was steady, almost soothing.

"All right." She nodded to Mr. Garbot, then with a small lift of her hand had Rochelle and John standing too. She stepped toward the door with the two a beat behind her. With a quick backward glance at the men sitting around the table, she paused. "I'll be in my office when you need me."

With that she stepped out of the room and, after her clients exited, closed the door with a soft click. She held a finger to her lips and leaned against the wall, curious to hear what Reggie would say.

CHAPTER
EIGHT

How much time would Garbot need to bring Reginald Nash and his client around?

Why wasn't Addy responding to her messages?

Savannah rubbed her forehead as she contemplated the questions.

She set her files on the desk and then sank onto her desk chair. She'd use this time to work on the stack of documents resting on her desk.

Three clients had matters at varying stages of litigation. Another was less than two months from trial if it didn't get moved or settled. Three were weighing the costs of filing suit, and another was evaluating whether settlement was best. None of that counted the run-of-the-mill matters that came up on a daily basis, the blips that felt like emergencies to clients but weren't necessarily . . . until they were.

A pop-up announced new emails. The first subject line read, "Follow-up question."

Savannah clicked on the mail icon.

From Jglover@WASource.com.

Really? That reporter was contacting her again? Didn't he get the hint when she didn't respond to his prior email?

The image of his chiseled jaw and direct blue gaze filled her mind before she could press it to the side. A movie-screen-worthy face wouldn't sway her. It was tempting though.

Men didn't love her. They were intimidated by her or overlooked her. She didn't even long for love. Not really. It wasn't something she could expect in this life. It was for other people, but not part of her destiny. She'd had her shot at it and lost.

The fact she was wasting time thinking about it was a sign of how much she needed to delete the message unread.

She hovered the mouse over his email address, then clicked without thought. What would it hurt to see what the man wanted?

Did you see the article? He included a link as if she wouldn't know where to find it if she wanted to read the drivel. Comments coming in. Outrage like expected. Any comment to add to the story now?

Short. To the point. Rude. A question she'd already answered.

She'd known better than to read it. Next time she'd trust her gut. It was wiser than she was. She hit delete and returned to her files.

Her phone rang, and she answered it as she picked up the remote for the small TV Bella had insisted she keep in a corner of her office. "Hello?"

"Aunt Savannah?"

"Addy Jo? Why did you 911 me and then not answer my call? I've been worried."

"Mom's passed out on the couch." Addy didn't add it was the third time that week. She didn't have to. Savannah and Addy monitored Stasi's addiction issues with the same seriousness. "I'm going to need a note."

Savannah pressed her free hand to her forehead as she tried to imagine why it had taken Addy this long to call her back. It was after two o'clock. She wouldn't need a note for school today. "What's the real reason you aren't in school?"

There was a huff on the other end, but Savannah let the silence lengthen. "I had a headache this morning and turned off my alarm.

Mom didn't wake me. When I got up, Mom was crashed on the couch. It took a long time to wake her, but she's out of it, Aunt Savvy."

Unfortunately, Savannah could imagine the entire scene. It had happened too many times before. She had called the school for Addy each time Stasi was too high on her pain meds or combined them with alcohol to make a noxious cocktail. As the TV flickered to life, Savannah couldn't look away from the image of smoke spilling from the fuselage of a plane sinking in the waters of the Potomac. "Addy, have you seen the news?"

"No. I've been trying to wake Mom. I need help." Her niece sounded too old and worn out for a high school freshman.

"Don't worry." Savannah could do enough of that for both of them. "I'll call the office. Let them know you won't be in."

There was a moment of silence instead of the quick thanks she expected. "I really needed to be at school this afternoon. Finals are in another week and a half." Addy sighed. "When do I get to be the kid and worry about normal things? I had a test in geometry I shouldn't have missed."

"You'll reschedule it."

"With finals? That'll be fun." Addy huffed, then seemed to relent as she sighed. "But what do I do about Mom?"

"Is she awake now?"

"Yes, but out of it."

"Any different than the other times?"

Another sigh. "No."

"As long as she doesn't get worse, let her rest." Based on the number of emergency vehicles at the crash site, there wouldn't be any available for nonemergencies. "I'll come by tonight after work. Try to talk to her."

"Talk doesn't work." The *duh* in her niece's voice would normally earn a mini-lecture, but not today.

"Promise you'll stay home."

There was a pause. "Why?"

"There's been a plane crash. Stay put until we know more, okay?" Images of the chaos of 9/11 fired through Savannah's mind. The cell phones shut down. The subway silent. Traffic gridlocked. If chaos erupted, Savannah needed Addy to be safe where she could find her. "Promise."

There was a pause as if Addy was considering her options. "Yes, ma'am." There was a meekness in her voice that clued Savannah in.

"You're online?"

"I am now." There was a hesitation. "Are you safe?"

"Absolutely." She infused the word with all the conviction she could muster. "It's a tragic accident. I'll see you tonight." She rubbed her forehead and tried to infuse her voice with a smile. "Stay out of trouble until I get there, okay?"

"Sure. I'll work on something in my room. How much trouble can I find there?"

"None if you aren't looking." Savannah didn't mention her sister had found a long list from the safety of her room as a teenager. Trouble followed Stasi like a puppy. So far Addy had avoided it, but Savannah wouldn't take that for granted. As long as she could, she'd be there to fill the gaps left by her sister. She said good-bye and hung up.

Bella stepped into her office. "We've got a problem."

———

The gangway overflowed with business travelers striding quickly toward a gate, and harried parents tracking children who yanked brightly colored suitcases as they plodded down the walkway. Jett sat like a stone at the edge of a stream of pulsing water, his cracked chair tucked against a wall at a United gate in Boston Logan International Airport. Noise-cancelling headphones were perched on his head, a Chick-fil-A bag with a late lunch sat next to him, and his laptop lay open on his legs. He hoped anyone walking by would assume he was a bored businessman killing time, but with a clear do-not-disturb vibe. His rescheduled flight was already running an hour behind.

The snow system that was working its way across the Eastern Seaboard was the given reason. He wasn't sure he bought it. Not when his phone lit up with alerts about a Western World Airways plane that crashed into the Fourteenth Street Bridge crossing from Virginia into DC.

He hadn't wanted to believe it when the first alert popped up, but then he confirmed it with the paper.

He checked his phone for an update on the status of his flight. So far just a delay. Maybe he should have the paper's travel guru change the flight to Dulles. Taking a taxi from the other airport wouldn't be fun in the snow. He also checked for a message from his mystery caller.

When he'd started the article, it had felt . . . well . . . blasé. Everyone knew the wealthy lived by a different standard. Okay, not all of them, but enough that it felt like a truism.

Secretly, he'd hoped to disprove that.

But when he landed on Logan Donnelly, a starting pitcher with the Virginia Colonials, a tingly spidey sense told him this was the story. He'd convinced his editor to let him dive deep, and he'd landed in mud. Turned out Logan partied in Asia like it was a job.

No foul there.

But when you included young girls in the partying?

Now this call. It made him wonder what he'd missed, if anything. He'd nailed the details. Those were easy. It was the nuances, those elements on the fringes, that made a story resonate, but they could be elusive.

The lines of text on his laptop screen represented the interviews he'd conducted plus the new information from this trip to Donnelly's hometown. The guy should be playing for the Red Sox but found himself south of his stomping grounds.

In this anybody-can-post-news-online world, people understood others were rarely what they seemed.

He shifted against the hard vinyl seat.

He'd had a clear picture of Logan Donnelly. It had been crystal clear. One more spoiled playboy who dropped his restraints when he was on the other side of the world.

The ballplayer was a cardboard persona. A buzz in Jett's pocket startled him from his thoughts. He slid his headphones off and glanced at the check-in desk as he shifted to dig out his phone. The uniformed woman standing there was frozen and pale, a growing murmur building in the crowd lined up in front of her.

Words began to stand out from the jumble.

. . . how do we get home . . .

Not again.

Accident?

Terrorism . . .

He put the phone to his ear. "Glover."

"We've got a rental car for you." How like Ted to launch into details without common courtesies.

"Why?"

"What kind of reporter are you? The plane crash means no flights in and out of National at least for a day."

"What about Dulles?"

"Nope. It's closed up tight too."

Jett felt the stillness, the flashback to 9/11 and sitting in his graduate classroom learning about the attacks with a host of classmates. "They thinking terrorism?"

Ted snorted. "Too early, you know that. Get back here. You're on the story, along with everyone else. It'll be round-the-clock coverage. At least initially."

"Any idea who's on the plane?"

"Not yet, but I expect big names."

"Yeah." It was DC. Any flight could see key government employees or elected officials filling the plane. On 9/11 Barbara Olson, the political commentator and wife of Solicitor General Ted Olson, had been on the plane that hit the Pentagon.

"Alice sent the details in an email. Get that car and drive."

"It takes seven hours on a perfect day."

"Longer if you hit the snow and rush hour in one of the I-95 cities, so get started."

"Yes, sir." As soon as he hung up, Jett opened his email and gathered his carry-on. Good thing he hadn't checked luggage.

CHAPTER
NINE

Bella stood in Savannah's doorway, a frown on her normally placid face.

"What do you mean 'we have a problem'?"

"Garbot left."

"Left?" Savannah hadn't had time to check his status before getting Addy's call. "He never came for us."

"Stormed out like a man on a mission." Bella held up the tablet she carried around when she wasn't at her work station. "What do you want me to do?"

"Nothing . . . yet. I'll go see what we can salvage." As she walked past the doorway of their small conference room, she saw John and Rochelle nose deep in their oversized phones.

When she reached the larger conference room, Reggie was throwing files in his oversized briefcase, and Mr. Garbot was nowhere to be seen.

"I need to get back." The man looked distracted.

"Where's Mr. Garbot?"

"The moment he heard the Western World plane was Flight 2840, he was gone. Said he'd call us to reschedule."

"Why?" The man was too professional to leave like this.

"Said his wife was on that flight. Off to see a new grandchild."

Savannah's stomach bottomed out. "That's terrible."

"Yeah, well, my client's gone too. We'll talk and call." Reggie locked his case and strode from the room with a nod.

Savannah sank to the nearest chair.

Garbot's wife was on the plane?

The fear must be crippling.

Bella hurried into the room. "Mr. Nash left."

"Yes. Mr. Garbot's wife is on the plane."

Bella's hand covered her mouth as she inhaled sharply.

Savannah pushed back to her feet. "The mediation's postponed. I'll have to push Mr. Garbot for another date. But not until he knows if his wife is okay." Or convince Nash to settle. She wasn't sure how to break that news.

She wandered back to her clients' conference room and updated them. They weren't out of options, but she knew they couldn't pay her next bill. "Y'all okay?"

John nodded without glancing up. Rochelle's face was paler than normal when she met Savannah's gaze. "I don't know what to do."

"We'll reschedule."

"You think Mr. Nash will negotiate without immediate mediation?" Rochelle set her phone down and leaned toward Savannah.

"I'll work to reschedule as quickly as possible." What her clients didn't understand was that all of this was a business strategy. If they won, they'd keep her as the company's primary attorney for years. If not, well, she'd been paid in part. "I'll call as soon as I hear from the other side."

"Thanks." John squared his shoulders.

Her clients left, and it was tempting to follow them. Grab a cup of overpriced coffee and clear her head. Instead, she headed to the small kitchenette to make a single cup. She stared at the Keurig as it brewed.

"Savannah, you all right?" Emilie's brows were knit with worry as she entered the kitchen.

Savannah startled. How long had she stood there without seeing a thing while Emilie saw right through her? "Sure."

Emilie quirked a perfectly shaped eyebrow.

"Guess I got lost in my thoughts."

"Anything I can do?"

"Not unless you can salvage my mediation."

"Not likely. Need me to gather the girls?" Emilie crossed her arms as she considered Savannah. "I didn't think the mediation was guaranteed to work, but I thought it might."

"I know." Savannah sighed as she remembered the look of defeat that had glazed Rochelle's face when she and John left. "But what can we do?"

"Work hard and leave the rest to God. I'll see if Hayden is free."

A few minutes later the team gathered in the conference room that held the large TV. Savannah had thought it an extravagance when Hayden insisted they add it for conference calls, but today it allowed them to monitor the crash coverage while meeting.

Bella hurried in with a box of Kleenex and a basket of bottled water. "In case anyone's thirsty." Then she sank onto a faux leather chair, the best Savannah could afford at the time. "Those poor people."

"William Garbot's wife was on that flight." Savannah felt the weight. "We need to pray for him and others waiting for word."

"Absolutely." Emilie shook her head. "It's awful. So many lives changed in an instant."

The news channel had live footage playing next to footage from a similar crash that occurred near the Fourteenth Street Bridge in 1982. The Air Florida flight had taken off with ice on the wings and skidded across the tops of vehicles before crashing into the river.

Bella swiped at her eyes. "I'll never forget that day. Used to drive the bridge to my job at the Department of Agriculture. After that crash it took me months to drive across it without looking for a plane first."

"This is probably a tragic accident like that one." Emilie pushed a strand of her blonde hair behind her ear, but her blue eyes belied her concern.

Hayden ignored the TV as she leaned forward with an intense gaze. "We need to figure out what role your clients have in this mess."

Savannah frowned as she focused on Hayden. "What do you mean?"

"Their company worked on the new black-box technology."

"Yes." Savannah had told them all about the tech when brainstorming the best angle for the case. "So?"

"Western World Airways is the one that agreed to allow them to test the software."

"But not now. The injunction stalled the tests." Savannah knew the case inside and out but could tell Hayden thought she was missing something.

"Remember when that brand-new plane model had several high-profile crashes?"

"Yes."

"We won't know for sure until all the lawsuits settle, but early speculation was the crashes were caused by problems with some of the autopilot codes. Codes very similar to the ones in Mnemosyne's black-box technology. The plane's systems overrode pilots. What if that happened here?" Hayden pointed at the screen. "What if something like that was part of today's crash?"

Savannah couldn't shake the feeling that Hayden might be on to something that could cost her clients greatly. Then she shook her head. "The case came with an injunction against further tests. They've assured me they're complying. If that's accurate, then there's no way their tech was on Flight 2840."

Hayden considered her words. "I hope you're right."

"I am." Savannah called Rochelle's cell. The moment the woman picked up Savannah asked, "You aren't running any tests on planes right now, correct?"

"Of the black-box technology?" Rochelle's voice sounded bewildered. "No. The injunction suspended it."

"And John's complying as well."

"Of course." Now a flicker of outrage edged into Rochelle's voice. "We're a team."

"Okay. Good."

"Can you tell me what this is about?" Rochelle huffed. "We followed your advice."

"A random thought that could give me nightmares." Savannah leaned back in her chair and closed her eyes. "Sorry about that."

But as she hung up, something niggled at her thoughts. Hayden couldn't be right.

———

The thermometer on the rental car steadily dipped as the miles slowly slipped away as Jett drove south. I-95 was an artery that connected the East Coast's major cities in a steady flow of concrete and traffic. The car was so small that the driver's seat practically ate the back seat, but it had been the only available choice. He shifted his uncomfortable body. At least he could keep up with the latest on the crash while he drove out of New York City toward Baltimore and eventually the District.

The phone rang, and he clicked to take the call while keeping his eyes on the fast-moving interstate traffic. "Glover."

"Hey, Jett. I've got something for you." Chase Matthews sounded excited, and Jett could picture him bouncing in his desk chair like the recent college grad he was.

"All right."

"It's the passenger list from 2840. It's not public yet, but we got a copy from a contact with Western." The newbie reporter spoke so fast, Jett's ears struggled to keep up.

"Anything interesting?"

"You could say that. The list is what you'd expect for a plane taking off from National. Not all of the names are recognizable, but staff are googling them." As if Chase wasn't one of the staff tasked with that.

"Why'd you call?" *Spit it out, kid.*

"There's a couple you'll be interested in."

"Who?" *Get to the point, Chase.*

"Logan Donnelly. Economy class. What happened to private planes?"

"He keeps a low profile here." It was part of what had made the private flights to Asia so noteworthy.

The kid snickered. "Yeah. And get this, his pilot had a seat near him."

That tidbit had Jett shifting in the confined space. "Dustin Tate?"

"Yep."

"Have a casualty list yet?"

"No. From the video feed we know some survived, but no way everyone did. And it's hard to identify people from the grainy videos." He paused, then rushed on. "Check out CNN for footage. Coast Guard helicopter's there pulling people from the water. I'll get you more details as they're released."

"How many on the passenger list?"

"One hundred eighty-five."

"Okay. Anyone else interesting on the list?"

"Off the top of my head an undersecretary of state and a chief of staff for the ranking member of the Senate Armed Services Committee."

Jett let out a whistle. "And that's early?"

"It's a flight out of National. It'll be a who's-who list, but I thought you'd want to know about Donnelly and Tate."

"You were right. Thanks." Jett was finally nearing Baltimore. He'd be in DC in a couple of hours, and then he could assess what Ted needed him to do. Sounded like Chase and others were already doing the important groundwork.

As he continued through Baltimore gridlock, Jett ran through what he knew.

After his stint in the military, Dustin Tate had shifted to commercial piloting with Western World Airways. Logan seemed to be his only private client, probably due to their friendship. Evan Spencer's relationship with Logan had made the three easy to identify. It was the fourth that remained elusive. The plane tickets and hotel information had been useless, the fake name too common to trace. If he didn't have the paperwork and a few photos with a shadowy fourth figure, he'd wonder if this person was real or some sort of smokescreen.

He'd done his job well. He did every time. It was too important to not do everything he could to track down the truth.

When Jett's father died, the blame lay at the feet of the reporter who had published a groundless article that smeared his father. The reporter had alleged Jett's father was the mastermind behind a scheme to defraud his company and its pension fund of millions. The company collapsed, putting hundreds out of work, and as a result of that and ensuing articles, his father had been unable to defend himself. It was only weeks after his death that the truth came out. His father had been framed by the CEO and CFO, the real masterminds. After his mother sued the reporter and paper and won, Jett determined he'd become a reporter, a Clark Kent fighting for truth and justice. He'd used his portion of the settlement to pay for a master's in journalism at Columbia.

He approached his job like a calling, understanding how much harm could be wielded by the pen or keystroke. He had vowed to protect the innocent, which is exactly what this story did.

The first step in protecting was revealing those who had evil intent.

Logan Donnelly was one more two-faced individual to expose.

Interestingly, not one ballplayer or agent associated with the article had denied a thing or expressed outrage. The silence was deafening.

As Jett drove through the north side of the Maryland suburbs, he plotted out next calls, his energy for the story recharged. He'd start by finding out if Tate and Donnelly were still alive.

CHAPTER
TEN

That evening Savannah swung by her town house in Cherry Blossom Estates long enough to change. Then she wound her way along King Street to Bailey's Crossroads and her sister's small apartment. The bag of takeout sub sandwiches didn't seem like a great offering to bring Addy, but it was the best she could do after an exhausting day. Somewhere with the passage of years, her gourmet cooking had yielded to takeout bags. It wasn't worth the effort to grocery shop for one. Her snug clothes let her know how much those seemingly simple choices impacted her. Another thing to attack when life let up.

She pulled into a visitor spot at Stasi's apartment but stayed behind the wheel.

She didn't want to go in.

Savannah had worked hard to find a safe place that Stasi could afford, but still her sister lingered one month from default on her payments. If she didn't stop drinking, she and Addy Jo could find themselves homeless, which meant they'd end up with Savannah. While she didn't want to facilitate Stasi's addiction, she couldn't let Addy Jo's life spiral into further chaos. That's why Savannah kept a bedroom for Addy at her townhome, but not for Stasi. Her sister had already taken too much from her.

God, help me be there for Addy, and continue to heal my relationship with Stasi. She sighed. Who was she kidding? They didn't have much in the way of relationship. *Lord, I'll keep forgiving her—every day, even— but it's a miracle only You can complete. I don't have the strength. Or the will.*

She cringed at those last words. She wanted to be stronger and better than this. But she couldn't. Not in her own strength. However, she'd keep showing up because that's what Addy Jo needed, and Savannah didn't quit.

A curtain moved at the third-floor apartment's window. She'd been spotted.

Savannah grabbed her purse and bag of sandwiches as she climbed from the car. She used her copy of the apartment key to enter the building, then trudged up the stairs. Another day without time to go to the gym meant she'd take every stair in front of her. At least her watch told her those steps mattered. A light had gone out on the landing, making the hall dimmer and shadow filled. A small wreath with a polka-dot-painted D hung on Stasi's door. Savannah had one just like it.

She knocked once before letting herself in. With two bedrooms, one bath, and an open living area and kitchen, the place was tiny yet adequate. It met the small family's needs while also keeping them in a relatively safe neighborhood with access to decent schools.

Addy Jo hurried from her room. "Sorry, Aunt Savvy. I was in my room."

"It's fine." She waved her key in the air. "I let myself in." Savannah pushed aside her fatigue and smiled as she held up the food. "I brought supper."

Addy stepped forward and her shoulders relaxed. "You came."

As the door closed behind her, Savannah pulled her niece into a hug. "Of course I did. I always will."

As many times as needed. Addy took a shuddering breath, and

Savannah made a mental note to respond faster next time. Addy needed to know one adult in her life was there for her ... any time and all the time.

Savannah glanced around the room. "Where's your mom?"

Addy Jo stepped back and wrinkled her nose as she placed her hands on her hips. "Where do you think?"

Savannah groaned. "Really? After this morning?"

"It's getting bad, Aunt Savvy. She can't seem to stop drinking anymore."

"The mom is here." Stasi's words were tart as she pushed up from the couch in the flickering light of the television. "You didn't need to come. We are fine." She tried to make her words punchy, but they fell flat.

The couch had seen better days, but the slipcovers they'd found at IKEA hid the worst of the wear. In fact, the small space could qualify as a showroom for the Swedish company. It had been the best Savannah could afford, and it worked. At least Addy Jo never complained. The girl survived with a serious air and occasional smile when Savannah could get her to forget the challenges with her mother.

"Well, I brought supper." She turned to Addy. "Grab a few plates and some cups of water." Her stomach grumbled, and she tipped her head to the side. "Guess you'd better hurry."

A minute later Addy was back balancing cups on the plates. "Happy birthday, Aunt Savvy."

It was still her birthday? "Thank you."

The phone rang, and Stasi held her head and groaned. "Someone make it stop."

"We wouldn't need to if you'd stop drinking." Savannah bit her tongue. So much for extending grace to her sister. It had taken all of five minutes to lose her cool.

She wished that was a record, but as Addy answered the phone, Savannah knew it would take a miracle to get through the evening well. That thought was still running through her mind when Addy exited her room, phone in hand, cheeks devoid of color.

"Addy? Are you okay?"

"Dad just called. He's in the hospital." Addy shuddered as she clutched the phone.

Stasi shot to her feet. "I'll go. You're too young to see him."

Addy turned even paler as she focused on Savannah. "Please don't let her go alone. Please."

"But that means leaving you." Savannah glanced from mother to daughter. Which needed her more? Savannah took the phone from Addy, but all she heard was a dial tone. "Tell me what he said."

Stasi slipped into her room as Addy leaned into Savannah. "That he's at the hospital and hurt. He was on the plane that crashed."

The information sank into Savannah. "Okay. He survived the crash, so that's good. And he could call you, so that's better. Which hospital is he at?"

"Arlington." Addy wiped under her eyes and then straightened. "Please don't let Mom go on her own. She can't drive, but she'll do it anyway."

"I can drive. I'll be fine." Savannah turned to see Stasi posing in her doorway. "How do I look?" She wore clean jeans and a white oxford that even looked ironed. The buttons were misaligned, but other than the crooked collar it would be hard to tell she'd been passed out on the couch most of the day. Until one stepped close enough to see her bloodshot eyes and the tight lines around her mouth. "I'm going to the hospital."

Addy was right. There was no way Savannah could let Stasi go on her own. "I'll drive."

Fifteen minutes later Stasi stared sullenly out the passenger window of Savannah's late-model Mazda SUV. The hospital wasn't far away in the Arlington suburb. Still, when she reached it, it took a few minutes to find parking in the garage. The cold kept frosting her window, and Savannah cranked the defroster. The silence felt as stiff as her body in the cold air. "There must be several crash victims here."

Stasi shrugged. "I only care about one."

"Why care about him?"

"Other than the fact his child support is keeping us in that over-priced apartment you put us in?"

"If it's so bad, move." She really should keep quiet, since Stasi was the one person she couldn't win an argument with.

If she got the chance, though, she'd give Dustin a piece of her mind.

Piloting spoiled, uber-rich athletes to the other side of the world for out-of-control parties on his off time? Her blood boiled at the idea. If she had her way, he'd never get near Addy again. If he thought those kinds of weekends were okay, what else was?

She shuddered at the thought.

After finally finding parking, they hurried toward the hospital entrance, where several satellite trucks hovered beneath white Christmas lights outside the front doors. The brick and stone building stood eight stories tall, and photojournalists were set up outside the door under the large silver letters that read Virginia Hospital Center. They crowded around a man in dress pants and FBI windbreaker. Savannah and Stasi slipped into the hospital behind him. Savannah stopped when they entered the lobby. Clusters of people and large Christmas trees decorated with various themes were scattered around the space.

Stasi looked lost as she slowly pirouetted. "What now?"

"I'm not sure. Give me a minute." She hadn't expected so many people at this time of day. Visiting hours had to end soon. How many victims had been brought here?

A young woman, blonde hair pulled into a messy bun, approached them. She wore a pair of khakis and a Red Cross polo with a name tag that read Cecilia. "Are you here to check on someone from the crash?"

"Yes." Savannah cleared her throat. "Dustin Tate."

The woman checked her iPad. "Are you family?"

"I am." Stasi stepped closer.

"Your relationship?"

"His wife." Stasi said the words without hesitation or shifting gaze.

Savannah startled while trying to keep her mouth from gaping.

Cecilia stared at Stasi for a minute. "What is your name?"

"Stasi Daniels. I kept my maiden name, since that was easier than messing with all the paperwork. Do you know how many documents have to be changed?" She made a waving motion like she couldn't be bothered.

She certainly wasn't concerned with the truth. Stasi pressed a hand to her chest. "I've been so worried. Could you tell me where he is?"

"I'll check with the nursing staff." Cecilia gestured toward a series of vending machines that stood against a far wall. "Why don't you get something to drink while I see what can be done."

Stasi shook her head, copper curls springing wildly around her face. "I want to wait right here." She pressed a hand to her stomach and made a squeamish expression. "I can't imagine eating."

Savannah glanced around the lobby and noted a couple of empty chairs tucked next to a sign advertising a Christmas bazaar that had been held earlier in the week. "Let's sit there." As soon as Stasi eased down, Savannah joined her, then wrapped an arm around her. "I'm sure he'll be fine."

Maybe.

"You can stop the act." Stasi pushed Savannah away. "I don't see how he can be all right. How often do people survive plane accidents?"

"The news coverage showed survivors. And he was well enough to call Addy."

"He would have called me next." She huffed.

So like Stasi to make it all about her. Savannah turned away and focused on the fact that at least for now, it was a miracle anyone had survived.

Clusters of people watched the televisions hanging from the ceiling in different spots around the lobby. Each was tuned to a different news network, broadcasting images of the crash and various talking heads. Floodlights had been placed along the edge of the Potomac and on the Fourteenth Street Bridge. The lights illuminated the bare outline of the plane through the swirl of snow flurries. It looked like floats of some sort encircled the fuselage to keep it from sinking farther into the murky waters. Even so, the investigation into the crash would be wet, dangerous, and could take weeks.

Planes taking off in the background surprised Savannah.

"They haven't closed the airport."

"No." Cecilia walked up with a sad twitch of her red lips. "It reopened about an hour ago. Guess the powers that be decided Flight 2840 wasn't a risk to other planes. The bridge, though, remains closed as engineers test its structural integrity."

"Hmm." Savannah watched as another plane skimmed over the lights on the bridge. "I think I'll fly out of Dulles for the foreseeable future."

"You won't be the only one." The volunteer turned to Stasi, who slid her chair closer to Savannah's. Guess they were back to being sad. "You can see your husband in fifteen minutes. A nurse will come get you when he's ready."

"Would it be better if we waited on whichever floor he's on?" Savannah didn't like the idea of a nurse having to find them.

"You are welcome to, though I've heard it's crowded."

"I want to be closer, don't you, Stasi?" Especially as the doors opened and a reporter with her photographer entered the lobby.

Cecilia bristled and took a step away. "They've been told they can't come in." She gestured across the lobby to a hallway that extended to the right. "Take that hallway to the bank of elevators, then proceed to the fifth-floor lobby. I'll let them know you're on the way."

As she and Stasi stood, a man entered, skirting around the reporter and photographer. He was wearing rumpled clothes that looked like he'd slept in them, but Savannah had no doubt it was that reporter Jett Glover. He walked their direction, so she urged Stasi to move. "Let's get upstairs."

In the hall, a more antiseptic smell assaulted them. Savannah wished she could hold her breath. Instead she inhaled through her mouth as Stasi pressed the elevator's up button. Footsteps behind them had Savannah looking over her shoulder.

When her gaze collided with Jett's blue one, she grimaced.

Had he recognized her?

It felt like it took hours for one of the elevators to open. Before they could enter, an orderly pushed an older woman in a wheelchair from the elevator. The reporter lingered on the edges of the lobby. What or who was he looking for?

She had a terrible thought.

Had he somehow got word Dustin was here?

As soon as the wheelchair was clear, Stasi slipped into the elevator, Savannah a half step behind. The doors closed and Savannah exhaled. It was silly, but she felt the urgency to get away.

Jett turned from the elevators back to the lobby and Chase, who had followed him like a puppy. "You take the Red Cross volunteer, and I'll try the information desk. Between the two of us, we should be able to find out something about which crash survivors are here." At least he hoped they'd find someone who would cooperate. He was banking on Chase's eager young face to work some magic on a volunteer who'd look at him and see her grandson.

"Yes, sir." Chase gave him a mock salute and then trotted toward the young Red Cross worker.

Guess that left him the other volunteer. Jett's own efforts to coax information from the silver-haired matron at the information desk were met by a firm commitment to HIPAA.

"I don't care if you're the president himself." She gave him a look over her glasses that said she was on to him. "Though you're a sight better-looking than he is, you'll get no information about the patients without asking about a specific one."

Jett wished for a venti black coffee. He couldn't pull out his phone and start running down the passenger list the paper had acquired, but he could ask about a specific name. "What about Logan Donnelly?"

The woman clicked at her keyboard, one slow key at a time. "No."

All right. One word was better than nothing. "How about Dustin Tate?"

More hunt-and-peck typing. "Yes."

"What room?"

"Nothing doing, young man. You can smile at me all you want. I won't be charmed." Something about her tone made him think of Ms. Novotony, his stern third-grade teacher, who had driven long division into his head one repeated step at a time.

"I believe you." He gave her his best Cary Grant grin and turned toward the elevators. Was that Savannah Daniels? The doors slid closed almost before he could be sure, but there was a self-confidence in her bearing that set her apart somehow.

Savannah Daniels might be forty, but she didn't look it. In fact, he'd been tempted to call her for non-work reasons since their short interview. He was intrigued about how the woman he'd researched matched the woman he'd interacted with in a display of fire and ice. She'd exhibited a core strength that made him want to know more in a way not reserved for interview subjects. He wanted to know what made her tick.

He noted the floor her elevator stopped on.

It had been a long day, and it wasn't going to end anytime soon.

He'd tried unsuccessfully to reach his mystery caller a couple of times. He rubbed the back of his neck as he wished for even twenty minutes to catch a power nap. He hadn't always embraced the need for sleep, but man, he was beginning to understand how important it was for his brain. It would take some kind of serious sleep to clear his thoughts.

Chase hurried up to him. "She didn't tell me much of anything."

"Yeah, I had similar luck."

"Now what?"

"We go upstairs."

"Where?"

"I've got an idea." Jett pushed off the wall and walked to the elevator. It was taking a long time to get a list of the fatalities. Supposedly they were holding it until families were notified, but that shouldn't take more than twenty-four hours, unless it was hard to identify some of the victims.

Okay, so the story demanded he cool his heels here. He'd see what he could learn.

Chase punched the elevator's up button. "You okay, Jett?"

"Sure, why?"

"You seem on edge."

"Let's just say hospitals aren't my favorite." Hadn't been since his dad died. He would never forget his mother crying and driving as she followed the ambulance. Then waiting at the hospital for hours for news he'd known would be bad. Even at twelve, he'd understood no one could survive what his father had done.

It didn't make it any easier. Just made it real.

He leaned against the wall while he waited for the elevator. If he closed his eyes maybe he could trick his mind into believing he was anywhere but here.

Unfortunately, his eyes weren't his only sense that could identify his location.

The elevator was taking forever.

He pivoted and looked back at the lobby. Chase watched him curiously but didn't say anything else.

When the doors finally opened, Jett's attention zinged to a security guard wearing a baseball hat, who stepped out of the bay. Jett walked into the elevator, Chase beside him.

"Which floor, boss?"

CHAPTER
ELEVEN

Stasi glanced around the fifth-floor waiting room, then turned toward a vending machine. "I'm going to grab coffee. Want anything?"

"I'm good. Thanks."

"Can I have a couple dollars to get something?" Stasi waggled her fingers from an open palm. "Please?"

Savannah bit back a retort. "There's always an angle."

"So said Bing Crosby in *White Christmas*." Stasi looked like she'd stand there all night with her hand out, so Savannah dug into her billfold as always. "Thanks, sis."

Savannah sank onto a vacant seat in a corner of the room close to the hallway as the "Sisters" song from the movie played through her head. Had more perfect lyrics ever been penned to capture the complications of sisters' relationships? *Please don't let the nurse take too long.*

Her patience for Stasi was about to break. There was too much Savannah needed to do, from protecting Addy to catching up on work. She couldn't divert energy to ignoring Stasi. Her phone dinged and she pulled it out to see a text from her mom.

Happy birthday, sweetheart.

Thanks.

Do anything fun?

Had lunch with the girls at Il Porto.

You love that place.

I do.

The flashing ellipsis indicated her mom was still texting. You safe?

Yes, it's just a tragic crash.

But the Fourteenth Street Bridge? That's close.

It is. But I wasn't on it. Unfortunately, others hadn't been so lucky.

Will you come home for Christmas?

I don't know yet. Maybe she should invite them here. Can you and Dad come here?

There was a pause, and Savannah had to resist retracting the invitation.

I'll talk to him. Well, love you. Tell your sister hi when you see her.

Sure, Mom.

Her mom refused to give up the naive hope that someday the two would be bosom friends again, like they had been decades ago as preteens. Maybe Mom's distance facilitated her belief in that fantasy, but it wasn't going to happen except in the dreams of a mother.

Stasi sauntered up. "The coffee's not much other than warm."

"Can I have my change?"

Stasi thrust a single at her, then took a sip. "Who was that?"

"Mom wishing me a happy birthday."

"Oh, that's right. Happy birthday."

"Thanks." Savannah forced herself to ignore the ire those words generated. "Why pretend to be married to Dustin?"

"For tonight at least, he can't deny me. If it gets us in to see him, then all the better."

"You shouldn't lie about things like that."

"It's not a lie. He will. One of these days." Stasi punctuated the last words with her finger.

A nurse approached them. "Are you Dustin Tate's family?"

"Yes." Stasi stepped forward with a little shuddering breath. "Can we see him?"

The nurse glanced at the tablet she carried. "I have to warn you he may not be himself. He claims he's not married."

Stasi's hand flew to her mouth and the other reached for Savannah as if she needed the physical support. "Is he badly injured? He must be if he doesn't remember me."

"I can't tell you much more than we're keeping him for observation. The doctor wants to be cautious."

Stasi looked uncertain as she let go of Savannah and wrapped her arms tight around her coat. "Should we go in?"

"For a few minutes. If he gets tired, you'll need to leave sooner."

The nurse turned and started toward the locked double doors, but Stasi stayed frozen in place.

Savannah squeezed her arm. "Want me to go in for you?"

"Yes. No." Stasi lifted her chin. "I'm his wife." She latched on to

Savannah as if clutching a lifeline, and they followed the nurse to the door. The woman keyed them through.

Stasi hesitated again. "I'll wait here." The nurse frowned, but Stasi wore a pleading look. "Please let my sister confirm he's okay first. I'm terribly squeamish. Our daughter goes to him when she's hurt." She gave a small shrug as if her words explained everything.

The nurse considered her a moment, then her expression softened. "All right." Then she turned to Savannah. "You can only stay a few minutes since you aren't family."

"But I am." Now she understood how Stasi could pretend to be his wife for the day. Too bad Savannah had actually filled that role. The nurse stared, so she continued. "We were married years ago, and I will always be his daughter's aunt."

"Sounds like a messed-up situation."

Savannah gave an uncomfortable chuckle. "That's an understatement." The scab was off, but the scar would always be part of her.

The nurse led her farther down a hallway with rooms off each side, most with closed doors. Christmas hadn't entered this wing, probably because of the germs that could get captured in decorations. The woman stopped at a door across from the nurses' station. "Mr. Tate was very lucky. He could go home as early as tomorrow."

"Will he require assistance when he's released? He lives alone." At least he did the last time Addy mentioned spending time at his apartment. The woman considered her, and Savannah caught her mistake. "I meant if he'll need help during the day when Stasi works and their daughter's in school." If Stasi even pretended to have a job.

"We'll see what the doctor says when he's released. Situations like his are usually fluid." The woman nodded toward the station. "I'll be there if you need anything. Please limit your time to ten minutes."

"That won't be a problem." She wouldn't spend that much time with him other than to give Addy peace of mind.

She peeked into the room without entering.

Dustin lay against the raised bed and pillows, his dark hair flopping starkly against the white pillowcase. He looked weak in the blue and white haze of light that flickered from the TV mounted on the wall. She glanced at it and noted the football game.

"I see you still like sports."

He rolled his head in her direction. "Ah, Savvy."

"You don't get to call me that."

"Addy does."

"Yes. You don't." Savannah tried to calm her tone. "I see you survived."

"Hope you aren't disappointed."

"No." She shook her head. "I wouldn't wish an accident like that on anyone."

"It was . . . rough . . ." An IV had been shoved into one hand. He dragged the other down his stubbled jaw. "It was a blur."

"What happened?"

"Did you know the Fourteenth Street Bridge is only fourteen hundred meters from the end of the runway? With the snow at takeoff, I wondered about deicing. But it's a blur. Crazy kaleidoscope of moments." He rolled his head gingerly, and she noticed a bruise forming along the right side of his face. "Why are you here?"

She gestured toward the door. "Your call terrified Addy, and someone had to let her know you're okay." She studied him, and he met her gaze a moment before shifting away with a grimace. "Stasi's here."

"Ah no." Age lined his face.

"Yep." She searched for something in his expression, though she wasn't sure what.

"Don't look at me like that."

"Like what?"

"Like you're x-raying my soul."

"Do you still have one?" The words burst from her, and she didn't care.

"Don't tell me you believe the article."

She simply stared at him.

"Come on, Savvy, you know me better than that."

"The man I knew said he loved me. Promised to never leave me. Then he went after my sister." She stepped closer and lowered her voice as she bowed her head to get closer to him. "Don't tell me what I can't believe. I used to believe the best about you." She wouldn't make that mistake again. Not without proof he was worth the risk.

"I didn't do anything that reporter said." His eyes flashed with a life that hadn't been there a minute before. "I don't know where he got his information but it's wrong. Dead wrong."

"Then fight back." The words burst from her.

"I can't. There's more happening."

"More than working for athletes too rich to be told no? Do I even want to know how much of that article is true?" She stood and stepped back. "You disgust me."

"There's a lot you don't know, and if I explained, lives could be in jeopardy." His hand grabbed her arm with startling force.

"Let go of me." She pushed the words through gritted teeth, but he ignored them.

"You have no idea." His hold eased enough she tugged free. "Savvy, we're doing something good. But it has to be kept under wraps or people could be hurt."

"If that were true, you'd still say something. Where's the man who fought for justice?" She bit off the words, her sophisticated edge long gone.

"Still here." He sounded like he'd given up. "You can't believe everything you read in the paper."

"I don't need the paper to tell me what I already know."

"Get off your high horse long enough to think, Savannah." His pulse-rate monitor took off at a gallop.

"You forget." She paused. "I *know* you."

"Well, if you believe that bunch of lies, you knew some fake person."

"Now, those are true words."

He lay back, pale, spent. "You have to believe me. Each trip is honorable. When I get out of here I can show you. I have proof stashed away."

"Show it to the reporter or tell me what it is now."

"I have to talk to Donnelly first."

"Why?"

"Because he's got more at stake than I do. No one cares about me. He's got a career in the limelight. Without his money, we can't do this."

Savannah bit her tongue. She needed to think about what Dustin had said. He spoke with a quiet fervor that defused some of her anger even though she still didn't understand what he meant.

A man wearing an FBI jacket stuck his head in the room. "Logan Donnelly?"

Savannah frowned at him. "No, this isn't his room."

The man's face firmed into a mask. "Do you know where he is?"

"No."

Dustin held up his hand. "Can you let me know when you find him?"

The man nodded, then moved out of the doorway.

"What's this proof, Dustin?" It was too easy to believe he was just sandbagging her.

"When I'm back home you'll see. I'll show you. I'm completely innocent."

"Keep telling yourself that." As a nurse rushed in, Savannah stepped back. "I'll tell Addy you'll survive and she can see you when you're home."

"Give me time to get the proof." His words faded. "I have to talk to Logan first."

Stasi stepped into the room and pressed her body against the wall. "What happened?"

What little color remained in his face leached away. "Why are you here?"

"I'm your wife." Her words held a little energy, then she sagged.

"I don't have a wife." His gaze drifted to Savannah. "Anymore."

Savannah felt like she was trapped in the Twilight Zone or her worst dream. How could she escape?

Stasi ignored the attention Dustin gave Savannah. "You're alive."

"Yes. Addy's check might be a little bit late this month."

The nurse turned from the monitor, where she was clicking away on a keyboard. "Is she bothering you, Dustin? Sounds like she's claiming to be someone she isn't."

"It's all right." The words were weak, almost listless. "It's a mess I created."

Stasi eased closer. "I can take care of you."

Dustin's laugh was bitter. "You don't like blood or other bodily fluids."

"Well, no, but they aren't anyone's favorites."

"Not happening." Dustin's words were harsh, and Stasi turned and fled from the small room.

Savannah couldn't stand to listen to them anymore, but what if Dustin had proof? She wanted to flee but was rooted in place.

CHAPTER
TWELVE

The lights were dim, the machines quietly whirring and dinging in the background as Jett stood in the hallway. Dustin Tate lay against the stark white hospital sheets, eyes closed and face pale where it wasn't bruised. Savannah Daniels stood in a corner, looking ready to bolt, yet frozen.

Jett wouldn't march into the room without knowing what he was walking into.

Dustin opened his eyes and studied Savannah, somehow missing Jett standing just outside. "I was awful to you."

"What?" Savannah took a step back as if unprepared to hear him.

"After 9/11. I needed you and you were busy with everything else."

"Law school claimed too much of my life." She eased onto the edge of a chair beside his bed. "I guess it was how I coped."

"Still, you didn't deserve me turning to Stasi. I should have fought harder for us." He reached for her hand and she took it. "I'm sorry."

Her face blanched and she tugged her hand loose. "It's too late."

"Never." He shook his head. "I won't believe it's too late to make us right."

There was a longing on her face, like she wanted to believe him, but then she stood and spun through the door, bumping off Jett without seeming to register who he was.

But Dustin did. His brow furrowed and he sighed. "You."

The man looked tired and battered, with harsh bruises appearing on his face and arms.

"What . . ." He swallowed hard, then tried again. "What are you doing here?"

"Color me curious." Jett tilted his chin as he took the seat next to the bed. "Heard you survived today's flight. That must have been something."

The man stared at him. Then his vision seemed to cloud as if he was seeing the short flight in his mind. "Couldn't have been in the air a minute."

"What do you think happened?"

"What?"

"You're a Western World pilot. Surely you have an idea."

"No way I'm talking about that with you."

"Why not?"

"I don't trust you." Dustin's expression took on an exhausted intensity.

Jett glanced away from the glare and noted the TV was on an ad about some kind of medication only old people needed. He eased his hands into his pockets and forced his attention back to the bed. "How did you get out?"

"It doesn't matter."

Jett leaned closer to hear. "What?"

"It doesn't matter. A lot of people died today. The fact I somehow survived doesn't make me news." He swallowed hard as if fighting emotion. "I knew the captain. She was skilled and had a clean record. Her kids are in elementary school."

Jett rubbed his neck as he wrestled back his own thoughts of how many families had been changed forever by the accident. "Where were you headed today?"

"A meeting." The words were clipped and short.

"With Logan?"

"Yep."

"And you didn't fly?"

"No." He snorted. "Even pilots get the day off."

"Tell me about the crash."

Color flared into Dustin's face and his fingers stretched for the call button. "Nothing doing."

Jett was running out of time before he had a nurse racing into the room. "What do you want to know? You've been stuck here since you were found at the crash. There has to be something you'd like to be updated about."

Dustin rolled his eyes, then seemed to stare into the distance. Jett was about to give up when he spoke. "Did Logan make it?"

Jett leaned back. "You haven't heard?"

"No. The chaos was . . . intense. The water started rushing in from every direction. It was . . . chaos."

Jett pulled out his phone and pulled up the manifest Chase had given him.

Jett sighed as he slowly scanned the list of names on his small screen. So many souls on that plane. He glanced up to find Dustin's gaze riveted on him. "We don't have a list of fatalities. Was the flight full?"

"Probably two-thirds."

"That's good. It could have been worse."

"Not for the folks who got bumped up from standby." Dustin cleared his throat. "We're all one choice from a life change."

Jett let that bounce around his mind, locking it into his memory. "Can I quote you?"

"Like you need permission."

Jett stiffened. "What does that mean?"

"Do you understand the harm your lies have caused? Unfortunately, people still believe what they read in newspapers. You'd think fake news would cure everyone of believing anything. I won't believe anymore." He grabbed the call button and pushed it. "If the airline fires me over your article, I'll be suing you and that newspaper."

Jett pushed to his feet but couldn't leave. Not without asking one more question. "What's the fourth man's name?"

"What?"

"The fourth man who joins your Thailand trips?"

There was a flash of something like incredulity on Dustin's face, but Jett couldn't identify it before it was gone. "I'm done talking." He reached for the jug of water on his bedside table. Took a sip while Jett waited . . . for something, hoping the silence would encourage Dustin to keep talking. Dustin finally said, "Have you ever walked up to someone's door with news you know will destroy their lives?"

Jett's brow wrinkled as he tried to connect the words to what they'd been discussing.

"You knock on it while you pray to God no one answers, but He's not merciful enough to have them be away. Instead, you're the one who has to break the news their loved one is gone. It's the kind of thing you never want to do, but you don't always have a choice."

"I'm sorry." Jett wanted to pretend the strong hospital smell was getting to him, but that was a lie. Instead it was the image of coming home and finding his father in the garage. The man hadn't wanted to leave a mess for his wife, but he hadn't minded killing himself in a place his twelve-year-old son would find his body when he got home from school.

Jett tried to shake off the memory that still haunted his nightmares. He'd learned some memories never disappeared. They could destroy waking moments as often as sleep.

"Do you understand the way my daughter looked at me when I dropped by last night? She believes you over what she knows about me."

"Every word is true."

"No. Remember, it's my life you're destroying." Dustin flung the jug at Jett. The lid popped off, dousing Jett with water.

He sputtered and wiped the water from his face. He stepped toward the room's sink and grabbed paper towels. His gaze landed on a purse, one he'd seen hanging on the back of Savannah Daniel's office door. She must have left it.

"Savannah left her purse."

Dustin growled. "How do you know it's hers? Have you been spying on her too?"

"Not spying." Just being observant. Noticing the details. "I'd better get it to her."

Dustin rolled his eyes. "Sure."

"Why didn't you two last?" Jett stopped himself before he could say anything else ridiculous. "Never mind."

"She was a bulldog. Didn't have the ability to step away from a challenge. I was tired of competing with that." He sighed and then his eyes slid shut. "It was exhausting."

There was a sound outside the room, and Jett turned in time to see a swirl of color as a woman headed down the hall.

CHAPTER
THIRTEEN

Dustin's words, so different from the ones he'd said to Savannah, knifed through her. Was he trying to spin things for the reporter? Make it look like everything had been her fault, leaving Dustin as the victim? The thought hurt, and she should be glad she was free.

Yet the words pierced.

All she'd wanted was to slide in and sneak her purse out without another interaction. She needed space and rest, but now she'd have to engage with Jett Glover again. She didn't have the reserves.

She did not want to spar with anyone. She just wanted to get home to her cat, Rhett, and put the day behind her.

Out of sight of Dustin's room, she slumped against the wall. What now?

Jett stepped out of Dustin's room. His charming smile would dazzle someone who wasn't as worn as she was. Would anything remove his smiling veneer before she decided he was as perfect as the image he portrayed?

———

A war of emotions flashed across Savannah Daniels's face as she spotted him.

"Hey, just the woman I was looking for." Her purse swung from his fingertips like a pendulum.

She sort of grimaced but then smiled, a little forced around the edges. "The words I wanted to hear."

"I think you left this."

"Thank you. I was headed to get it." Her eyes were hooded and her shoulders sagged. She looked exhausted. "Dustin might be telling the truth."

Jett studied her. So she'd overheard part of their conversation. He shrugged like it was nothing important. "What do you mean?"

"He claims he has proof." Her lips quirked as if she knew something he didn't, which, considering the topic, was likely. "We'll see."

"Will you let me know if he does?"

She considered him. "Maybe, but he has to have something first."

He nodded but felt weighted like a barbell had been placed across his shoulders, pressing him down. "Would you tell your niece I'm sorry?" The words slipped out before he'd formed the thought.

She seemed to catch his surprise and gave a slow nod. "I'll tell her, but I wouldn't expect any more from her than her dad. As much as I'd love to listen to that conversation, I'll spare you the fireworks."

"The what?"

"Intense emotions. She's a fourteen-year-old girl. Emotions all over on the best of days, and your article ruined that for at least a week."

Fair enough. Time to restart this conversation. "We've gotten off on the wrong foot." He waggled his fingers in front of the attorney and applied his best cocky, trust-me grin. "I'm Jett Glover, a man who's obsessed with the truth."

She left his hand hanging there as she looked away. "I've heard more convincing lies from defendants. You really need to work on your technique."

Her words stung. "Thanks for the tip."

"Well, thanks for bringing me this." She held up her purse. "Good-bye."

He watched her walk off. He had the desire to follow her, but she'd take it as hounding. The beauty had no interest in him. Not that he had an interest in her. He wanted to slap that idea from his thoughts.

Time to do anything else.

He glanced at his phone, but still no return call from his caller. He left another message in case this one generated a response.

When he got home, he headed immediately to the woodshed. The only way to focus would be to run the plane along the wood. If he calmed his body with steady motions, maybe his mind would cooperate. After ten minutes of deliberate movement, his thoughts continued to swirl as if he had an IV of caffeine flowing straight into his bloodstream. At this rate, it would be a long, sleepless night.

He tried to direct his thoughts along the length of the board but cycled through the interviews he'd conducted over the last two days.

Logan Donnelly and Dustin Tate had grown up in the same neighborhood, but Dustin had been friends with Logan's older brother, Tyler. Tyler had joined the military with Dustin, then died on a tour of duty in the Middle East. At that time, Dustin stepped into the role of big brother for Logan, who had been eight years younger than his hero brother. Jett had seen a couple of photos of the two together when he'd tracked down Logan's old Sunday school teacher. The sixtyish woman had taught the same class to thirteen-year-olds for twenty years. Her stories about Dustin and Logan had been entertaining.

Typical boys.

Then he'd tracked down a couple of guys Logan had played with in high school. Same story, different voices.

Everything indicated the move to the major leagues and an extravagant lifestyle changed the man, though he maintained a facade of good character.

Jett himself hadn't believed the story until he received the USB drive with video of Donnelly negotiating with a pimp.

It validated other evidence that Logan had changed. He had a ream of paper filled with flight manifests and other details he'd put together while in Thailand. He'd retraced the team's itinerary on two of their trips. Each one followed a disturbing pattern. Purchase the penthouse suite of a hotel that catered to rich foreigners. Throw an extravagant party. Watch the girls come in. And then it got hazy.

Until the video.

Then the truth was in pixelated black and white.

Dustin's fall had been more circuitous.

Jett's wood plane skipped on the board as he thought of the man's ex-wife.

Dustin had started well. He married the moment he finished undergrad while his new wife was still a student. Then she'd gone to law school while he was deployed as a pilot. It seemed 9/11 undid him. He headed out on another deployment and left the divorce paperwork for her to deal with.

Dustin lost his way for a few years as he completed his commitment to the Air Force. He rebounded after that, getting the job with Western World and seeming to fly a straight if lonely course.

The plane skipped again. Jett straightened, then twisted to ease the tension in his back. His attention had wavered, and now he'd have to resmooth this area. If he was lucky, he wouldn't have to replane the entire surface. If he did, the plank could end up being too thin.

He had mounds of evidence.

He thrust the plane away.

Time to get some sleep before he ruined the plank.

———

SATURDAY, DECEMBER 12

The next morning Jett headed in for another Saturday at the *Washington Source* offices.

A weekend in this city could either be sleepy or overwhelmed with news. This was the nation's capital after all. Even without a plane crash in the heart of the city, there would be the pressure to complete legislative work before both houses of Congress adjourned for the holiday season.

He planned to settle into his cubicle, put on his headphones, and make progress on crafting the follow-up story from his trip to Boston and the crash. First, he needed more coffee.

Chase sat in the small breakroom, but popped up the instant he spotted Jett. "Need some coffee?"

The kid had eager beaver written all over. *Wonder how long it will take for that to be beaten out of him by the cutthroat pace and business of journalism.* "I can get my own. Thanks." He gave the kid a wry grin and stepped to the old-school coffeemaker.

As it hissed and brewed, Chase didn't return to his seat. "I've been wondering something, Mr. Glover."

"What's that?"

"Where's Logan Donnelly? He hasn't turned up since the crash."

"Hopefully he's in a hospital recovering." He wouldn't wish anything else on the man, no matter what he'd done in Asia.

"I thought so too." Chase pulled a notepad from the table. "Except I've called all the local hospitals. Nothing doing. Can't find him."

"Or you're reaching people who are concerned about violating privacy."

"Sure. But all I'm finding is this." The kid took his cell phone from his back pocket and pulled up a video. "Watch."

Jett stepped closer and leaned forward. Jett had driven on the

Fourteenth Street Bridge earlier in the week and could imagine the scene clearly. The bridge had three spans, each with multiple lanes. As a main artery into the capital, it usually had heavy traffic with planes taking off and landing at Reagan National in the background. The video had been filmed from the bridge, and showed a man helping survivors out of the plane into the river. One woman floundered in the water, and he pulled her to the surface and secured a life vest on her. Looking heroic.

No, being heroic.

Jett squinted as the video played again. Yep, it was Donnelly.

The short video ended with Logan still in the water, but it was clear he had survived the crash. "Have you checked his social media accounts?"

The kid rolled his eyes as if that was a dumb question. Maybe it was. "Of course. No activity since your article broke."

"All right. I'll keep digging too. We'll find him." After he filled a coffee mug with the fresh brew, Jett wandered through the hive of cubicles in the newsroom. The cacophony that buzzed around him indicated it would be a busy news day. The aroma of too much perfume blended with a locker room assaulted his nose. Seemed like a few had come straight from the gym, something Ted wouldn't like. It might be Saturday, but that didn't slack the normal workday expectations.

After he reached his cubicle and booted his laptop, he pulled up notes on one half of the monitor and a blank document for the new story on the other half. Then he did a quick search of Logan's social media accounts. It was possible Chase had missed something important. After twenty minutes of clicking around, Jett had to admit the kid was right because he couldn't find a post made in the last two days. Logan's last post had been immediately after Jett's story hit the web on Wednesday. That one had been a quick tweet that the story was inaccurate and incomplete. A flash of frustration climbed Jett's neck. He'd tried to interview Logan prior to the release of the story, but the man had been obstinately silent. He clenched his jaw as he sent a direct message to the man with what must be the tenth invitation to tell his side of the story, but as he clicked send, he didn't expect a reply.

He went back and did a general search on Twitter. He noticed a recurring tweet with a link to his article. The tweet was odd but had the same weird tone and misspelling of the one he'd noticed earlier.

> Harm the innocent and you'll get your due. If not from God then from those who avenge the damaged and abused. The crash was God's judgment, but next time it will be mine. The trueth will be revealed.

Jett sank against his seat back. That tweet contained a lot of angry emotion. He clicked on the handle, UndergroundVigil486, no one visible using it. No picture, no mini-bio.

Was it a simple troll?

Maybe, but the anger reflected in the words felt connected to a living, breathing person. The questions were who and if it even mattered.

The background of clacking keys and voices ebbed, and Jett looked out of his cube to see Ted had stepped out of his office. "Editorial meeting in five."

Good. That gave him time to try his mystery caller's number again.

The call bounced to voice mail. Maybe it was a burner phone or something similar that the man didn't check often. Jett left a message anyway.

"Glover." Ted did not sound happy. Great.

CHAPTER
FOURTEEN

Jett double-timed it to the conference room. The force in Ted's voice warned today was not the day to stroll into the meeting just on time. A large walnut table anchored the space, with sixteen chairs crammed around it. Jett decided to stand. He'd spent too much time sitting in the car or at his desk. Leaning against the wall felt good, and he liked the vantage point that allowed him to see every facial expression and movement.

Sometimes what wasn't said revealed more than what was. Those nuances were key and could give him an advantage.

"Jett." Brett Sanderson, the walking Pulitzer prize, leaned against the wall next to him. The man was in his late thirties and had the glow of a career that had been touched by journalism gold. As a graduate student at a top journalism school, he'd been part of an investigative team that won a Pulitzer. Then lightning struck again when the man stumbled onto a Wall Street scandal that bled onto Capitol Hill and turned into that award last year.

Jett wasn't jealous. Much. He forced a grin. "Whatcha working on?"

"Flight 2840. My contacts in the agencies are tight-lipped about causes."

"Can't say I'm surprised." He maintained a nonchalant air as he studied Brett from the corner of his eye.

"Sure, but usually I can get a whiff of which way they're leaning. This time nothing."

"It's only been forty-eight hours. These investigations take weeks. Any thoughts?"

"Not sure. Just glad it wasn't terrorism. Have you seen a fatality list?"

"No. Thinking it's long since it hasn't released yet. Bet it has a few politicos and local celebrities."

Brett snorted, a rough sound that belied his urban air with a goatee that was perfectly trimmed and tortoiseshell glasses. "What plane flying out of DC doesn't?"

"You've got me there."

The man crossed his arms and shifted as Ted strode into the room. So much for hoping Brett would take the last empty chair at the table. "Lance thinks you've got an award hinging on the Donnelly piece. Good work."

"Thanks." Jett didn't want to acknowledge how much he hoped the same. "Can't control the awards."

"You can write a story that screams 'recognize me.' You've checked that box."

"Maybe." He wouldn't hang his hat on it even if he held a spot on his wall for the picture of him receiving his Pulitzer. Would that get Savannah's attention? He froze. Why did he care? Other than she was accomplished and he wanted to catch her eye. "Not all of us are lucky."

Brett's shoulders tightened and his eyes narrowed. "Luck didn't have a thing to do with it."

"You're right." Jett covered a yawn. All he had for his time at the hospital last night was an exhaustion hangover and time with a spitfire. "What's your working theory?"

"Not sure. Maybe human error."

"Really? Not ice?"

Brett stroked his goatee. "Maybe, but don't think so. Call it a feeling."

"Not buying it." No way would Brett say something that certain without evidence.

The man tipped his head closer to Jett. "My source in the State Department let it slip last night over drinks. The only person who talked. Off the record of course."

"Always." This was too important not to press hard for confirmation.

"He said it while bemoaning the loss of the beautiful undersecretary, who had a seat on the plane. Guess they were close." He waggled his eyebrows in a way that made it impossible to miss his meaning.

"You mean they had an affair."

"If you need it spelled out, yes."

The woman had been reckless to get embroiled in something that could compromise her career and security clearance. "Where does your source work?"

"Terrorism task force. Says the crash is definitely not his area. No groups claiming credit, so pilot error or equipment failure."

"Sounds like he'd know."

"Yep. But look at the passenger manifest. That dictates a comprehensive and fast response."

Jett nodded, but fast also meant margin of error. Something that couldn't be allowed on a disaster like this. It was tragic as an accident. It was response worthy as terrorism. With both Donnelly and Tate on the flight, he'd leave the actual crash investigation to other reporters. Unless assigned by Ted, he'd investigate the angles related to the passengers that featured in his investigation. He still had a week for follow-ups.

Ted cleared his throat and placed his hands on his hips. His expression was stern, especially for a Saturday where he'd called in a large number of the team. "I appreciate you coming in on the weekend. Good thing none of you signed on for a regular nine-to-five job. Let's go through assignments for today. It's going to be fast and furious as we work through plane crash coverage along with our regular slate of weekend news."

The next fifteen minutes were filled with the routine of schedules and story ideas. In a city as big and multifaceted as DC there were always events waiting to be covered and investigated. International affairs, domestic squabbles involving the three branches of government, run-of-the-mill crime, and local, national, and state politics. It was the city to be in if you wanted to be at the heart of the stories that impacted the world.

"Glover, I want you working with Sanderson on Flight 2840. You'll keep following Donnelly and Tate, and work with Sanderson on anything else that comes up related to the crash. Have Bowers and Penny help as needed."

Penny Sheldon bristled, and he didn't blame her. Lance consistently used the guys' last names and her first. Nothing like calling out her gender in a word.

"On it." Sanderson nudged him. "You and me. We got this."

Penny looked up from her phone. "Rumor has it Donnelly didn't survive." She showed the screen to Jett. "Guess he died to save the woman in the video."

———

MONDAY, DECEMBER 14

Over the snowy weekend news headlines and social media had lit up with the news that Logan Donnelly had perished in the Potomac. Savannah had repeatedly watched the dramatic footage of him helping a woman escape the sinking fuselage. Posts all over social media were calling him a hero who laid down his life for another. Her gut had clenched as she watched him thrust the woman onto a flotation device while it was clear he was worn out by the cold waters.

Who was he?

She couldn't reconcile the man in Jett Glover's article with the man in the video. Maybe it would make more sense when she had whatever proof Dustin had mentioned at the hospital.

The morning coffee conversation at the firm had surrounded those who'd died, a list of eighty-five souls including the undersecretary of state and the chief of staff for a congressman, someone Hayden knew thanks to Andrew, her fiancé. Savannah had watched a video put together by one of the news outlets of the names and images of those who had perished with tears in her eyes. Early speculation was that many had died on impact, while those closest to where the plane broke apart may have died from drowning.

Divers were still searching in the icy Potomac for the black box that would explain what had happened in the cockpit in the minutes leading up to the crash.

This was why the technology her clients were developing mattered. If Flight 2840 had used Mnemosyne's black-box alternative, maybe the cause would already be determined. The case needed to settle.

She picked up her phone and placed a call to Reginald Nash. The man wasn't thrilled to hear from her.

"Come on, Reggie. Let's get this resolved so both our clients can get on with their core work." She crossed her fingers but didn't harbor high expectations.

"Not now. My client is adamant. They won't do anything until mediation is complete."

"We're two smart attorneys. We can get them to settlement without Mr. Garbot."

"They're adamant, Savannah. No deal." There was no margin for argument in Nash's voice.

"But Garbot is unavailable." Indefinitely, according to his assistant, but Savannah would let Nash figure that out on his own. Since the man's wife was on the list of those who died, Savannah couldn't press for him to resume the mediation, not yet.

"I'm sorry, but no meeting. If you want to send a settlement offer over, I will convey it to my client as I must, but short of your client giving them the patent, it won't go far."

Savannah bit back a sputter. Did Nash think he had something on Garbot that would make the mediator take his client's side? It was the only thing that made sense. "Expect something in the mail."

A moment later he'd hung up, and Savannah stared at the phone. A quick call to Rochelle and John, and Belle was drafting the settlement offer. Savannah wanted to believe the settlement offer would be considered but feared it was just another delay tactic. If it was, it added to the story of their competitor's unreasonableness they'd eventually tell in mediation or court.

At lunchtime she slipped on tennis shoes and walked across Old Town to Founder's Park along the Potomac. She needed to feel the sun on her face and the breeze off the river. Across the water's expanse she could make out the joint Navy and Air Force base at Anacostia-Bolling. Then she kept walking until she reached a bench from which she could barely make out the Fourteenth Street Bridge. She'd heard it would fully reopen by the evening rush hour. It had taken several days for the Army Corps of Engineers to confirm the structural integrity of the bridge after the plane careened off it, and now the sides were being strengthened in a couple of places. Thanks to diverted traffic, her Monday-morning commute had taken twice as long as usual even though her route was only five miles.

As she sank onto a park bench and let the sounds of chirping birds and lapping waves roll around her, she was overwhelmed with gratitude. She was blessed to live in this city. She should be content with her life. Then why wasn't she?

The question ricocheted around her mind as she walked back to her firm and slipped inside the back door. Before she could take off her sneakers and replace them with her usual low pumps, Bella paged her phone.

"A client is here to see you."

"Did I forget an appointment?" Savannah woke up her computer and pulled up her calendar. "Calendar says I'm free until three."

"Rochelle is here and says it can't wait."

"Okay, send her back. Is John with her?"

"Not this time."

"Thanks." Savannah finished changing her shoes, slid the sneakers back in their bag, then put them in the bottom drawer of her desk. She was slipping her lipstick back in the top drawer when Rochelle knocked on her door. "Come on in."

Savannah appraised Rochelle as she walked into the room. Today, Rochelle was wearing jeans with strategic rips and lace along with a maroon hooded sweatshirt emblazoned with University of Siena. Her hair was pulled back in a messy bun, and she wore a floral backpack slung across her shoulders. The combination made her look like an undergrad at one of the many local universities rather than a forty-something start-up executive.

The woman perched on the edge of one of the chairs in front of Savannah's desk and then slid the backpack off.

Savannah waited to hear why Rochelle had come without an appointment.

Rochelle unzipped the top of her bag, pulled out a folder, and slid it across the desk. "We got this today."

The world was smiling on him.

It felt like a sign.

The scum may not have been part of his daughter's disappearance, but he participated.

The article made that much clear.

Men like him were the reason his baby had been stolen, broken, destroyed.

Now it was his turn.

He forced his thoughts to harden, hone in on a plan. This was not the time to let emotion overcome him. No, it was time for iron-clad logic, the kind that led from point A to B to C all the way to the inevitable conclusion.

Care was needed. Deliberate pacing. This opportunity wouldn't come easily a second time.

He must be quick. But he must not be reckless.

This man was the one he could reach. And if he died, the others' pursuit of evil would be slowed. They wouldn't be able to harm other girls so easily.

He could not protect his Gracie, but he could protect others.

He would.

His resolve hardened. This was right. It was his call and he would answer. It was the least he could do and the most. Gracie was lost. But the others weren't, not if he acted now.

First to find the man's residence.

When the pilot was released from the hospital, quickness would matter while the man was still weak. Surviving the crash might mean he'd sidestepped God's judgment for the moment, but he wouldn't avoid it again.

When he executed his own judgment.

CHAPTER
FIFTEEN

Savannah eyed Rochelle's envelope before picking it up. "What's this?"

"A subpoena. The FBI wants access to our code."

Savannah frowned as she opened the folder. "Why?"

Rochelle shrugged, her blonde bob swaying as she looked away. "I think it's related to the crash."

"The Fourteenth Street Bridge crash?" Rochelle nodded, and Savannah pulled the subpoena from the envelope. "Why?"

Rochelle rubbed her hands together as if trying to get warm, not hard to imagine with the threat of snow in the forecast again. "I think they're fishing for information."

"What kind of information?"

"John and I aren't sure."

Savannah pinched the bridge of her nose. "There must be a reason. Help me speculate."

"My guess? They want us to recreate what happened on Flight 2840. They don't have the flight's black box yet. In theory we could shadow a flight and simulate what really happened."

"Can you do that if the technology wasn't on board?"

Rochelle shrugged but still didn't make eye contact. "John insists we can. Before the injunction we tested that capability on a few flights for Air Express. In theory it wouldn't be hard to reverse engineer modeling to determine what could have caused the crash. It could be as simple as lack of proper deicing. The weather changed over the course of the morning, creating an urgency to get flights off before the airport could be shut down."

"It closed because of the crash."

"Yes, but it might have closed anyway because of the weather. Dulles was closed, and so was BWI."

Savannah sped read the subpoena. The language left little room for evasion. "The FBI wants your software."

"They can't have it. That software is our business. It's why we've been sued. If that's released we're done." Rochelle's words were sharp. "If we comply, our competitors won't have to reverse engineer our software. The government can hand deliver it to them. At that point we might as well lock our doors and send our employees home."

Savannah leaned forward and studied her client. "Rochelle, do you understand how crazy that sounds?"

"Yes." The woman didn't elaborate, letting the word hang in the air.

"You're responding to a government demand. If you don't, you're breaking the law."

"And if I comply, then our code is public."

"It's not."

"There's nothing to prevent its release through a Freedom of Information Act request. I don't see grounds under that to keep it secure."

Savannah pulled up a quick search on FOIA exemptions. "That's not true. There's an exemption for anything related to trade secrets and commercial information obtained from a private source that would cause competitive harm. That's this exact situation. You have to turn it over."

Rochelle crossed her arms but didn't say a word.

Savannah didn't rush to fill the void, but Rochelle remained stubbornly silent. Savannah shook her head and picked up the subpoena.

It was standard except for the demand time. "You only have until Thursday to comply. That's three days."

"We can't respond that fast."

Savannah reread the subpoena. "I'll call the listed attorney. See if we can negotiate more time. Since this request is part of an active investigation, I'm not sure we'll be successful."

"I can wait."

Something was . . . off. Savannah considered her client. "What aren't you telling me?"

"I'm telling you all that I can. At least right now." Rochelle looked away, and her fingers plucked at her sweatshirt's hem.

Savannah cocked her head. "Something is bothering you."

Rochelle's gaze snapped back to Savannah. "This whole mess is about to kill the company I've invested my life savings in, not to mention many of my family members' savings. That allows me to be on edge."

If she could have, Savannah would have taken a step back to create space between them. "I'll call and see what I can do." She picked up the phone and dialed the number listed on the subpoena. She left a voice mail for the attorney, then turned back to Rochelle. "I'll let you know as soon as I hear back, promise. Until then, I need you to start compiling the documents listed in the subpoena. Collect everything and then we'll go through it all here. I don't want you to self-select what you exclude."

"We can't comply in time."

"You'll have to." Savannah waited a beat. "We'll start in the morning. Bring the code here, and we'll prepare the response."

Rochelle stood and gathered her large bag. "Thanks for your time. I'd better get back to work."

Savannah stood quickly, bumping her shin against the desk's leg. "Let me make a photocopy of this before you leave."

"Already did. You get to keep that one." Rochelle headed out the door without a backward glance. After she disappeared into the hallway, Savannah kept watching, her thoughts spinning.

Something was going on because Rochelle had become hostile, and that wasn't like the woman. There was no getting around it. Savannah needed to talk to John and get his take on the impact of the subpoena. She picked up her phone and dialed his number.

He answered without preamble. "You talk to Rochelle?"

"Yes." She paused. "The live tests of your software stopped with the injunction."

"Just like we told you." She could almost hear his eyes roll. "Why are you still asking?"

"Then why is the FBI subpoenaing your code?"

"They're desperate for answers on what caused the crash. If they get our product, it can run simulations."

"But other products exist for that."

"Sure, but not as good as ours."

She had to smile. Confidence wasn't an issue for John. "Then complying helps."

There was a rustling sound. "No. It'll kill us. That piece is tied to the code the black box feeds directly to the satellite. We can't separate the two."

"All right." Savannah bit her lower lip as she tried to evaluate what she'd heard. "Thanks. I'll see you tomorrow when we start going through your production for the subpoena."

"You can't get it extended?"

"Not yet."

"Then what are we paying you for?" He slammed down the phone, and she jumped.

Why were her clients giving in to the stress now? This behavior from both was out of character. She rubbed her temples and then pulled the subpoena back in front of her. It didn't matter how many times she read it, the words couldn't be clearer.

Mnemosyne had to turn over the requested documents and information.

Late that afternoon, she got a call back from the agency's attorney, and then relayed the message that her clients had until Friday. The government had graciously agreed to extend their deadline by one day. Rochelle objected, but Savannah told her to be at the office at eight in the morning with all the paper documentation they had. As soon as the code was clean, they'd walk through that too. These document requests were huge time drains that had to be managed well so the right documents and information were released without inadvertently sending items that were outside the scope of the subpoena.

Savannah left the office at six. Ready or not, it was time to check on Stasi and Addy and then maybe relax a bit.

She called and Addy informed her she'd already placed the to-go order for their supper. Savannah was to stop and pick up Mexican from their favorite hole-in-the-wall on her way.

"Please." Addy's assured tone communicated she knew Savannah would do whatever she asked. "It'll be ready at six thirty."

"Really?" Savannah couldn't help smiling at her niece's pleased tone. "Why did you pick that time?"

"Because you said you'd check on us right after work. I knew you thought that would be fiveish, but we'd be lucky if you left at six."

The words stung. "Guess I get caught up in my work a lot, huh?"

"It's okay, Aunt Savvy. You do important work. Besides, I'm used to waiting."

Savannah rubbed over her heart where it felt like an arrow had zinged her. "You aren't holding anything back."

"And it won't stop unless you add guacamole to the order. Mom said I couldn't."

Savannah chuckled. "Nothing like a little extortion."

"But avocado is good for you."

"So they say."

"Please?"

"All right. Avocados are good fat."

Twenty minutes later Savannah ordered guacamole and settled in to wait at the bustling restaurant. Despite Addy's valiant effort to order ahead, the food hadn't been ready when she arrived. She enjoyed a Coke while she scrolled through her Instagram feed. She really needed to add some shots of Rhett, but that would require her to catch her shelter kitty doing something adorable, which necessitated being home. She inhaled the aroma of spicy food and listened to a soundtrack of "Feliz Navidad," hustling servers, and happy patrons.

Fifteen minutes later she carried two bags of steaming food to her car, and it was still piping hot when she got to Addy and Stasi's apartment. With her hands full, she leaned into the doorbell, and a minute later Addy opened the door. Her eyes had purple splotches underneath them as if she hadn't slept well. Still, they lit up, whether at the sight of Savannah or the food, Savannah wasn't sure.

Addy gave her a quick squeeze and then grabbed the bags. "I'll put these on the table."

"Thanks. Where's your mom?"

"On the couch." Addy said it with a where-else-would-she-be air.

Savannah stepped toward the couch and noted the heavy floral scent hanging in the air. A candle flickered next to the TV, lending ambiance to the space IKEA built. Savannah spotted Stasi crashed on the couch with a blanket their grandma had crocheted pulled over her shoulders, her eyes closed. The blanket signaled it had been a rough day for Stasi, but Savannah couldn't wait for a good day for the conversation they needed to have. "Someday you have to get a job, sis."

Stasi shifted, but didn't open her eyes. "That's why I've got you and Dustin."

"That doesn't leave me feeling used."

"No need to be sarcastic." Stasi stretched and sat up. "Am I smelling food? Took long enough."

Savannah held back a hard response. "Addy ordered enough for a platoon."

"Did not." Addy's voice came from the small galley kitchen. "I'm a teenage girl."

"And that explains everything." Stasi smiled. "You are the best thing that ever happened to me, kiddo."

"I know." Addy leaned out of the kitchen with a smile before disappearing again.

"Humble too." Stasi patted the couch next to her. "Savannah, you have to quit worrying about us."

Savannah eased next to her sister. "That's not easy to do when I get calls like I did from Addy." She hadn't made time to call Stasi on it when they were at the hospital, but Stasi had to stabilize.

"She worries too much."

"She shouldn't have to think about whether you're okay." Savannah studied her sister, noted the wrinkles that feathered her face, a signal of a life lived hard. "You aren't okay."

"The doctors aren't helping manage my pain." It was an old story about how she'd never recovered from a back injury at work.

"But you can't self-medicate at the expense of your daughter."

"Don't forget I'm the mother. You chose not to have kids." The words hit. Hard. "All that matters is she'll always be fine."

"What does that mean?" Stasi wasn't making sense.

"Dustin has a life insurance policy on each of us for Addy's benefit. He might not have married me, but he's made sure she'll be all right."

"That's a morbid thought."

Stasi rolled her eyes. "You should be happy, Miss Risk Adverse Attorney."

"I will be when you start acting like the mother Addy deserves."

"We aren't all perfect. Oh, wait. You aren't either or you wouldn't have chased Dustin off. Then Addy would be yours instead of mine." The I-won tone made Savannah want to walk out and leave.

Addy stepped out of the kitchen precariously carrying three glasses of water. Savannah watched her, heart aching.

"Have you heard from Dustin today? Is he out of the hospital?" She wished she could reclaim the words the moment she spoke them.

Stasi stayed quiet, but Addy shrugged her thin shoulders. "Not today."

"That must mean he's fine."

Addy put napkins on the table as if it was no big deal that her dad had survived a plane crash and hadn't called, but Savannah knew how much the girl wanted time with him. The man wasn't perfect, but he was her dad.

"Let's eat while it's still hot."

Stasi waved her away. "I'll join you in a bit."

Savannah turned to Addy and mouthed, *Is she okay?*

Addy glanced at Savannah. "While I was at school Dad called and asked if I could spend the night at his place tomorrow."

"On a Tuesday?" A school night. That didn't seem like a great idea.

"I know how to get to bed on time and get up for school. I can even order an Uber if I need a ride."

"Or call your aunt to get you. You know I don't like you getting in a stranger's car." She'd read too many articles about people getting into what they thought was a car share, only to have something terrible happen.

Addy rolled her eyes as she ran a chip through the queso. "I'll be fine. I can get a ride."

Savannah sighed. "I can do that." She just wouldn't go inside.

They were cleaning up dishes when her phone rang. The reporter? She sighed and may have rolled her eyes, though she'd deny it if Addy asked.

"Hello?"

"Savannah, Jett Glover. Wondered if you'd meet me for coffee?"

"Coffee?"

"Yes."

"Why?" She couldn't fathom why the man would be calling her. It wasn't like she'd been friendly or helpful.

"I know this great coffee shop near your office." He paused, then hurried on, and there was a confident assurance in his voice that she would say yes. If only he understood how much that assured she'd say the opposite. "They have a great pain au chocolat. Want to meet me there at eight tomorrow?"

"I'm at work by seven."

"All the better to take a coffee break at eight."

"I have a client coming in." A client who still had a lot of explaining to do about why they hid the fact that their tech would be interesting to the FBI.

"I'll bring it to you then. At seven thirty. Before they arrive. Have a great night."

Before she could say a word, he hung up. She stared at the phone as Addy grinned at her.

"You have a date." The girl's smile was big enough to crack her face in two.

"Why is that so amusing?"

"Because you avoid men, but this one you like."

Savannah wanted to pretend it wasn't true, but truth was a high value to her. So she said nothing but pulled Addy into a side hug and then tickled her niece until she squealed.

Jett might come, but that didn't mean she'd let him in.

CHAPTER
SIXTEEN

Front or back?

The lobby looked locked down, so Jett walked around the building and through the parking lot to the law firm's rear entrance. The lone car indicated that Savannah was the only one inside, which didn't bode well for him getting in. But if she really did have an appointment at eight, someone would arrive soon. He balanced the drink carrier and bag in one hand and used the other to bang on the back door, but no one came.

Fine.

She'd learn how determined he could be. He tapped out a message on his phone with one hand, then waited a minute before calling her.

Her answer was exasperated. "You don't give up."

"Nope. I've got coffee and pastries." He tried to infuse his voice with a smile. His phone buzzed but he ignored it.

She sighed. "I don't have time."

Was that a hint of longing in her voice? A car pulled into the parking lot. He turned and watched a fiftyish woman—had to be the receptionist—get out of the sedan. She watched him closely, then shook her head with a smile. Yep, she was becoming an ally.

"At least let me give you the coffee. I shouldn't drink both." Or eat

115

both pastries, though he'd find a taker for one. Savannah sighed, but his attention was focused on the receptionist.

The woman pulled out her keys as she neared the door. "You have chutzpah." She unlocked the door and waved him in. "You remember where her office is?"

Not from this door, but it had to be the only one with its light on. "Thanks."

The woman rolled her eyes. "I don't know why I let you in, and if I lose my job, you'll hear from me."

"I'll make sure you don't."

"Sure you will. Be good to her." The woman straightened her black jacket and headed to the front, but paused. "She doesn't trust easily, so be gentle. You've got fifteen minutes until her clients arrive."

"She said eight."

"Let's just say they're early. Always." Without another word or a backward glance to see where he headed, she walked up the hallway to the reception area, turning on lights as she went.

He took a couple of steps toward the light-filled doorway. A moment later the stately attorney stood there. A beautiful authority about her made her intriguing but not hardened. "You know you didn't end the call? I heard every word."

He shrugged. "Guess I let you." He handed her the pastry bag emblazoned with the logo for Sips and Sweets. "If you've never had one, you'll love the pain au chocolat. Nothing like a fresh French pastry."

She quirked an eyebrow. "How long do you think I've had an office here?"

"No idea."

"Long enough to have tried every coffee shop in a two-mile radius. Trust me, I've been there multiple times."

"And you love the pastries."

She finally cracked a smile, though she kept it contained. "I guess I do." She opened the bag and took a whiff, then sighed. "This is perfect for this morning. Thank you."

"You're welcome." Jett resisted the urge to fist pump. "Where would you like the coffee?"

"My office is fine." She stepped back to let him in and eyed the carrier but didn't help herself to a cup. She was the picture of restraint. Interesting. "The name's always been a little odd to me. Like they should serve wine rather than coffee. Sips and Sweets." She rolled her eyes. The lady was really letting her guard down and he liked it.

"It fits." He lifted his cup in a silent toast. "Sips away." As he took a drink, he absorbed her office. The surfaces were clean except for one file that lay open on her desk. And the creamy yellow walls reminded him of fresh butter. There was something soothing yet energizing about the color, and the scent. "Are you diffusing oil?"

Pink tinged her neck as she glanced at her hutch. "Wild orange. It helps me wake up in the morning. Also makes me happy." She bared her teeth at him in a hideous grin that couldn't mask her quiet beauty. She'd have to try harder to discourage him from coming around. She sank into her chair and nibbled at the pastry. "Why are you here?"

Her look warned that she wouldn't tolerate anything but the truth.

"I got a call from a man on Thursday."

"So?"

"He claims I didn't get the article right." That still bothered him, because the article and its supporting research were rock solid and some of his best work.

"I'm still not sure why you're here."

"Do you mind if I sit?" She shrugged, so Jett handed her a to-go cup of latte and then sat on one of the chairs. "My article is accurate. I did all the research, and I was thorough. I can't reach the man who called me. Now that Donnelly's dead, that means Tate is my only bet for figuring out what he meant when he said I got the article wrong."

"He mentioned something similar to me."

"Did he tell you anything more?"

"No. It was a basic assertion he could prove the truth was different than your article."

His phone vibrated, the silent signal someone had left a message. "There are odd tweets too. Probably mean nothing, but I'd like to ask Tate his opinion."

She raised an eyebrow in a skeptical look but said nothing.

"They've got a misspelling."

"That makes them odd? You haven't read many tweets."

"How do you spell truth?"

"T-R-U-T-H."

"Right. These tweets spell it T-R-U-E-T-H."

"So the author thinks he or she is Shakespeare."

He chortled. "I had the same thought."

"Scary."

"Yeah." He sighed. Now came the ask. Always the hard part. "Dustin hasn't returned my calls."

She snorted. "You're surprised?"

"No, but I'd like to know what he thinks he has that proves there's more to the story."

"All you want me to do is smooth the way?" At his nod, she looked away.

What was going through her mind? Was there something else he could say that would convince her? Rather than speak he took a sip of his black Americano. He'd opted for a latte for Savannah, guessing she was neither a black coffee gal nor a frou-frou drink person.

Time ticked by, and he wondered if she'd simply stay silent. Then she nodded as if affirming her decision.

"All right."

"That's it? No demands?"

"It wouldn't change anything." She grabbed a pad of paper and scribbled a note. "I'll call Dustin when I can."

"Thank you." He wanted to press but her phone beeped. "Today would be helpful."

She nodded and held up the pastry. She mouthed *thank you* as she picked up the phone.

Hopefully that meant she'd have an answer from Tate today. Now to find a way to keep the investigation moving. He pulled out his phone and listened to the voice mail as he left her office.

"Look into the agency Light Comes After Darkness. CEO is Bernard Julius." The caller didn't leave a name, but it sounded like his mystery caller. He checked the number. Yep, the same. He called it back but again no one answered. He pushed through the firm's back door and resisted the urge to pound something. Fine, it would take more than that to deter him. And he had two possible leads to chase down.

———

Savannah barely had time to finish her pastry before Rochelle and John arrived, each carrying a couple of file boxes into the conference room where Emilie waited for them. Savannah texted Dustin a quick note while the trio got their boxes organized.

> Reporter really wants to talk about the evidence you have.
> Call him?

Then she shoved her phone in her pocket and turned off notifications on her watch with a vow to ignore it. She had a much larger problem in front of her.

Emilie wore a sheath dress the clear blue color of the spring sky and a chunky statement necklace in an effortless style. She eyed the boxes as John and Rochelle plopped them on the table. "How much did you bring?"

"About half of it." Rochelle wiped sweat from her forehead. "We're not sure how much of this we can keep from the FBI, but it's critical to keep as much of it as possible here."

"What do you mean?" Savannah leaned forward, an uncomfortable tingle warning her this wasn't going to be good.

"You're our attorney, so if we bring the code to you, you have to protect it." John gave a smug grin. "Attorney–client privilege."

"Do not replace my law degree with your Google search." Savannah stared at him, then at the boxes.

"What did you expect us to do? Bring you a bunch of random letters and files?" John snorted, and she resisted telling him that was exactly what she'd expected.

Savannah rubbed her eyes, but all the boxes were still there when she reopened them. "John, you are too smart to think I'll play games with the FBI." She turned to Rochelle. "If you want me to guide you through this, then you will handle this as I tell you. That will include giving up crazy ideas." She counted to ten. "Attorney–client privilege covers our communications. It covers what you say to me and the documents we use to communicate with each other, not every piece of paper you bring to me." She gestured to Emilie. "The two of us will go through these boxes with you. Then we'll determine what can be sent to the agency and how it will be framed. Are we clear?"

She stared at John until he nodded and then at Rochelle, who looked desperate. "Are you firing us?"

"Tempting as it is, no."

Rochelle's shoulders collapsed in relief. "We've got our chief tech guru working on the code while we're here. Tell us what to do."

"You're going to tell Emilie and me everything we need to know about what's in these boxes." She took a breath to steel herself. People assumed she loved confrontation because she was an attorney, but she hated stirring it up. "I need to know you are both being fully truthful with me. If I get any sense you aren't, you will work with the FBI on your own." She sank back into her seat. "Are we clear?"

"Yes." John nodded with a quick affirmation.

Rochelle studied her so long, Savannah wasn't sure the woman would comply. Then she straightened the bottom of her shirt and shifted on her seat. "All right. This subpoena has to be dealt with because it's dangerous to our business."

Emilie kept her hands placed lightly on top of her legal pad as she smiled at them. "Y'all have no idea how much Savannah understands. You aren't her first clients to find themselves in this position. It's why you chose this firm." She smiled in her sweet way, the one that cloaked her resolve. "Would you mind starting at the beginning so I'm up to speed?"

With thoughtful questions, Emilie probed the edges of their technology, and Savannah noticed Rochelle and John were getting better at clearly explaining it, a skill that would help them in future hearings.

"The system is designed to track flights via the satellite network. Data is streamed consistently throughout the flight, unlike current black boxes."

Emily looked up from her note-taking. "So entire flights are recorded?"

John nodded. "Well, most of it. It won't usually start until after the captain and first officer run preflight checklists." He ran his hands through his hair and then tapped the box closest to him. "Here's where it gets interesting."

Rochelle grimaced. "That's not the word I would use for it." She wouldn't meet Savannah's eyes as she continued. "Our test isn't supposed to be on big airlines yet."

"Right. Because of the injunction." Savannah had a bad feeling as she noted the awkwardness between the partners.

Rochelle swallowed hard. "We think Flight 2840 was recorded." She shook her head. "No, we're certain it was. But we don't know how."

"What do you mean?" Savannah didn't understand for the first time in the explanation.

Rochelle glanced at John and then at the box he was tapping. "We have data from the crash, and we shouldn't."

"You shouldn't have data from any flights."

"I know." Rochelle rubbed her forehead as if a headache throbbed there. "I was up all night trying to figure out what happened, but I can't."

"And the FBI knows." Lights were now dawning in Savannah's mind. "That's why they sent the subpoena."

"Which doesn't make sense either. If we didn't know, how could they?"

John rolled his eyes. "Which conspiracy theory would you like me to launch into?"

"None." Rochelle's words were sharp, like a mother speaking to an unruly child. "In addition to trying to figure out how this happened, we downloaded the flight data and ran a quick analysis."

Savannah held up a hand. "Back up. How did your tech get on that plane?"

John shrugged. "We don't know."

"Someone stole it, but I can't prove it yet." Rochelle looked miserable and exhausted.

Savannah stared at John and then at Rochelle, but neither blinked. What was she supposed to do with this information? "We will have to figure it out, because that's a violation of the court's injunction. But setting that aside for the moment, what's your conclusion about what caused the crash?"

John glanced at Rochelle, who held his gaze for a moment before turning to Savannah and really looking at her for the first time. "There's indication in the audio transmissions that the captain was distracted."

"What kind of indication?" It had better be good or they'd better be wrong.

"It's subtle. More than she missed rechecking the deicing. The plane was on the ground too long between deicing and takeoff." John's eyes almost glowed. "I'd bet money that when the investigation is over, the cause of this crash will be that simple."

Rochelle shivered. "Listening to the back and forth between the captain and first officer in the last minute is something I'll never forget."

Emilie glanced from Rochelle to John and back. "So it's not a function of stripping the code anymore. What we're doing is giving the FBI a transcript of the flight."

"And the code." Savannah tapped her pen against the table. "The subpoena was clear."

"Yes. And because this transcript could impact the investigation, I don't know how we can keep it from them." Rochelle grimaced and looked away.

"Does that really matter?"

John looked at Savannah like that was a crazy question and took over answering. "If our competitors realize how we've digitized everything and analyzed it so quickly, they won't give up on the infringement lawsuit. Instead they'll attack harder because this is the kind of disruptive tech that makes them irrelevant. If we win, they're done."

"I'm still not tracking." Savannah would play the dumb card if it meant getting a clear answer.

"There are indications the captain left the cockpit in the middle of the preflight check."

"That's unusual?"

Rochelle nodded and pulled a file from her top box. "Very. Once the flight check starts, protocol is for the captain and first officer to finish it without an interruption."

"And that led to eighty-five people's deaths?" This time the yes was much more reluctant. "How do you reach that conclusion?"

"The first officer was talking to himself about whether the weather required a second deicing. But he didn't mention that when the captain returned."

And then the flight crashed.

His credentials and access to resources would have made it easy enough to find Dustin Tate's home. But the pilot did nothing to secure his privacy. A fifth grader on a school computer could have found the address in a matter of minutes.

Security was lax at the building as if the pilot had nothing to fear and felt above all accountability for his sins.

That was fine. It had made it easy to substitute sleeping pills for the drugs the doctor had prescribed. Tonight the pilot would have a few moments of feeling weak, and then suffer the consequences for his evil.

He had considered everything. How to enter. How to exit. What to do. How to force Tate's hand to hold the blade. The man was just another weakling taking out his frustrations and appetites on those who were weaker still. But this time he would be faced by something stronger.

A father's rage.

While people talked about the protectiveness of a mother bear, it was nothing compared to the rage that churned through his veins. What had been bottled up for so long had reached volcanic levels.

He would no longer sit back and wait for someone else to act.

The release tonight was months too late, but it would come.

And when it did, justice would be served.

Truth would be unleashed.

He patted the envelope.

It contained a single sheet.

That's all he'd needed to itemize the man's crimes and his self-imposed punishment.

And when he was found?

Well, then the world would know the depths of this man's depravity and why a death sentence was the only justice.

CHAPTER
SEVENTEEN

Savannah dropped her work bag next to the door and kicked off her kitten heels, then leaned down to rub first one arch and then the other. She stepped into the slippers she left by the door each morning.

She felt . . . worn.

The document review with John and Rochelle had taken all day, and she had the clear sense her clients were lying to her. The question she couldn't answer was why.

Frankly, she'd been stunned by what the two had revealed.

They had a serious security breach if their tech was on that plane and they really didn't know how it got there. She wasn't sure she could defend Mnemosyne if she didn't understand what had transpired to get their software on that flight.

And she only had two days to figure out how much of their data had to be released to the FBI and what she could fight to keep hidden.

Life bordered on a tsunami that wanted to drown her in its waves.

Her phone rang from the depths of her purse. She didn't want to answer. Still, she dug for it and glanced at the screen.

Addy. The sight of her niece's goofy photo tugged a smile free. "Hello?"

"Hi, Aunt Savvy. You're still coming to take me to Dad's, right?"

Savannah's body sagged. "What time?"

"As soon as you can. I want to spend as much time with Dad as I can. It'll already be too short since I have school in the morning. You don't think . . ."

"No. You can't skip."

There was a small huff but nothing else from Addy.

"Give me thirty minutes and I'll be on my way. I just walked in the door."

"Thanks!" Her niece's voice vibrated with gratitude and enthusiasm, and then Savannah listened to nothing.

There was something to be said for having a strong persona, one that let people know she could handle life on her own. *Got something hard? Throw it at me. I can handle it.* But as she walked into the kitchen, she felt like she slogged through thick mud, and she couldn't pretend she was strong. A tear trailed down her cheek as her tuxedo cat meowed her way down the hallway. Another leaked out as Rhett stopped in front of her and raised to her hind legs, a plea to be picked up.

If only everything could be solved by reaching down and cuddling a cat.

Maybe that's what God wanted her to do.

She stroked Rhett's silky fur. There was something soothing about the simple motion. The feel of the smooth coat and the rumbled purr. Stopping at the Humane Society shelter to look at kittens with Addy had been an inspired decision.

Her phone rang again, and Savannah answered it without looking. "I promise I'll leave in fifteen minutes, Addy." She was just going to sit for a couple minutes. She sank onto the small leather love seat in her living room. Rhett settled in and placed her paws on Savannah's shoulders, then stared into her eyes, as if trying to communicate a deep truth.

"That's great, but I wondered if you could grab a gallon of milk on your way." Stasi's voice sounded like a command rather than a request.

"Not tonight." Stasi sputtered, but Savannah didn't care. "You can walk to the corner mart if you need one before the morning. See you soon."

She hung up, and Rhett licked her cheek. Something shifted in Savannah at the realization she'd said no. It felt so irresponsible, and good. Rhett hopped down and meowed before taking a step away, then meowed again.

She stood and followed the cat to the empty water bowl. "Looks like you're thirsty."

The cat wound between her legs, and Savannah high-stepped to avoid crushing her. After Savannah filled the bowl and set it down, she crouched next to her happily licking kitten. "Now what?"

The cat ignored her as she took delicate licks from the bowl.

"I'll go give Addy that ride I promised her. I'll be back as soon as I can." Savannah gave her one more long stroke down her back, and then pushed to a standing position.

WEDNESDAY, DECEMBER 16

What time was it?

The thought barely registered as Savannah's hand scrabbled across the top of her bedside table, groping for her phone. The chiming bells jarred as she tried to free herself from the tangle of blankets. It felt like she'd been swaddled, she was twisted so tightly into the sheets.

There.

Her fingers finally gripped the phone.

"Hello?" She cleared her throat and tried again. "Who is this?"

"Aunt Savannah? I need you."

At the panic in Addy Jo's voice, Savannah pushed to a sitting position against the fabric-covered headboard and brushed hair from her face. "What's wrong?"

"Dad's dead." The girl's voice broke. "Please come."

Savannah pushed her legs over the side of the bed, toes reaching for her slippers. "Where are you?"

"Still at his place." The girl's tone rose.

"Right. I knew that." She tried to clear the sleep from her mind. Catch up with what Addy said.

"There's so much blood." The last word dropped away, and Savannah prayed she hadn't heard correctly.

"What?"

"Blood. It's everywhere."

Savannah lurched to a seated position with her legs over the side of the bed. "I'm on my way. Have you called 911?"

"The police are here." Her voice faded, and Savannah heard a thump like the girl's arm had dropped to her side.

Oh, God. What on earth had happened? *Be with her until I can get there. Please.*

Savannah rushed to her closet and pulled a pair of jeans and a sweatshirt from a pile on the floor. She tucked her phone into her back pocket, then slipped her feet into moccasins and dashed to the hall. At the door she grabbed her keys and purse from the small table.

Rhett reached up to be held.

"Not now." She eased the cat to the side with her foot and then hurried out the front door to her parking spot. What had Addy stumbled into? What did she mean there was so much blood?

Her car clock said it was one thirty in the morning. As soon as she turned onto the road, she activated her phone's assistant and had it call Stasi. The call rolled over to voice mail, so she placed another call. "Come on, Stasi. Answer the call." When the second call also clicked to voice mail, she pounded the steering wheel.

Poor Addy. It was going to take twenty minutes to get across Arlington to Dustin's home. She pushed the speed limits as much as she dared. It would cost precious time if a police officer flashed his lights in her rearview mirror.

Finally, she turned on the road that ran in front of his apartment complex. The red and white swirling lights led her to his building. Her heart stuttered as she spotted the ambulance and pulled into a parking slot. People had spilled from their apartments and gawked at the action.

A police officer kept bystanders from approaching the scene. However, the officer's presence wasn't keeping reporters from edging closer, and Savannah watched for a moment as she wondered how to get to her niece.

There was only one way.

Through.

She sighed and then pushed her glasses up her nose and wished she'd taken a minute to brush on basic makeup, just enough to feel like she had her battle armor affixed. As she watched the officer guarding the building speak into her radio and then gesture for someone—a reporter maybe—to back away, Savannah knew it wasn't going to be a simple process to talk her way in.

She locked her car and then with a cautious smile approached the woman. "My niece called that she was inside her father's apartment and there was a lot of blood. I came immediately to make sure she's okay. Her name is Addy Jo Tate." She swallowed as the officer considered her.

Time seemed to stretch before the woman pressed a button on her radio. "I have a woman who claims to be the child's aunt. Says she got a call from an Addy Jo Tate."

The answer was so garbled Savannah wasn't sure how the woman interpreted it.

"All right." The woman met Savannah's gaze. "An officer will walk her out in a moment. Stay right here."

Addy's call hadn't been part of some crazy waking nightmare as she'd hoped. "Thank you. I'll wait here."

Jett stood in the shadows of the building. He'd sent a quick video from his phone to the paper. Ted hadn't been overly interested, but Jett knew something big had happened here. The address called in had matched Dustin Tate's. It seemed too much of a coincidence.

The ambulance and three or four police vehicles emphasized the serious nature of whatever had happened.

The other thing that struck him was the lack of urgency.

No one was rushing.

Paramedics had entered the apartment building but hadn't hurried back out. It had also looked like there might be a body bag on top of the gurney they'd carried up the stairs to the front door.

While he hadn't loved being roused from sleep, it was part of the job. When Phil, the night assignment editor, heard the police scanner sending multiple units to an address related to one of Jett's investigations, the call had been automatic. If he hadn't gotten it, he would have been ticked in the morning when he'd rolled into the office.

Things didn't look good for Mr. Tate, and that didn't sit well with Jett. He might think the guy was scum of the earth, but that didn't mean he wanted the man to get this kind of assistance off of it.

He edged along the shadows trying to find a way around the policewoman guarding the sidewalk. She took a step in his direction, and Jett froze.

"There's no crossing the line." Her hand rested on her gun in her utility belt.

"Yes, ma'am." The woman was good. He'd have to wait, but that didn't mean he wouldn't look for another access point.

He turned and took a few steps toward the street where he'd parked his car. After he glanced over his shoulder and confirmed the officer was distracted by another reporter trying to cross the line, he angled toward the line again, but this time farther away.

Then he noticed another officer escorting a girl from the building. The girl looked small inside an overlarge jacket, and he couldn't tell much about her other than she looked to be a young teen. Then she spotted someone and took off running through the halo of a streetlamp light with what sounded like sobs. He shifted to better see who she ran toward and froze when he realized it was Savannah Daniels.

That woman kept turning up in relation to her ex-husband. For a woman who claimed there hadn't been anything between them for years, she appeared a lot. The image of her looking at Dustin while he apologized from his hospital bed flitted through Jett's mind.

A man in a trench coat, shoulders hunched against the drizzle, approached the officer guarding access to the scene. The man looked like a detective or supervisor, so Jett reversed course and edged closer while trying to appear nonchalant.

"We caught a reporter sneaking around back, so be alert." Jett slid into the shadows. The man glanced around and paused when his gaze slid over Jett's position. "We'll be here awhile. It's a messy one. Not good that his kid found him." He shook his head and turned back to the building. "If you need backup, let someone know."

"I've got it handled." The officer stiffened and returned her attention to the parking lot.

The girl had to be Savannah's niece. That girl had already endured more in the last week than any young teen should.

It seemed eerily ironic that two of the men he'd discussed in his article had been on Flight 2840 just days later. How many planes flew across the world every day without incident? Now one of the men had died in the plane crash and the other appeared to have suffered worse.

He didn't like it.

Didn't like it one bit.

CHAPTER
EIGHTEEN

Savannah had to get Addy away.

Addy clutched an oversized jacket around her shoulders as she raced into Savannah's arms. "You came!"

"I always will, Addy. Every time." No matter when she called. What she needed.

"I'm so scared, Aunt Savvy." The teen trembled against Savannah with a pallor to her skin. Was there a way to get Addy someplace she could collapse?

Savannah glanced around and noted a man in a trench coat talking to the female officer who had let her through. When the man turned back to the building, Savannah waved to get his attention while keeping Addy tucked within the circle of one arm.

The red and white lights flashed across his face, illuminating the detective's frown as he stepped toward her. "Yes?"

"Can I take my niece home? I'm concerned about her."

His gaze shifted to Addy, and she noted a slight loosening of the tight lines around his eyes and mouth before his mask slipped back in place. "She's a witness."

"To what kind of event? She's fourteen years old."

"A suspicious death." The tactless words thudded into the space between them.

"A death?" Savannah's heart sank as her fears were confirmed, and she pulled Addy even closer as if that action would shield her niece.

The man rubbed a hand over his face. "Look, we don't know what happened, other than there's a man's body in the apartment and this young lady called 911."

"That man was her father. And my ex-husband." Savannah swallowed back a sudden rise of bile.

"I'm sorry for your loss." Again, there was a slight softening around his eyes. "I need to talk to her about what happened."

"I'll bring her wherever you need tomorrow." She pushed an edge into her words. "But right now she's shattered, and I need to get her someplace where she feels safe. This isn't it."

"Is there any reason to think she isn't safe?"

Addy stiffened and wrapped her arms tighter around Savannah's waist.

"I don't know. But this isn't the place for her to be." She tipped her chin up, so she could better meet the taller man's gaze. "I'm an attorney. Again, I will bring her anywhere tomorrow." She fished a card from her purse and swallowed against the sudden clot of emotion. "This isn't the time for an interview."

The man took the card and considered her. "Let me check that we have what we need for now." He took a step back to the house, then paused. "Stay here. Please."

She nodded, wishing she could click her heels twice and transport them to her home. Addy could try to relax in her bedroom next to Savannah's. And maybe then Savannah could learn what Addy had seen and help her process it. Because right now it was clear whatever had happened was a typhoon across her soul.

She'd also need to alert Emilie that she was now lead on the Mnemosyne discovery for the FBI subpoena. At least for a day.

It felt like an hour passed before an officer approached. The woman wore a sympathetic look. "Detective Jensen said you can leave, but first

I need to confirm your contact information." After Savannah gave it to her, the officer handed her a card. "Call if you have any questions."

"Thanks." A minute later Savannah led Addy down the parking lot to her car. A shadow moved as she unlocked it, and she swiftly got Addy seated before she closed the door and squinted to spot what had moved.

"Who's there?"

Jett Glover edged into the pool of light, his defined jaw clear as the shadows hid his expression. "What happened?"

"I don't know yet."

"But your niece knows." The man looked worried and worn.

She crossed her arms and kept the car between them, not that she was afraid, but she felt the tug toward him and couldn't decide if he was someone she could trust. "He never got back to me. After I texted or called."

The man nodded. "That's what I gathered. But it's not what I'm asking."

"Now is not the time to chase a lead for some story." She went around to her side of the car. "I have to make Addy my priority." She paused as a thought hit her. "He was going to prove your story was wrong."

"Did he give you anything?"

"No."

"Then how was he going to prove me wrong?"

"I don't know. He'd just gotten home, and I wasn't racing to his side." Now it was too late.

"Savannah, we can work together. Figure out what he meant."

His words stopped her where she stood. "Why?"

"Alone, we might not get much information. Together, though . . ." She fought the urge to lean in and hear what he hadn't voiced.

"You want to use my niece."

"No. I would never do that." His stance was relaxed, his gaze sincere . . . still.

She snorted and didn't care that it wasn't prim and proper. "You wouldn't know the truth if it smacked you between the eyes."

"Then help me."

She glanced in the car. Addy hadn't moved, a vacant expression on her face. "I have to get Addy away."

He stepped toward her, and she had to fight to stay where she was without moving away. He reached into his pocket and pulled out a small card. "Call me."

"I already have one."

A ghost of a smile slipped across his face. "Now you can't claim you've lost my number."

She took the card, and he held on a minute.

"I'm not the enemy."

Part of her wanted to believe him. Why? She had no idea, but before she could formulate any sort of reply, he tipped his chin toward her SUV.

"Do me a favor and call me the minute you turn the car on."

"Why?"

He shrugged in a nonchalant yet tension-laden way. "Call it a hunch that there might come a time you need help."

"Why would I call you?"

"Because you need options."

"Fine." If that's what it took to get him to leave her alone and return to the shadows, she'd do it.

He didn't slip away until after she called. Then she realized she'd given him her private cell number. *Brilliant move, Daniels.* She sighed, but put her car in gear. Time to get Addy to safety and figure out how to help her.

Addy curled into the passenger door and didn't say anything. She also didn't move. She looked like a ghost.

Should she try to pierce the cloak her niece had pulled around herself or give her space until they reached Savannah's town house? Right or wrong, she opted for waiting, praying for her niece as she wound her way back home.

Constructed when the Pentagon was built during World War II, the historic neighborhood had once served as officer housing but now was filled with civilians. When she'd bought her end unit tucked in a back corner a couple of years out of law school, she'd shared expenses with a roommate. Today she cherished her privacy. At the same time, she knew the families near her and the widow next door. They were a surrogate family who helped one another. In a city of military and government jobs that tended toward transience, she appreciated finding a pocket that was more constant. Watching for kids on bikes and scooters was a reasonable price to pay to feel removed from the hustle of the city while remaining a short drive from Old Town and the city.

But Cherry Blossom Estates didn't feel homey and safe tonight. Instead, as a cloud slid in front of the moon, it felt like whatever had happened at Dustin's had followed her car.

She pulled into the parking lot in front of her unit. Maybe she should have asked Jett to follow her if for nothing else than to convince her they were safe. She shook the thought off. She didn't need a man to ensure she was all right, but there were days it would be nice to have someone to lean into.

After parking, she turned to her niece. "What can I do, Addy?"

"He's dead." Addy's voice was as lifeless as the words.

She wanted to offer her niece hope, but couldn't. "I'm sorry."

"There was so much blood." Addy threw herself across the console until she was sobbing against Savannah's shoulder.

Savannah hugged her fiercely but wanted to get her inside, somewhere sheltered where her niece could sob as long and hard as she needed. "Oh, sweetie. I'm so sorry. You should never have been there. I'm so sorry I gave you a ride." She stroked Addy's long blonde hair while the girl sobbed. "Let's get you inside where you'll be more comfortable."

"What am I going to do?" Addy pushed back far enough for her gaze to search Savannah's face.

"Live one moment at a time until you can go one hour at a time." Savannah opened her door and then walked around the car to help Addy from the vehicle. "And I'll be with you every step of the way."

Later, after Addy had fallen into an exhausted sleep on the couch with her head resting against Savannah, Savannah's mind wouldn't release the image of all the lights and emergency vehicles, or the intense spurt of adrenaline she'd felt when she'd known Addy was somewhere in there . . . alone.

What was she supposed to do with all the thoughts and emotions flaring through her?

She needed information. Needed to know what had happened so she was prepared to help Addy or get her professional help. She reached into her pocket and pulled out two cards. She set Jett's aside and punched in the detective's number.

The phone rang so long she was about ready to hang up when he answered.

"Jensen."

"Detective, I'm Savannah Daniels. The woman who picked up her niece at the apartment."

"Yes?"

"Is there anything you can tell me about what happened tonight? My niece is hysterical but can't tell me much other than there was a lot of blood."

The man sighed. "There's not much I can say while we're in an active investigation."

"Detective, anything will help." She didn't want to sound so desperate. "I can't hear about whatever happened on the news. Is her father dead?" She froze at the blunt words, and glanced at Addy, who didn't even shift.

"Yes. Looks like he slit his wrists. Now I have to go. Call in the morning to set up the time to interview your niece."

She stared at the phone after he hung up.

Dustin was dead. Suicide?

That did not match with the man she knew at all. But why else would a man slit his wrists?

She felt the weight of the implications. She toyed with Jett Glover's card and studied the number. Could the reporter help her figure out what had happened?

It was worth considering, though she decided not to make another call while Addy slept against her. But she could text.

What happened?

It took a few moments, then three dots started flashing on the screen. He was responding.

Still unclear. Suicide?

Impossible. There was no way the man she'd known would have done that. Surely the police aren't buying that.

Actually, they seem to be leaning that direction. At least right now.

She frowned at the phone as if he could see her. Push them. He would not do that with his daughter in the next room. He would never let her find him.

He didn't reply. She set her phone down and leaned her head against the couch. It was all too much. How could she help Addy accept that her father was gone? How could she cover the ache in the girl's heart too?

It shouldn't matter to Savannah that he was gone. But it did. She wanted to believe it was because she loved this young woman who had filled a hole in her heart. A hole her father had a direct hand in creating.

But she knew it was a lie.

There was a part of her heart that Dustin still inhabited. She hated it, but what was she supposed to do with it? He hadn't loved her in fifteen years. If she was honest, he may never have loved her the way she loved him. That reality made her sick and mad and angry.

Savannah eased Addy's head up and then slid aside as she tucked a couch pillow beneath the girl's head.

Savannah picked up Rhett, who stiffened, then snuggled in with a purr as she headed to her small kitchen to make a mug of tea. Did Jett have a pet? It wasn't like it mattered. He wasn't any concern of hers, and she needed to remember that. But on a night that had surreal overtones, she wanted to think about something normal.

Even if her heart whispered there could be more.

No. Maybe she wanted there to be something more.

That made her a fool.

CHAPTER

NINETEEN

Ted wanted a story for the online edition, so Jett poured a coffee, opened his laptop, and pounded one out. After emailing it in, he opened a search engine. It had been too late last night to look for Light Comes After Darkness, but now he could. The first page of results was links to pages of quotes about light or darkness. He kept clicking. Then came a page of eclectic links to sermons, songs, and other random pages. This wasn't working.

Next he popped over to the Virginia Secretary of State's website and searched for a business with that name. Nothing. Same after searching in Maryland and the District. He sank back. Time to let a cub reporter take this on.

A quick call to Chase Matthews had the kid agreeing to visit the other secretary of states' websites as well as GuideStar to search through 990s from recognized nonprofits.

A quick search for Bernard Julius wasn't any more productive, unless a German spy the FBI caught helping the Japanese during WWII had some clue to offer.

Jett would have to get creative.

Time to call a police contact about Tate's death. Detective Ethan

Lorenze had hung in his group of friends in high school, but this morning that didn't seem to count for much. Jett pressed.

"Let me take you to coffee. We both need it after last night."

"Are you trying to get me fired, Glover?"

"Nope. I'll only take ten, fifteen minutes. I'll buy breakfast."

"Fine."

An hour later Jett stood outside the Arlington police headquarters on Wilson Boulevard. He'd spent the night thinking of Savannah's niece and what she'd seen. Few people understood that trauma like he did, so he was here at eight a.m. to do what he could for her. Addy Jo Tate didn't know him from Adam, but fortunately he knew the value of truth. And he would get that for her if it was in his power.

Ethan strode across the lobby toward him, face haggard from what had likely been a sleepless night. His wrinkled suit indicated he hadn't made it home yet. That meant Jett needed to ask his questions fast and let the man go before his patience expired. The detective stopped in front of Jett and looked him up and down. He'd aged in the job.

He made a follow-me gesture and exited the building. "You owe me a good cup of coffee. Looks like you need it too."

Jett nodded and fell in step with his acquaintance. "Can you tell me Dustin Tate's cause of death?"

The detective opened the door to Bayou Bakery. "Coffee first."

"I can live with that."

After the detective ordered and Jett paid, he led the way to a booth by the plate glass window. A minute later a young man brought a black coffee and a plate of beignets to the detective. Jett's Americano arrived next with a breakfast bar. Jett waited to see how the detective wanted to proceed.

Ethan downed half his mug in a long drink. Then he set the mug on the table and closed his eyes. He leaned forward and closed the space between them. "Off the record?"

"Sure." It was too soon to have more than a direction. "What's your gut about Tate?"

"Early signs are suicide."

"In front of his daughter?"

The man shrugged but met Jett's gaze. "It's early. I wouldn't report that."

"This is off the record."

"Good." Ethan took another sip. "Glad to know you haven't forgotten." He sighed and picked up a spoon to stir his black coffee. "Look, it's not my case, but a couple things make us suspicious."

"Like . . ."

The detective sighed and then his bass voice dropped lower. "There's nothing official, but the assistant medical examiner said it wouldn't be a quick turnaround on the autopsy."

"Any word on when they'll release the body?"

The detective snorted. "Really, Jett? The man hasn't been dead for twelve hours. It could be suspicious. It'll be a while."

"If he was killed, how did the girl survive?"

"It's a good question." Detective Lorenze paused. "Look, I can't say more, but we'll be talking to her today."

"Anything else you can tell me?"

The detective shook his head. "You reporters are all the same. Always think we'll have results as fast as one of the TV shows. You're lucky I gave you that. It'll take weeks to have all the tox screens back."

"You think drugs are involved?"

"He did it with his daughter in the apartment." As if that said it all.

And maybe it would, if Jett hadn't seen what he had as a twelve-year-old.

The man met Jett's gaze unflinchingly. "Look, it's too early to know one way or another. Suicide. Accidental death. Murder. It's all in the mix until we know more."

Jett slid his card across the table. "Call when you can say more?"

"Not likely. I don't have time to babysit the press." He leaned back against the seat.

All right. Jett clearly got that the detective wasn't fond of media. That was fine.

As Jett walked away, he couldn't shake the image of Addy clinging to Savannah. She would live with the image of her dead father imprinted on her mind for the rest of her days. If God was kind, it would fade to a hard moment, not a permanent shadow over her days.

Maybe he could help.

He needed to try. The question was whether he should call first or drive over and ask for forgiveness after.

Half an hour later he entered Cherry Blossom Estates, noting the stately trees lining the sidewalks. He'd always liked the all-brick facades of the town houses and condos and had considered purchasing one, but the prices had accelerated beyond what he could afford.

Savannah's unit was on a cul-de-sac at the bottom of a hill. A male cardinal twittered from the crepe myrtle near her front stoop, his bright red feathers standing out against the bare branches.

The house looked quiet, but it was a little after ten, so he hesitated only a minute before rapping on the door.

Nothing.

He rapped again, then glanced around to confirm her car was there. The gray Mazda crossover SUV rested in the spot closest to her sidewalk. She must be home.

He knocked again, a bit firmer, then stepped back when he heard footsteps coming from inside. A moment later a haggard Savannah opened the door. Her brunette hair was pulled up in a messy ponytail bun that somehow looked elegant, and she wore a pair of yoga pants and flowy top. It was so different from her professional attire, and he liked seeing this side of her, even as he regretted the reason for the circles under her eyes.

She leaned against the doorframe and considered him. "What are you doing here? How did you get my address?"

"I have my sources. I wanted to check on Addy."

"Why?" Suspicion tightened her eyes, and she crossed her arms over her chest. Mama Bear had arrived.

"Aren't you going to ask me in?" He tried to cajole a smile from her. Even a grimace would work. "You don't want to let all the cold air in."

She shivered at his words. "No. I can't." She disappeared for a moment, then reappeared with a coat.

He rubbed a hand over his heart. "Ouch. I thought we'd decided to work together."

"I don't have time to spar right now." She glanced back inside, and he noted the crack in her strong facade. The woman was about to break. "Addy's whole world was upended last night, and I'm still trying to figure out how and why." She rubbed a hand across her eyes. "Please go."

"I can help her."

This time when she looked at him, there was fire in her gaze. She stepped onto the porch and her breath puffed out. "You can't. You'll only hurt her more. She'll draw the connection that you wrote the article about Dustin. I can't guarantee what she'll say when she does."

"I know." His words were much softer than he'd intended. He'd try a different tack. "I found my dad."

His four words landed like twenty-five-pound weights in the space between them. As a softness replaced her anger, he wished he could go back to her disdain. That was better than sympathy.

"I'll come back later, but let her know I'll talk if she wants to. She can call me on the number I gave you last night. Any time of the day or when the nightmares come in the middle of the night." No need to mention that they still chased him from bed on occasion. "I'll get out of here, but I want to help make this right if I can."

"There isn't a way to do that."

"I have to try." He turned to go, feeling the weight of his foolishness in coming.

———

There was something almost endearing about his uncertainty as he took the three steps from the small porch to the sidewalk. The snow had melted over the weekend, and now the grass looked dead and abandoned. She should step back inside, close the door, and let him leave, but instead her mouth opened of its own prerogative. "How old were you?"

"Twelve."

Her heart wanted to go out to him, but she knew he hadn't come for her sympathy. In his own way he was offering understanding to Addy, and Lord knew the girl needed it.

"You can come in." He turned around in an instant and she held up a hand, palm out. "There are conditions."

"Okay."

"You don't make her say a thing. If she wants to be silent, she is."

He nodded and took the steps to the small concrete porch. As she held the screen door open, she could feel the heat from his body. Could she really let him in? The man she barely knew? A reporter who might say anything for a story? She started to close the door but hesitated.

She swallowed but met his gaze. "She's so broken and wounded, and I'm not sure how to pull her back from wherever she disappeared to last night."

His blue eyes were serious as he studied her. "Has she cried?"

"Buckets." Savannah had felt more helpless with each tear.

"Good. She's letting herself feel. I didn't cry for more than a month."

"What changed?"

"My hamster died, and that triggered me. My counselor had a heyday with the idea I couldn't cry about my own dad, but could about a tiny piece of fluff." He shoved his hands in his coat pockets, and there was something vulnerable in the action.

"And you grew up to be a productive member of society."

"Most of the time." There it was again, the slight, self-deprecating shrug. If he kept it up, she'd let him in and ply him with coffee and cookies in an attempt to take care of him. Something he did not need and wasn't asking for. She needed to create space. Fast.

Savannah held on to the door as he edged inside. "Please don't hurt her."

"Understood." He paused, and she was frozen in place. "The police will want to talk to her today. Try to figure out what she saw and why she wasn't also hurt."

Savannah nodded. It had been all she had thought about as she stroked Addy's hair through the night. "I don't know that she can talk."

"They'll try to make her."

She huffed. "I know. I deal with these sorts of matters, but never with people I love." She willed her tears not to fall. She would not show him that sort of weakness. "She will be okay."

"I agree." Jett glanced past her into the living space.

Like many of the townhomes in the community, the first floor was fairly open, with stairs moving up from the entryway, and a living and dining area flowing into the galley kitchen. Upstairs were two bedrooms and a bathroom, and the basement held a den, laundry room combined with a bathroom, and a small bedroom she used as an occasional office. Right now he would find Addy curled up in the twin bed in her room upstairs, one that Savannah and Addy had spent a Saturday painting a girlie lilac. The bedroom was designed for the times Addy needed to escape home chaos, but with Savannah's work hours, Addy couldn't get away as often as either wanted.

Today Addy had barely moved within her nest of pillows and blankets.

Savannah would leave her there as long as she felt safe. That had to be the primary focus right now.

Jett must have read her thoughts, because he glanced up the stairs. "She's up there?"

"Yes."

Jett started up, keeping his steps surprisingly quiet for a man who must be 180 pounds. She followed because she didn't know what else to do, and she still wasn't sure she should trust him. Was he here for the story or her niece? Would he drive here for someone he didn't know?

It had to be about the story. About worming his way into her home and up the stairs into her niece's life.

The man hesitated at the top of the stairs in the doorway to Addy's room.

"She's asleep."

Savannah nodded. "It was late when I got her home, and even later when I could talk her into bed. At first she slept curled next to me on the couch." Savannah felt the weight all over again, the pressure of how to protect Addy.

He stood in the doorway and watched Addy, almost with fatherly concern. "We'll let her sleep." *For now* unsaid.

"You seem certain the police will need to talk to her today."

Jett nodded, then headed back downstairs. "That's what my source indicated earlier today. You can't be surprised."

"I'm not. I just wish it wasn't necessary." Savannah followed him down the stairs, though part of her wanted to sit beside that girl and defend her from anyone who approached.

She needed to be here and she needed to be at work, but she'd have to trust Emilie to do her work today.

"It is," Jett said.

"What?"

"Necessary for her to talk to the police."

"I know." Savannah sighed and led the way to the dining room table. "Would you like something to drink? Iced tea? Water?"

"I'm good."

Yes, he was. Fine even, but she still couldn't reconcile the man standing in front of her with the man who wrote the article about Logan Donnelly and Dustin.

He met her gaze with his own, steady and determined.

"What?"

He shrugged. "I was going to ask you the same thing."

"Then it's a good thing I asked first." The bantering had to stop. It was ridiculous in light of everything that had happened. She sank onto a chair and put her hands on the top of the table. "I can't get ahold of Stasi."

"Your sister?"

Savannah nodded. "She should have gone to Dustin's by now to collect Addy for school. At the very least she should have called to see what happened."

"Crime scene tape and police everywhere."

"That's what has me worried."

"Call her again."

"She never answers unless she needs something from me." Savannah dialed anyway and listened to the phone ring.

CHAPTER
TWENTY

Jett watched Savannah's expression darken as her call went to voice mail. She frowned and set the phone down but didn't say "I told you so." She eyed him, then stepped to her coffeemaker and made a cup. "What does your source at the police think was the cause of death?"

"I got a lot of caveats, but he said likely suicide." He rubbed his hands over his head trying to get his brain to think. Fatigue weighed the edges of his thoughts. "He kept saying it was too early. You know he's right."

She studied him over her coffee cup, then shook her head. "You think it's possible." The words were a whispered accusation.

"Maybe Dustin did decide to end it."

"Then you're at fault." Savannah scrubbed her face with her hands. "He would have never considered something like that before his name was dragged through the ink in your article."

Jett crossed his arms, tried to imagine all she'd been through and extend a little grace, but all he could do was bite back fighting words. "There's a lot you don't know."

"I could say the same." A sound on the stairs made her turn.

A moment later Addy stood on the landing. She rubbed her eyes and looked from Savannah to him. "Who is he?"

"A friend." Savannah's expression indicated it pained her to say that, but he'd take it.

"I'm Jett Glover."

"The reporter?" Addy's nose wrinkled like she'd smelled something terrible.

"Yep." Might as well own his name.

"Why are you here?" The girl crossed her arms in a replica of her aunt.

"I want to help." Two sets of eyes bored through him. He held up his hands in a placating matter. "Figure out what happened to your dad."

"That's easy." Addy crossed the room into Savannah's arms and started to wail.

"I think you need to leave."

She was right. He should leave and let her do whatever aunts did in situations like this. But that didn't mean he wouldn't work in the background.

Logan Donnelly had died on Flight 2840.

Now Dustin Tate had died at his home.

It was a tight time frame. Jett would dig into the two seemingly unrelated events and see what he could uncover.

Questions cycled in his mind as he left Savannah's home and headed to the newsroom. He'd interview witnesses and write an article on Logan Donnelly's heroism after the crash. Then he'd turn his attention to the question of Dustin Tate.

The man had claimed he had evidence that would clear him. Now he was dead. But maybe the evidence was still out there. To find it he might need Savannah's help, but he'd see what he could learn on his own first.

———

The knock at her door came too soon after Jett left. Savannah wanted to ignore it but found herself at the door peeking through the peephole and regretted it. Now that she saw the badges, she knew she had to answer the door, no matter how reluctantly.

"Can I help you gentlemen?" She tried to press the weariness from her voice as she held the door.

One man's face was long like his body. He wore a trench coat over khakis and a white button-down shirt. She squinted to take in his name. "Detective Ethan Lorenze?"

"May we come in?" His voice had a high tenor that surprised her considering his large frame.

"Can I ask why?"

His cohort stepped up. "We need to talk to your niece."

"And you are?"

The tall man looked vaguely familiar as he flashed his badge. "Detective Mark Jensen. I was at the scene last night."

Savannah nodded as she remembered his name and their interactions from the prior night. "Why come here instead of to her home?"

"Her mom said she was here."

Huh. Stasi wouldn't return her calls but would talk to police. Savannah wished she could make her sister come field the questions and decide what was best for Addy, but of course that would be left to Savannah, as would caring for Addy's emotional needs. "I don't think she's ready to speak with anyone about last night."

"We don't have the luxury of waiting." Detective Lorenze even sounded apologetic. "The option is to have her come downtown or talk here. My understanding is you're an attorney. You can protect her interests. Or everything can take longer than it needs to and we can interview her at the precinct." His mien was serious as he studied her. "I don't like taking kids out of the familiar if possible."

Savannah considered the two men. "Can you wait a minute?"

Detective Lorenze looked grumpy at the suggestion but acquiesced. "No slipping her out the back."

"Course not." No, what she needed was a minute to get Jaime Nichols on the phone. Her former student specialized in criminal defense, and Savannah needed to know she wasn't making a mistake because she was too tired to think straight. Fortunately, Jaime answered on the second ring, and Savannah quickly caught her up.

Jaime was silent a moment, and when she spoke her words carried authority. "It's a calculated risk to let them talk to her there. It will be less formal than at the precinct. Addy will still be nervous but should be more comfortable. If they start pressing her, stop the interview and ask if they plan to Mirandize her." She sighed. "That poor girl. All we can do now is try to keep her from more trauma."

"If I need you . . ."

"Call. It would take me an hour to get to the precinct, but I could meet you if you decide to move the interview location."

"Thank you." Savannah took a minute to consider her options. "So it's best for Addy to at least start here."

"Probably." Jaime paused then sighed again. "The best would be to avoid it altogether, but from their perspective, they need to know what she saw."

Savannah heard the shifting steps on her small porch. The detectives wouldn't wait much longer in the cold. "I've got to go. Thanks for the advice."

"Just remember criminal law 101. She doesn't have to talk to them today, so don't let them force her to do so."

"Got it. Thanks." She clicked off the call and then leaned her forehead against the wall. Even two days ago she couldn't have imagined this turn of events. She returned to the front door. "Can I have a minute to prepare Addy?"

Detective Jensen shrugged as he glanced at Detective Lorenze. "Sure."

"Thank you. You may come in, but wait here." She trudged up the stairs to Addy's room. The twin bed was covered with a soft gray comforter that usually lay straight and smooth across the mattress. This morning it was clutched around Addy's shoulders.

"Who's down there?" Addy's words were quiet.

Savannah eased onto the edge of the bed and stroked Addy's hair from her forehead. "There are two detectives who need to ask you questions about last night."

Addy lurched into Savannah's arms. "I can't."

"I know, sweetie. If I could keep this from you, I would."

"I'm scared."

Savannah squeezed her more tightly. What else could she do?

Ten minutes later, Addy was curled into the corner of the couch. The detectives had grabbed chairs from the dining table. Detective Jensen leaned forward and tried to look into Addy's eyes. There was something calm yet intense about his presence as his coffee-colored eyes bored into her.

"Miss, I need to talk to you about what happened last night." He glanced at the other detective when she didn't answer, and then resituated himself as if to appear less threatening. "We're trying to understand what happened to your dad. You're the only person who was there, so we need to talk."

Savannah felt Addy tremble as the girl covered her ears. "Addy, can you talk to them?"

"Do I have to?" The words were the barest whisper.

"I know it's not easy, but if you answer their questions, they will leave faster. I promise I'll stay with you."

"I can try." She struggled to sit up, and the purple circles under her eyes emphasized all she'd been through.

"Thank you for agreeing to speak with us, Miss Tate." Detective Lorenze set a small device on the table. "I'm going to record this to make sure we don't forget anything you say, okay?" He arched a dark eyebrow as he exchanged a glance with Jensen, then proceeded. "Addy, can you tell us why you were with your dad last night?"

"He asked me to come over. I think the plane crash scared him." She swallowed hard. "It scared me."

"What time did you get there?"

She frowned and then glanced at Savannah. "Aunt Savannah dropped me off about seven. Usually Dad picks me up, but he was on painkillers."

"Do you know why?" This was from Detective Jensen.

"No."

Savannah leaned forward. "Don't you think it's likely because of the crash?"

"We'll check." Detective Lorenze scratched a note. It should be easy for police to gain access to Dustin's medical records if they hadn't already. He set his pad down. "What did you do with your dad that evening?"

"We ate a pizza. Played games, but Dad said he was tired and went to bed about nine. I watched TV until ten, and then went to bed."

"Did you hear or see your dad after he went to bed?"

Addy shook her head, blonde hair flowing around her face. "Not until I got up."

Detective Jensen settled against his chair. "When did you get up?"

"I'm not sure. There wasn't a clock in the room I slept in."

"Why get up? Did something wake you?"

"I don't know." Addy shifted in her seat, a strained expression on her face. "Maybe I heard something. But when I got up and went into the bathroom there was blood. Everywhere. I was worried so I checked his room. That's where I found him."

"Found who?"

"Dad, but I don't know if he was alone. There was a shadow." She covered her face with her hands. "Maybe if I'd gone closer I could have helped Dad." She shuddered as she cried, and the detectives waited while Savannah rubbed her back.

"Do you need to take a break, Addy?"

"Only if I'm done."

The detectives exchanged a look, then Detective Lorenze leaned forward. "We have a few more questions."

"Tell me about this shadow." There was an edge of excitement to Detective Jensen's voice.

"It was a shadow."

"Size?"

"I don't know."

"Shape?"

"It was a shadow."

"You have to know something, Addy." His voice was pointed.

"I don't. All I know is I didn't help my dad." Her voice had a hysterical tone to it that had Savannah sit forward between Addy and the men.

"I think that's all, detectives."

Detective Jensen stared at her with an incredulous expression. "We need to know what she saw."

"Yes, but she's getting upset, and that won't help anyone." Savannah stood and the detectives reluctantly followed suit. "I promise when she's ready she can talk more."

Detective Lorenze's jaw firmed. "How will you decide she's ready?"

"I honestly don't know, but I promise if she says anything that seems like it will help you, I will communicate it." What else could she do? Her heart ached as she looked at Addy curling back into the corner. Her niece was a turtle pulling from danger into her shell.

"Fine. Walk us to the door." Detective Jensen's words weren't an invitation but a demand.

"Yes." She followed them the few feet to the front door, the calm gray-violet paint on the walls failing to infuse her with its usual peace.

Detective Lorenze leaned closer and pointed a finger to her chest. "If we learn you're keeping anything from us, we will have the Commonwealth's Attorney consider obstruction-of-justice charges. Understood?"

"That's ridiculous." She bit out the phrase. "I have done nothing but cooperate from the moment you arrived." She shoved her fisted hands on her hips. "I will gladly continue to do so, but only if Addy and I are treated with respect." She looked from one detective to the other. "She has experienced a terrible trauma, and it is my prerogative as her aunt and her attorney to call a time-out."

Detective Lorenze stepped back. "You're right, and I'm sorry I got out of line. Here's my card. Call me anytime. I promise we'll learn what happened to her father."

Savannah gingerly accepted the card. "I want to know even more than you do. If she saw something, then Addy is in danger. But if Dustin did kill himself, then we're worried about nothing."

"Maybe. That's the question we will answer."

CHAPTER
TWENTY-ONE

By the early afternoon, Addy was beginning to ask questions Savannah wasn't sure how to answer. They had moved to the basement and *Captain Marvel* played on the TV in the background while they sipped homemade hot chocolate and ate kettle corn from a Pinterest recipe. A space heater whirred in the corner, but each of them had cuddled in a fuzzy blanket in cool pastels. A few drops of chocolate had slipped from Addy's mug to the couch, but Savannah didn't care. Not with everything that was spinning through their lives.

The girl pulled her knees up and placed her feet on the narrow coffee table before readjusting her blanket. Savannah watched her out of the corner of her eye and braced for the silence to be broken. She held the remote under the blanket to turn down the volume or stop the movie in an instant.

"Can we have the funeral this week?" The teen hiccupped at the end of the words as if barely holding back tears.

"I don't think so, but I can check." She made a mental note to call the police to get an idea of when Dustin's body would be released. "We could have a memorial service though. Maybe as early as Monday."

"Do you think anyone will come?" The words were so quiet, Savannah almost missed them.

"Why would you say that?"

"People will believe he was evil based on what the newspaper said about him and how he died. What if he killed himself because of the article?"

"That's a hard what-if." Savannah considered how to answer the question in a way that honored the asking and yet helped Addy feel safe. "You have to understand, we may never learn exactly what happened."

"I need to know."

"Me too, kiddo." Savannah stroked her niece's hair and then began weaving it into a long braid that would hang down her back, sweet blonde strands curling around her face. "We'll do the best we can to find answers."

"Maybe they're in his apartment."

"I don't know." How could she convince the teen that there might not be answers, at least not any that would satisfy her? "We can look as soon as the police let us in."

Addy wrapped her arms around her middle as if she'd become suddenly cold or ill. "I can't go back."

Savannah nodded and tugged the girl closer. "You don't have to. That's something I can do for you." While she was there maybe she could find whatever proof Dustin thought he had.

They stayed huddled under blankets, quiet, and Savannah wondered if she should push or let the silence continue. Her phone dinged and she grimaced when she saw the number. Emilie. "I have to take this, Addy."

The girl barely nodded as she leaned her head back against the couch and watched a scene on some spaceship somewhere. Captain Marvel was running back to get her shoes. Savannah slipped upstairs and answered the call. "How's it going?"

"Definitely better than your day. I'm so sorry about Dustin." Emilie's voice was husky with genuine empathy. She knew what it was like to lose

people you cared about to violence. "I hate to ask, but we need you."
She sighed. "I'm trying to understand what this Mnemosyne technology
does, but they keep giving me the PhD version when I need something
closer to middle school. We need to frame what we give the FBI."

"Don't sell yourself short."

"I'm not. I just recognize my strengths. If I understood and loved
science, I would have specialized in patent law."

"Addy's still with me."

Emilie must have sensed her hesitation. "It's your firm." There was
a smile in her voice. "I think you can bring your niece to work. She'll be
safe, and you can help me salvage the subpoena production."

Addy wanted to go home and sleep, so thirty minutes later Savannah
dropped Addy at her apartment only to discover Stasi wasn't home. She
didn't like leaving Addy, but the girl insisted she would be fine.

"I'll call if I need anything."

So Savannah texted Stasi that Addy was home and then drove to
the office. She didn't like the subdued air when she walked in the conference room.

John and Rochelle looked like they hadn't slept. John's hair stuck
out in all directions, while Rochelle had circles under her eyes that
makeup couldn't hide. Sad thing was Savannah knew she didn't look
any better. "Looks like we're the walking wounded."

John startled and refocused as he looked at her. "Where have
you been?"

"Helping her niece, John. Emilie told us first thing this morning, and
if you subscribed to news alerts, you would have known even earlier."

"Why should I when I have you, Rochelle." He waggled his eyebrows at her in a Groucho Marx impersonation.

The woman didn't crack a smile. Instead she gave Savannah an
apologetic frown. "Here's where we are."

It only took a few minutes to unwind what had gotten tangled.

Savannah found herself translating their explanations of the technology as Emilie took rapid-fire notes. While she wasn't a scientist, she played one in a courtroom, a skill that helped her now. "Let's look for the information that is related directly to the testing of the device."

"Only? Didn't you say yesterday the FBI wanted everything?" John threw his hands in the air. "There has to be some way to protect our data. Without it—"

"We're done." Rochelle sank back against the padded executive chair. "The bigger problem is how our code got on that plane. I was up all night and can't divine the answer."

John crossed his arms but didn't add anything as the silence lingered.

"Do we have a corporate spy inside our company? That seems crazy, but it's about all I've got. We talked with our team about the judge's order. That alone was reason to ground the project. But we also had indications it wasn't ready to test on commercial aircraft." Rochelle rubbed the back of her neck as she watched John. Was that suspicion in her gaze?

That was new information. "Why not?" Savannah asked.

John shrugged but kept his gaze on the table. "We may never know. Don't we need to finish this?"

Savannah turned to Emilie. "Why don't you draft the response? Emphasize our concerns regarding the security of the technology in this situation and that it must be protected from FOIA requests."

"I can do that."

"John, Rochelle, and I will continue working through the documents to determine which we can give to the FBI without negative impact." While they did that, she'd keep probing for how the tech got on the plane. Someone knew, and if it was one of these two, she needed to find out.

They all got to work. After thirty minutes, Savannah stepped out to text Addy.

When Savannah reentered the conference room, Rochelle was on the phone.

"What do you mean?" Rochelle's face blanched. "You can't be serious."

In the silence that ensued, the woman mimed writing in the air. Savannah slid a pad of paper and pen across the conference table toward Rochelle. The woman frantically filled a page with notes, then paused.

"Can you say that again?" Her brow wrinkled as she started to write, then lifted her pen off the paper. "That doesn't make sense." She slid the notes toward John and he scanned them.

He shook his head. "That's not possible. Something is wrong with their data."

"Hold on a second." Rochelle put her hand over the mouthpiece. "That was a friend who works at NTSB. He said the Coast Guard found Flight 2840's black box earlier this morning. This is what's coming off it."

John twisted his flop of hair, then stroked his goatee. "No. There's an anomaly somewhere. We need to get to the office and analyze the actual data."

"He says the FBI is only one of a constellation of agencies that will want to talk to us."

"We've got nothing to hide." His words were right, but Savannah thought she noted a hesitation. "I mean, we're responding to the subpoena."

Rochelle rubbed her hands over her face in a sweeping heart motion. "But what if we missed something? We've spent so much time looking at it this week, but I'm just not sure."

Emilie pulled a stack of paper from the side. "This is what we have ready to go to the FBI. We've been through it carefully and are fully cooperating or explaining why we feel something can't be shared in a way that can be captured through a FOIA request."

"Be careful." Savannah gestured to the phone. "You don't want to say anything that could be misconstrued as an admission of guilt."

Rochelle shuddered. "That's scary."

"Scary?" Savannah frowned as she tried to read Rochelle's notes upside down. "Let's talk after the call." She had to protect her clients from potentially incriminating themselves.

Rochelle turned back to the phone. "Thanks for letting me know. I need to look into this." Then she set the phone on the table.

"All right. Time to explain what just happened." Savannah got her pen ready.

Rochelle exchanged a glance with John but quickly broke eye contact. "John's right. We need to get to the office and start running scenarios. There must be something they've missed."

Savannah held up a hand. "Wait a minute. I'm your attorney, and you need to fill me in. Right now. If the information you just received impacts what we're ready to tell the FBI, Emilie and I need to know. Now."

John looked at Rochelle as if seeking her permission to continue. She tipped her chin an inch, and he sighed. "One of the engineers thought there could be a problem. He's wrong, but he got Rochelle on his side."

Rochelle nodded. "He found a glitch where the program would randomly power cycle. Similar to what they think happened with the 737 MAX."

"Make this understandable for a layperson."

"If a sensor took in bad information, the code cycled up, sucking energy from other flight systems."

"It was just theory, never proven," John jumped in.

Rochelle frowned at him. "Until we could figure out the true cause of the power cycle, we agreed to delay testing. The injunction was just coincidental, but it reinforced our decision."

Savannah was starting to understand. "But now you think your code was on Flight 2840."

Rochelle nodded.

Savannah's stomach dropped. "Okay. So what's the worst that could happen if it cycled while on a flight? Would it cause a crash?"

John shook his head. "We aren't sure . . ."

Savannah's phone rang, and she swiveled from the table to take it. "Addy? You okay?"

"The police are here and want to call something called Child Protective Services."

CHAPTER
TWENTY-TWO

An Ode to Dustin Tate
Men hide from the trueth
because their evil will destroy them.
They harm children knowing that
destruction is coming. Vengeance is
mine.

Jett studied the tweet on his monitor. What did it mean, if it wasn't gobbledygook? But this post had 8,628 likes and several hundred retweets. It didn't make sense, but he'd checked the numbers a couple of times.

He checked the handle. UndergroundVigil486. That was familiar, so he flipped back through his notes on his tablet. Yep, there it was with an earlier tweet. What was this person's thing with the innocent and children? Was the first tweet connected to this one?

Jett scrolled through prior posts, but there weren't many. A few retweets of people Jett didn't know. Then he saw a retweet of InsiderWDCStyle. Yep, another one of the tweets he'd noticed. Interesting.

But that tweet hadn't taken off like this one. This one was gaining traction in the aftermath of Dustin Tate's death. He should check into them further. His leads were dwindling.

Tweets = not much to go on.

Agency = nada.

Bernard Julius = zilch.

The cacophony of background noise wasn't providing the soundtrack he needed to keep his thoughts focused.

What he needed was a combination square in his hand, so he could use the ruler and leveler to find the corners of the truth and gauge the importance of the tweets. In the careful placement of the ruler he might let his subconscious work on the problem.

Someone rapped on his cube wall, and he pivoted in his chair to find Chase standing there. The young reporter held a sheaf of papers. "Hey, boss. Wanted you to know I haven't found any nonprofits or other businesses with the name you gave me today."

"Hmm. Can you show me what you did?" He stood and followed the young man back to his small cube.

Chase looked a bit like a kid who was trying to make a spontaneous presentation. Was that sweat breaking out on his forehead? "I looked everywhere you told me to."

"I believe you. I just want to see, so I can figure out where to look next."

The kid sank onto his chair and then pushed hair out of his eyes. He began clicking through websites with running commentary. "See, I checked Guidestar and each of the secretary of states' websites. Do you have any idea how long that took?"

"I'm guessing a couple hours."

The young man's eyes widened. "Exactly. How do you do that?"

"I had these kinds of assignments when I started out. It's also why I decided to ask you to do it. Save my time for harder work." Like beating his head against a wall studying the language in a tweet. Such a great use of the time.

"What now?" Chase poised his fingers over his keyboard as if ready to launch into the next assignment.

"Hold up. Let's think strategically." He thought a minute. "You've checked all the obvious places. What about the IRS website?"

"What do you mean?" Chase grabbed a pad of paper and a pen.

"We can check the tax-exempt organization database. It's a record of all 501(c)(3)s that people can search prior to making donations. It might capture the information if the organization is using a DBA in the origination state."

"I'm not sure I'm clear."

"Just type it in."

Chase's fingers flew over the keyboard and he hit enter. "Nothing."

"All right." Maybe he'd gotten bad information from his caller. "We'll keep trying, but I need time to come up with an idea." Usually these kinds of searches would pull up the information.

"No problem." The kid handed a stack of papers to Jett. "Here's the printout from each state showing nothing." Then he picked up another stack. "While you think, Mr. Lance wanted you to have this."

"What is it?"

The kid shrugged. "Flight 2840 stuff. I cross-checked who survived and didn't based on where they were sitting."

"Sounds like you did the legwork. Why give it to me?"

"You're the established reporter." The kid did an admirable job of keeping whine out of his voice.

"Pull up a chair and let's look at it together."

They spent the next twenty minutes reviewing what Chase had mapped out. It was good. Insightful stuff. Essentially he'd showed that those in the front third of the plane hadn't stood a chance. Ninety percent of them had died, with the rest experiencing terrible injuries. The crash became survivable the closer to the tail of the plane one sat. With seats in row 30, it was no surprise that Logan and Dustin both survived. Logan Donnelly could have saved himself if he'd just swam away from the crash and let everyone fend for themselves. Instead, after his body was recovered, the coroner reported Logan had drowned, likely after the cold and fatigue weakened him.

The plane had broken apart, with the tail and nose cracking under the stress. It had taken a technological marvel to raise the fuselage and keep it on the surface until it could be safely removed.

"Let's think about the logistics."

Chase nodded. "Okay."

"What happens in the event of an emergency?"

The kid looked at him with big eyes and shrugged. "I don't know. Never been on a plane that crashed."

"Me neither, but every time you get on a plane they tell us the protocol. Follow the lights to the emergency exits. Obey the flight attendants' instructions."

"Yeah. All things I never want to have to do."

"But we all know the system if there's an emergency. The plane hasn't even gotten into the sky, and now it's in the water. What would cause that?"

"They found the black box today, but nobody's talking. Yet anyway."

"And the plane crashed so fast, nobody's expecting that. Bet the pilot didn't have time to warn the passengers." Jett made a note. "So we need to talk to someone at NTSB and figure out what they know." He tapped his pen against his notepad. "Something happened. A plane doesn't crash without a reason. Something failed."

"Or caused it."

Jett eyed the young man. "You thinking terrorism?"

"Not really, but like you said, something happened. The black box will help the investigators determine if it was engine or system failure." He glanced at the diagram he'd made. "But I know that it didn't just go down. The plane was only two years old."

"Nope. Think about the 737 MAX. Brand-new planes that failed."

Chase pointed to a spot on the diagram. "When you look at the video that was taken immediately after the crash, you can see a break here." He pointed along a line close to the forwardmost doors.

"Did any of the crew from the flight survive?"

"No, they all perished trying to get the passengers out."

A minute later, Jett headed back to his desk. The kid had promise. He showed a dogged determination and willingness to learn that Jett wanted to think was like him when he was a young reporter out of grad school.

There was something here. Something related to who made it off the plane and who didn't. Maybe it was dumb luck, but over one hundred people made it off.

He felt it in his gut, where his best ideas originated. He picked up his phone and dialed Brett Sanderson. "Who's interviewing survivors?"

"A few people are working through the list."

"We're interviewing all of them, right?"

"About twenty, I think. A few of the bigger names about town. Folks who work on Capitol Hill or other interesting context. Also talking to those in different positions around the plane. Trying to compile an overview of what happened in the minutes leading up to the crash."

"Makes sense."

Jett heard rustling as if Brett was picking up paper and pen. "What questions do you want asked?"

"Where were they, how did they get off the plane, etcetera. Pretty standard."

"I think they're asking those questions, but will confirm. Why?"

"Call it a hunch." He wished he could articulate what he was looking for. "Thanks."

He turned back and ran a finger down the sheets of paper filled with his scrawled notes. Some of the writing was so rough he could barely read what he'd written. It wasn't there. He knew the crash couldn't be connected to his article, but two of the subjects of his investigation had been on the plane and had died soon after. Had the unidentified team member been on the plane too? Those were questions he couldn't answer until he learned the identity. No one had responded to his social media requests with more than "good luck." He wasn't sure where else to look but would come up with something.

He could check on Brett Sanderson from the Thailand junkets, make sure he was still among the living. He placed the call and it went to voice mail.

A quick call to Savannah. That's what he needed. To see how Addy was doing. If she had talked to police. Maybe she could help him get into Dustin's apartment.

Wait.

She'd given him no indication she wanted anything more to do with him. Savannah was an amazing woman, but she wasn't his. He allowed himself just a minute to think about what it would be like to go from his solitary existence to one with a spirited, intelligent woman at his side.

CHAPTER
TWENTY-THREE

The edge of panic in Addy's voice had Savannah shooting to her feet and heading to her office for her purse and keys.

"Slow down, Addy. I can't understand you and I want to help."

"Aunt Savannah, the police are here to arrest Mom, and they're ready to call Child Protective Services. Please don't let them." There was a ragged edge and then a hiccup. "I can't go with them."

"Is your mom there?"

"No."

"Okay. I'm on my way. Can they wait for me to get there?" She glanced at her watch and groaned. It was four thirty, which meant rush hour would be well under way. It could take forty-five minutes for her to reach Stasi's apartment.

"I don't know. Hurry." Addy hung up before Savannah could ask her to put one of the officers on the phone.

She rushed from her office, stopping at Hayden's door long enough to fill her in. "Can you let Bella know I'm out the rest of the day?"

"Absolutely. Do you need anything?"

"Other than this month to stop?" She blew out a lungful of air. "Prayer would be great."

"You have it. Always." And the crazy thing was Savannah knew that was true.

"Thank you."

"Now go get your niece." Hayden's eyes were filled with concern. "Don't worry about anything here." As Savannah stood rooted in place, Hayden came around her desk and eased Savannah toward the door. "Really, we have it covered."

"You do." Savannah nodded and snapped back into motion. "Thanks, Hayden. I'm glad you're here." She clutched her bag closer and then moved toward the back door. She had to keep moving or she'd crumble. This was the final pebble that had filled her jar to overflowing.

She climbed into her car and reversed out of the parking lot. As she drove, one question tormented her. What was she supposed to do when she arrived at Stasi's?

Addy shouldn't be a ward of the state, but how had things gotten so bad that was even an option?

Had she failed her niece and sister that much?

Savannah felt the pressure crushing her until she had to remind herself to breathe. Her lungs had forgotten how to do the function on their own. At a red light she leaned her forehead against the steering wheel. Where had the nascent peace she'd felt gone?

Even in the absence of peace, she had a choice. Trust God or take control.

Her instinct was to take it herself, but she couldn't, not anymore. *You can handle whatever situation you're walking into, Savannah, because God is already there. Please, God, be there with Addy.*

A horn startled her, and she moved the car forward through the green light.

The rest of the drive passed in a blur of stop-and-go traffic as she traveled to Bailey's Crossroads and then turned along Carlin Springs Road to the apartment complex. When she'd found this place for Addy and Stasi, it had seemed perfect, right down to the pool where Addy could relax. It also wasn't too far from the shopping all around Bailey's, making it easier for Addy to navigate on her own if she needed.

That was probably why the officers were threatening to remove Addy from the home. She'd been left on her own one too many times. That had to be it, right?

The drive into the neighborhood was quiet. A couple of mothers with small children bundled in coats and mittens chatted at the pocket-sized playground. She followed the curve and neared the cluster of three buildings where the apartment was located.

Two Falls Church Police squad cars and an unmarked car sat near Stasi's building.

Savannah's lone hope that Addy had misunderstood disappeared like a mist. This was a real threat, one she had to address now. She pulled her car into a visitor slot and took a moment to pray before climbing out. It felt like a hundred-pound weight had settled across her shoulders, and she had to force herself forward. One cruiser held an officer, but the other two were empty as she walked past.

She used her key to enter the building and then climbed the stairs to the third-floor apartment Stasi had insisted on for safety. No garden apartment for her sister. Anyone could break in, Stasi had said.

Rather than let herself into the apartment, she rapped briskly on the door. A moment later she heard heavy footsteps followed by the door opening. A young officer who couldn't have been more than twenty-five stood there, hand on his gun as he gave her a quick visual inspection. "You are?"

"Savannah Daniels, Addy's aunt. She called and asked me to come."

"I'll need some ID." He held out his hand as she dug through her purse.

"I should have had it ready. Sorry about that." She kept her motions slow and hopefully nonthreatening. After she found her wallet and pulled it free, she showed him her license. "Her mother, Stasi, is my sister."

The man took her wallet and began talking into his shoulder radio. Then he waved her in while he continued to talk. Savannah scanned the living area with its couch, coffee table, and TV. Where was Addy? Her thoughts began to spin as her niece was noticeably absent. "Addy?"

The officer came back over. "Here's your wallet."

"What happened?"

The man considered her. "The minor's mother went to the girl's school and got in an altercation with the staff."

"What?"

"Her mother made a visit to her school today and threatened the principal. He's pressing charges, so your sister is coming down for booking."

"For a threat?" Savannah wanted to argue it couldn't be true, but unfortunately it was the kind of thing Stasi would do while out of her mind.

The man's attention didn't flicker. "The black eye the man is sporting indicates it was more than a threat."

"Can't she be released on her own recognizance?" Savannah rubbed her throat trying to dislodge the lump that was growing.

"If bail is low enough, but that doesn't fix the problem of a fourteen-year-old being alone."

"She won't be. I'm here to take her home with me if you'll explain why she can't stay here." Savannah tucked her wallet away and scanned the small kitchenette. Still no Addy. "Where is my niece?"

"Packing a bag." This officer wasn't a man of many words.

A door opened and Addy dashed to Savannah's side. "Please don't let me go." She held on so tight, Savannah couldn't see her face.

"Of course." She rubbed her niece's back. "Are you okay?"

"Mom's done it this time," Addy whispered. "She was drunk. Maybe more."

"Why was she at your school?"

Addy shrugged. "Can we please leave? I've seen too many police officers lately."

The officer's eyebrows shot up. "What do you mean?"

"She found her father's body. It may be a suicide, but the investigation is ongoing." She sounded like an attorney, even in the middle of a family crisis. What was wrong with her? She put an arm around Addy and pulled her back in. "It's all right if we leave?"

"Yes." He turned to Addy. "You shouldn't be left on your own." As Addy started to protest, he held up his hands. "I can tell you're mature, but you still have a right to have someone take care of you. Let your aunt do that when your mom can't." He focused his attention on Savannah. "Your sister could be out tomorrow. We took her in as much to help her get off whatever high she was on."

Addy leaned more tightly into Savannah's side, and Savannah studied her. "Why was your mom at the school?"

"I have no idea, but I wish she'd stayed drunk on the couch." She huffed. "I used to think that was bad enough. I was wrong. There's a whole other level of bad."

"All right." Savannah would deal with Addy's emotions later, because she couldn't do it with a police officer watching every move and listening to each word. "We'll figure this out as soon as we get to my place." She turned to the officer and handed him her business card. "Please call if you need anything further. Thank you for staying with my niece until I could arrive."

"Ma'am."

A woman walked out of Addy's room and eyed Savannah cautiously. "I'm starting a child-in-need-of-services investigation. You might warn your sister this kind of behavior catches our attention." She handed Savannah a card, then joined the officer and they walked out.

As soon as the front door closed, Savannah urged Addy back to her room. "Get as much as you'll need for school for the rest of the week."

Addy nodded, the fight in her evaporating.

CHAPTER
TWENTY-FOUR

THURSDAY, DECEMBER 17

Savannah woke up with thoughts racing about all that had to happen. Preparing for the subpoena. Planning a memorial service. Figuring out what else needed to happen related to Dustin. His parents had died several years ago, so she'd see about getting into his apartment to look for a will. If he was as prepared as Stasi claimed, he'd have a will and life insurance filed there. And while she was looking for that, she'd look for the proof of innocence he'd claimed to have.

Then, depending on what the proof was, she'd contact Jett Glover. See what he wanted to do with it.

Would their lives intersect today? They might not, but a woman could hope. Before leaving, she woke Addy and prayed for her. Then she called the school to let the administration know Addy would be out another day.

The morning sun was warming the sky as Savannah climbed into her car. Ready or not, it was time to tackle the challenges of this day.

Chilled from the short walk to her car, she turned on the seat warmer. There was something comforting about the heat slowly soaking into her back. She wanted the hope of a new morning and fresh day to rise inside her like the heat.

Instead she felt the weight of her emotional exhaustion, which was beginning to affect her physically and spiritually. There was so much tension bubbling around her and all she wanted was peace. She might be a litigator, but her heart's cry was reconciliation and unity.

This was a day she could own from beginning to end. All she had to do was turn the key in the ignition and get into the office. This early in the day traffic wouldn't detain her, and she'd have a quiet hour before the others reached the office. She needed the time. A few client files had been neglected as she worked on the mediation and then been derailed by the plane crash and Addy's needs. She'd take a minute to make sure she hadn't missed a deadline, and then get back to the file prep.

It was only when she realized she needed to turn down the heat that she pulled the car from its parking slot.

At a stoplight, she took a sip of the latte she'd made at home. The splurge on a nice coffee machine had been a great investment. She liked to tell herself she saved all kinds of money each week not stopping at various coffee shops, though the expense of specially roasted coffee beans and organic creamers might counterbalance the savings.

The light turned green, but as she started forward on King Street, she glanced in the rearview mirror and saw a vehicle barreling toward her. She tried not to brace, but before she could do anything, the SUV rammed into the back of her crossover.

The coffee mug flew from her hand as she was thrust forward.

Hot coffee splashed across her clothes and the windshield.

Her SUV rolled forward.

The seat belt cut across her chest, and her neck and head continued forward.

A scream echoed through the interior, and it took her a moment to register it was hers.

Her car slipped into the intersection, and she tried to think which pedal was the brake.

Then the car shuddered as it was rammed again.

What?

What was happening?

Her gaze darted from the rearview mirror to the side mirror and then into the intersection. She hammered her foot along the floorboard, desperate to find the gas. Maybe she could get through the intersection and pull into the T. C. Williams High School parking lot. There she could get help. Find her phone. Call the police. Anything to get the car behind her to stop hitting her.

There! She'd found the right pedal.

Adrenaline coursed through her, scrambling her thoughts in a jagged rush.

She rammed on the gas, and the car lurched forward.

She wanted out of the car.

She charged into the high school's parking lot, grateful few cars were there as hers surged up the short incline. When she looked back in the rearview mirror, the SUV took off down the street.

License plate.

She needed to be able to tell the police something. All she could make out was its dark color and SUV form.

That wouldn't help anyone ID the vehicle. She felt sobs trying to escape but she couldn't inhale enough to release them. She had to get out, go somewhere safe, but all her muscles could do was tremble. She hit the button on the steering wheel to activate her phone. Told the system to call the last number. Couldn't remember what the number was, but it was all she could think to do.

Jett needed the information Savannah told him Dustin had. What if Dustin had been Jett's mystery caller? It was a bit of a stretch, but one way to find out was to get into the man's apartment. Easy-peasy. He just had to find out if the police had released it and then get one of Dustin's close relatives to let him in.

He picked up his phone and placed a quick call to his old friend Detective Lorenze.

"Hey, Ethan. Quick question. Wondered when you planned to release Dustin Tate's apartment?"

"It's ready. Just need to get ahold of his daughter's mom."

"She not taking calls?"

"She is. Just not responding."

"Interesting. Thanks for the info."

"You're going to owe me after this."

"Yeah. Next Wizards game at B Dubs."

"If I'm not working, sounds great."

Once the call ended, Jett weighed his options. Call the mom and get stonewalled or call the aunt. He cocked his chin and grinned. That was easy. Call the aunt. Only she didn't pick up. He glanced at his watch and grimaced. Guess he hadn't realized it was before eight in the morning. Way before eight. He felt surprised Lorenze had taken his call.

All right. He'd turn back to the tweets while he waited to call Savannah at a more reasonable hour. The tweets he'd been monitoring were spreading rapidly, but he couldn't figure out why. Bots likely triggered the retweets, but who was behind them? He might not know, but he knew a guy. Jake Thorns had some serious private investigator skills.

His phone rang, and he closed the laptop before grabbing it. "Glover."

"Jett?" The word trembled, a quiet vibration.

"Who is this?"

There was a silence, long enough he almost hung up, but hesitated in case it was his mystery caller.

"I need help."

He straightened as he recognized the voice. "Savannah? Where are you?"

She paused again. "I'm in a parking lot. Let me check which one."

He frowned as it registered how disoriented she was. "Do you need medical help?"

"I don't think so."

He stood and shoved his laptop and other items into his backpack. "I'm headed to my car now. Tell me where to come."

"I was driving to work and a car hit me." The sound went in and out a bit like it did when coming through a car's audio system.

His skin flushed and he picked up his pace as he pushed through the coffee shop's door. "Is the vehicle still there?"

"No. It kept going after I pulled into the lot. I didn't get any information that will help the police."

He exhaled. "You called the police."

"I don't think so."

"Is anyone there? Anyone nearby?" Maybe he could get her to give the phone to someone who could tell him where to drive. He unlocked his Bronco and tossed the backpack into the back seat.

"Someone's coming toward the car." Her voice rose in pitch and he could hear her panic. "What do I do?"

"Roll down your window enough to talk. Ask them to call me with your location."

He could hear a muted conversation and prayed he'd given her good advice. What if that was whoever had rammed her? He thrust the thought from his mind. There was nothing he could do about that.

What he could do was start driving the moment he knew which direction to head.

There was a beeping, and he looked at his phone. Thank God it was a number he didn't recognize. "I think he's calling. I'm going to put you on hold while I talk to him." He clicked over to take the other call before she could reply. A moment later a man's voice came on. "She needs help. Looks dazed and her SUV is banged up good."

"Tell me where you are. I'm in my car ready to drive."

The man rattled off an Alexandria high school. "She's in the parking lot on the side as you approach from the west."

"Thanks. I'm on my way."

"Want me to stay with her?"

"Yeah. If you can."

"I'll try." The Good Samaritan hung up, and Jett put his car in reverse.

His fingers thrummed against the steering wheel as he drove. Was Savannah the victim of a run-of-the-mill hit-and-run, or something more sinister?

He feared the worst. A good person would have stopped. Called for assistance if it was a true accident.

———

Savannah tried to clear her thoughts. Was Jett still on her call? Or had he gone away? It felt like her mind had been dipped in molasses and her synapses couldn't fire right. She must have been hit harder than she'd thought.

She closed her eyes and willed everything to be okay.

Her car was just a thing.

It would be a pain to deal with getting it fixed, but it's also why she carried rental-car reimbursement on her auto insurance. It would be an inconvenience, nothing more.

"You gonna be okay, lady?"

She opened her eyes to see a man leaning close to the window. "I don't know."

"Here's a bottle of water. Maybe a drink will help."

She took the bottle from him and took a sip. The water smelled odd, but maybe it had just been in his car awhile. That had to be it because the liquid refreshed her, but a minute later when the man spoke to her, she frowned. "Who are you?"

"I called your friend like you asked."

"My friend?" What did he mean? Maybe if she could think, his words would make more sense. His expression wasn't exactly concerned, but he'd helped her, hadn't he? She glanced at the water bottle. Yes, that was help.

"Your friend is on the way."

"He's not my friend." But he was. Sort of. If she remembered right. She wanted him to be more of a friend. But how had she called him? She couldn't remember.

The man walked away, and Savannah tried to think. She should do something. But what?

The car accident couldn't have caused all this brain fog.

She'd just close her eyes again. Wait for Jett to arrive. Then she'd be okay.

CHAPTER
TWENTY-FIVE

Jett felt his shoulders unknot just a bit when he slowed to turn into the high school's lot and spotted Savannah's SUV. His car jerked up the ramp into the lot, causing his head to about hit the roof. He wouldn't do her any good if he gave himself a concussion trying to reach her.

Her car sat alone in the lot. He frowned. Hadn't the man said he'd stay?

That thought didn't slow him as he threw the car into park, jumped from it, and hurried around to the driver's side of her vehicle. Her head was leaning against the headrest, her eyes closed, her skin paler than normal. The window was cracked, and a slight breeze ruffled her hair. He glanced at the back of her car and noted the way her bumper was crumpled like an accordion.

No low-impact accident would cause that kind of damage.

He tried her door. It didn't open, so he rapped the window. "Savannah?"

She struggled to open her eyes and then turned slowly in his direction. It took a minute before her eyes focused. "Jett? You came?"

"I did. You asked, so I'm here." He reached into his pocket and pulled out his phone. He placed a 911 call while he tried to evaluate her. As soon as the operator came on, he told the woman they needed an ambulance and police for a hit-and-run. He urged her to send someone quickly, because the longer he watched Savannah, the more concerned he became.

"Savannah, I need you to unlock the door." His concern grew as she looked at him but didn't move. The ambulance arrived as he was considering breaking the window, pushing her to the passenger seat, and driving her to a hospital himself, except he wasn't sure her car should be moved.

An EMT hurried from the ambulance, a bag slung over his shoulder. "What happened?"

Jett tried to explain. "I'm not sure. She called me about thirty minutes ago. Said she'd been in an accident and the vehicle took off when she pulled in here. Her thoughts were jumbled, and she couldn't tell me where she was. I had her ask a bystander to call me with the location. When I arrived, he was gone. Now she just wants to sleep."

"Sounds like she could have a brain injury." The EMT glanced toward the back of the car, as his words hit Jett.

"Brain injury?"

"Could be as benign as a low-grade, mild concussion, but she'll need to be checked." He walked to the driver's side and set his bag down. "Would be consistent with the damage to her bumper. That can cause serious whiplash." He edged Jett to the side. "Let's check her out." He tried the door handle and frowned. "Why isn't it unlocked?"

"Because she hasn't gotten out of the car. I couldn't force it open or I'd have driven her to the hospital."

"All right." The man tapped on the window. "Ma'am, we need you to unlock the car."

Savannah didn't stir, though her eyelids fluttered.

"Ma'am." The man raised his voice. "I don't want to have to break into your car. Can you unlock it?"

Her eyes opened, but she didn't move.

The paramedic stood and called over his shoulder. "Dan, we'll need to break the window."

Jett winced. That sounded expensive on top of the damage to the back end of her car. A police vehicle rolled up and the officer was hustling their direction almost before she'd parked the cruiser.

"What happened here?"

The EMT gestured to the car. "It's locked. Have a way to pop it?"

"Sure." She hustled back to her car and popped her trunk, emerging a minute later with some kind of tube and bulb. She slid what looked like a deflated whoopie cushion into the space between the door and the car frame, and then pumped the bulb. It was similar to a blood pressure cuff, and in a minute, she had the car unlocked. She stepped back as the EMT knelt next to Savannah, who was starting to rouse.

The officer gestured for Jett to follow her as she stepped out of the way of the EMTs.

———

Savannah felt someone checking her pulse and something—maybe a blood pressure cuff—sliding around her arm.

Why couldn't she wake up?

It was scary to lack control of her body.

In what felt like moments, they pulled her from her car and put her on a gurney. An oxygen mask was strapped to her face and then the vehicle—an ambulance?—took off.

Who would take care of her car?

She should call someone to let them know where she was. Someone would worry. But her thoughts were clouded and her phone . . . she had no idea where it was. Had Jett grabbed her purse and phone?

She didn't remember much of the ride. Her thoughts began to clear as they reached the hospital, but it didn't stop the emergency room doctor from drawing what felt like pints of blood and then sending her back for an MRI.

After twenty minutes in the loud, clunking machine, her head still pounded, but her thoughts made more sense.

What had happened?

A nurse returned her purse and phone to her, and Savannah saw Jett's frantic texts, which had arrived like clockwork every fifteen minutes. He didn't know which hospital they had transported her to. Savannah asked a nearby CNA, then relayed the information to Jett.

Sometime later the clanking of the curtain that covered one end of the room caused her heart rate to pick up. When she saw Jett, a part of her that had clenched relaxed.

"You're here." She had a new appreciation for the relief Addy expressed when she said the same words.

"Have been." Jett's gaze scanned the machines, and she wanted him focused on her. "They wouldn't let me back."

She sighed and blinked to prevent the moisture that filled her eyes from overflowing. "What happened?"

"There are a lot of people who'd like to know." He finally looked at her. "Do you remember anything?"

"Just the jar of being hit, hard. Did I call you?"

He nodded. "Do you know why?"

She frowned as she tried to think. "I must have had the car call that last number." She looked at him. "But why would it call you?"

"The night Dustin died. I gave you my number and you dialed it so it would be stored."

That still didn't feel right. "Why?"

"Because I pestered you to do that in case you ever needed anything."

"We barely know each other." But she wanted that to change, didn't she?

"We can fix that." He sank onto the edge of a chair. "I'm glad I goaded you into it."

"Maybe." If his number hadn't been the one, who would her car have called? Addy? The firm? Neither would have been a good option in that moment.

He glanced away and she noted his hands were now clasped in his lap. "Do you want me to call someone for you?"

She tried to think. Who else would she call? Stasi wouldn't be any help, and Addy was too young and should be in school. No, she'd called the school for her. Her parents were in another state and the gals were at work. "There's no one."

"Then I'm glad I was your last number."

She nodded, then winced as a knifing pain sliced into her temple. She rubbed the spot.

He lurched to his feet. "I'll get the nurse in here."

"I'll be all right." She reached toward him, and he took her hand. "Could you call the firm and tell Bella what happened? I'll need her to have my car towed."

"Consider it done." He looked at her in a way that communicated more than a glance should. There was the promise of something deep, like he could see her weakness but also see her strength, and he liked the blend.

"Thank you for coming."

"Always."

His voice held a promise in the words that echoed those she had told Addy. She wanted to believe he would be the man who always followed through. The kind she could depend on in the days ahead.

That thought scared her and gave her hope.

A couple of hours later, the sight of her town house should have filled Savannah with peace. Instead she felt the flutter of unease as Jett pulled into the parking lot. She needed to be at the office helping Emilie, but he pulled to a stop next to the sidewalk that led to her front door.

"Thank you for driving me home, but I really need to go to the office."

"Not today. You have to trust the attorneys who work for you."

"I do." She sighed. "But these are my clients."

"What's so important you can't wait until Monday?"

She didn't trust him that much. "Bella insisted she'd get my rental car here and bring me dinner."

"Feeling managed?" His eyes were hidden by his sunglasses, and she wanted to push them up and see his thoughts. Instead, the tinted glasses formed a barrier she wasn't sure she should storm.

"A little, but after this morning's scare, I guess it's okay." The ER doctor had decided dehydration led to her severe disorientation after the accident. The answer felt too simple, but she didn't have anything to counter it. Nothing more than a hunch. Anyway, maybe it was a mild concussion. Maybe drinking two cups of coffee before leaving the house rather than a gallon of water had been a bad idea. But the man had given her that odd-smelling water. Too bad she couldn't see if it still smelled odd now.

"Do you want company?" He glanced at the dashboard digital clock. "I can come in for a while."

Jett tried to decide whether to help her inside.

"No, I'll be fine."

She might believe her words, but she barely staggered to her front door and slotted her key in the lock. She twisted the knob and then shuffled inside. Leaving her alone didn't seem right. She was not the in-command, strong woman he'd seen during every other interaction.

This woman was too intelligent to lose track of where she was and have her thoughts so twisted around. He didn't trust her by herself even if the doctor thought a bag of saline solution via IV was enough to hydrate her and fix her disorientation.

After sitting in his car watching her front door for thirty minutes, he exited his car and stood at the front door to Savannah's home. She wouldn't be thrilled to see him.

Who was he kidding?

For all he knew, she may have already forgotten how she got home and would hate knowing he knew where she lived. She may have forgotten he'd been here yesterday checking on Addy. He hadn't done anything wrong then or now to be here, but who knew if she'd see it that way. But he couldn't drive away, not until he knew she was okay inside.

He wanted to uncover who she was. She had a space where she was weak, where she didn't let others in as they relied on her strength. He'd seen her throughout the morning in a way that she hadn't let others see. She'd insisted her receptionist not tell anyone why she wasn't at work, but he doubted the woman would follow along. Still, no one had shown up to support her yet.

As she'd lain against the white hospital sheets and flat pillow, she'd looked so self-possessed and alone. But he'd seen a flicker of vulnerability, one she'd deny, just like she'd deny she needed anyone to stay with her now.

He'd use the excuse of talking to her about Dustin to step inside her home and make sure she was okay. He could do that without her knowing his real intent was to protect her.

As a confirmed feminist, she might not like that. But hopefully he could cajole her into lying on the couch while he got her tea and toast. Anything else she needed. He liked the idea of serving her like she served others. He rapped the door, then twisted the knob. When the door eased open, he stuck his head in the house. "Savannah, it's Jett. I'm coming in."

"You don't need to." Her voice was thready . . . and close.

"Thought I'd make sure you're settled before I leave. It's the chivalrous thing to do."

He heard a sigh but took the lack of protest as a tacit invitation to come in. He'd barely stepped inside when he stopped. She was lying across several steps about halfway up the flight to the second floor. He jumped toward her. "You okay?"

She didn't open her eyes as she answered. "I can't get the room to stop swimming, and then I thought I'd lose my breakfast." She blinked at him, then closed her eyes again. "It was easier to lie here."

"Maybe, but it doesn't look comfortable. Your bedroom upstairs?"

She gestured toward the landing. "Up there. Next to Addy's."

Without a thought he scooped her up and carried her upstairs. There was something so right about holding her in his arms. She wasn't some wisp of a thing that would blow away in the first wind. She turned into his chest and he took a side step until he regained his balance. "Careful there."

She didn't say anything.

One glance reminded him which room was hers. One bore a lilac color on the walls with a twin bed covered in an eyelet quilt. The other room was the palest blue that reminded him of spring and brightness. The queen poster bed was covered with a comforter in a swirl of gray, blue, and white. It looked like a Monet painting covered the bed. The dresser had a clean surface and the bedside table held a lamp, clock, and Bible. Everything was neat and organized and revealed an ordered mind.

He carefully eased through the door and tried to tug the comforter free of the mountain of pillows without dropping her. The moment he eased her onto the bed, she rolled over and snuggled into her pillow. He pulled the comforter up and then stepped back.

Maybe she didn't need anything right now other than rest. He'd stick around and make sure she kept breathing.

He went downstairs and called Bella. "I think she's going to need someone to stay with her."

The woman didn't hesitate. "I can get there about four. Can you stay until then? It's a chaotic day here."

"Should be able to. She'll probably sleep but might have a mild concussion." He paused. "I found her on the stairs."

"Thanks for staying with her. I'll get there as fast as I can."

After he ended the call, Jett grabbed a chair from the table and carried it upstairs to her doorway. He sank onto it and then considered her.

A peace in her features added a layer of beauty, the natural kind that couldn't be bought at a counter or applied from a tube. She had shadows under her eyes and her hair was a tangled mess, yet all he wanted to do was get closer to her, protect her, and show her she could be loved. That she could be cherished the way she adored her niece. That someone could see into her soul and love what he saw there, especially in the mess.

He'd learned a long time ago that the story trumped everything else.

He'd ignore the voice that reminded him it hadn't always been this way.

It's how it was now.

His phone dinged and he pulled it from his pocket, only to release a groan when he read the message. Got anything? We've got to file a story today.

Leave it to Brett Sanderson to pull him back to earth and his job.

At least his editor hadn't called.

He pulled out his tablet and stylus. Savannah's gentle breathing filled the small room, and he watched her a minute, monitoring the up-and-down motion of her chest.

Then he turned to a fresh page in his notes app and began a list that morphed into a flow of ideas. There was something with the tweets. Now he had the time to think about what that was.

He texted Brett back. Working on an idea. Get back to you shortly.

He pulled up the tweets and copied them into a document.

InsiderWDCStyle.

RightSideAllTheTime.

UndergroundVigil486.

There were two posts about Donnelly after the article appeared. Then two posts by UndergroundVigil486 that were retweeted by InsiderWDCStyle.

Was there something in the language? Something he could use to connect the tweets and thus the accounts? Did it even matter if there was no profile information to draw lines to the people posting the content?

He needed to reach out to the accounts. Learn what he could about them.

Then his mind ricocheted to something in the list of tweets he'd noted. The one from SoulFreedomThaiNow. What was it about that one that had made him think about the unidentified fourth man the first time he read it?

He smiled as he opened a new page to capture his thoughts and reach out to the tweeters.

CHAPTER
TWENTY-SIX

Savannah shifted against her pillow and sighed. Her head pounded but her thoughts were clearer as she opened her eyes.

How long had she slept?

"Careful there." The man's deep voice startled her, and then her hand flew to her head as she felt the pounding accelerate. "Easy."

She carefully shifted, then a man came into focus. Who was he? She sifted through her mind. The reporter?

Yes, the distinguished, rugged look was Jett's. The way he watched her, a mix of protectiveness and concern in his eyes, flummoxed her. Why was he here? The questions must have played across her face, because he eased back as if to give her space to feel less threatened.

"I drove you home from the hospital."

That simple sentence released a kaleidoscope of images. An SUV tailing her. The crash. Pulling into a high school parking lot. A man, but not this one. Then the ambulance ride. The CT scan. "You brought me home, but why are you in here?"

"I found you sprawled halfway up your stairs. Decided it would be a good idea to monitor you until backup arrives."

She grimaced. That meant Bella. "I don't need a babysitter." The words came out without the punch she'd imagined. They practically limped from her barren throat. She cleared it and tried again. "I might need a glass of water."

He stood and hesitated. "Downstairs in the kitchen?"

"There should be a pitcher in the fridge." She liked her water colder than tap, but the thought of getting up—she really should—made her queasy. She must have hit her head hard, but she didn't feel any bumps as she ran her fingers lightly over the back of her scalp.

Jett's heavy steps clomped down the stairs. Thanks to her wood floors she could follow his progress across the first floor and back. He'd found one of her Captain Marvel glasses and filled it with ice water.

"Thanks." She scooted back against the headboard. "How long was I out?"

"About two hours." He picked up a notepad and then returned to his seat. "You've had quite the day. Is there anyone I can call for you?"

Wait. She shouldn't have had an empty house. "Where's Addy?"

"She wasn't here when I dropped you off."

Savannah frowned. "Where's my purse?"

He went back downstairs and a minute later returned with it. Savannah pulled out her phone and looked at the texts. "She walked to the library. Crazy girl." She leaned back against her pillows. "I don't want to bother anyone."

"Bella will be here at four, and I'll stay until then. I can write on my laptop."

"That's not necessary." Especially if Addy were here.

"Says the woman who was crashed on her steps after being hit by a mystery SUV earlier in the day. It's a nonstarter." He shifted against the wooden back as if to emphasize he wasn't going anywhere. Then he gave her a self-satisfied smile. "This reporter only needs his laptop and power cord to work from anywhere in the world."

"What are you working on?"

"A follow-up article on Logan Donnelly and his friends. I think I found a new thread."

"The man is dead. Leave him alone."

"He wasn't the only one on the trips."

"That doesn't mean he's fair game now."

"No, but it does mean the investigation didn't die with him and Dustin. There's more to the story, including the fourth person I haven't found."

Her jaw was so tight, she couldn't speak. She rubbed it to ease the tension. "Don't waste your time on dead ends." She winced as her word choice registered. "That's not what I meant."

"I know, but what if there was more to the trips?"

"Like what?"

"I don't know, but as I was reviewing my notes I remembered a tweet that when I first read it made me think the person knows something. When I read it again, I couldn't help wondering if they might know who the fourth man is." He sighed as he leaned forward. "I just sent a direct message and now we wait."

"Maybe a fresh set of eyes will help." She clapped a hand over her mouth. She hadn't meant to offer that. The last thing she needed to do was spend more time with this man. He caused her to say and do things she didn't intend, and she didn't need the distraction. "What does the account show?"

He clicked a few buttons on his tablet, then flipped it around. He started scrolling down. "It's mainly images, but they're fantastic shots of Thailand and Bangkok." He stopped as he hit a series set in the city. "Do you sense a theme?"

Savannah reached for the tablet. "Can I look?"

"Sure." He handed the device over and she slowly scrolled down.

"It's interesting that so many of her posts include a photo."

Jett twitched as if he'd been shocked. "Why did you say her?"

"I don't know." Then she pointed at a post with exotic orchids and flowers. "I guess I can't imagine a man posting photos like this."

He leaned toward her bed, and she shifted, trying to sit up more. Next thing she knew, he stood and helped her, shifting pillows so she could be more comfortable. She eased back against the pillow and smiled. "Thank you."

"Sure." He took the tablet back. "I've posted photos like that."

She arched a brow at him. "Really? Of delicate orchids?"

"Okay. If I traveled to Thailand on vacation, I'd expect to post things like that. My trip was all business." He handed it back to her. "These are different from what we have here."

He grinned at her, and she found herself responding. There was something about the way he looked at her and immediately moved to assist her that drew her to him. She might take care of others, but no one had taken care of her in a very long time. Maybe working together to determine what had happened to Dustin and what the trips were really about wouldn't be so bad.

Maybe in the process she could clear Addy's father.

His trip through her town house had revealed much about Savannah Daniels. She didn't spend a lot of time in her home, because it felt like a showroom, perfectly staged but without much soul. Not one book was out of place on a bookshelf. Not one glass had been left on the dining room table. Instead, she had a leather couch in front of a medium-sized, wall-mounted TV. He'd bet she never took the time to watch it.

And there hadn't been a single dish in the kitchen sink. The marble counter was immaculate. With the subway tile backsplash, it was a kitchen that could be featured in *Southern Living*. Did she really live here or did she just land on occasion?

Right now, however, it was the look on her face that held his attention. He figured she hadn't intended to offer to help him with his research, but now that she had, Jett thought it was a great idea.

"How often did you spend time with Dustin after the divorce?"

He'd take notes in his mind even as he itched to enter notes on his tablet. No need to alert her to how much he wanted to know.

"Not any more than I had to with Addy."

He cocked his head as he considered. "Really? You seemed comfortable together at the hospital."

"You have no idea." She rolled her eyes and looked back at the Twitter feed.

"Do you have custody of her?" The girl cropped up often enough in her conversation that he wondered.

"No. But her mom isn't the most on top of it, and with his schedule, Dustin was gone more than he was around. I spend a lot of time with her." Savannah took another drink of water. "She makes it easy. And I could keep the distance I needed."

"I had a thought while you were out." She raised an eyebrow at him, but he ignored it. "Did you know Dustin and Logan went to the same high school?"

She shrugged. "Why does that matter?"

"It means they have history and a depth of trust."

"Maybe. I hardly stay in touch with anyone from school."

He could see that. The woman was so focused on work and her niece that she didn't seem to leave room for much else. "That doesn't mean they didn't. All the flights to Thailand were piloted by your husband."

Savannah drained the glass, then set it on the vintage nightstand. Her place had a cottage feel. Not quite antique, but chic that wasn't modern. "This is your epiphany?"

"Do you know what the trips were for?"

"According to your article they were pleasure excursions." She studied him like a teacher who was displeased with the efforts of her least favorite pupil. He tried to meet her gaze without flinching. "You can't make accusations like that without solid facts."

"I did months of research—time my editor still holds against me. Did you know I traveled there . . . twice? Once wasn't enough, because I had more questions after I got home. I spent time finding the taxi drivers, the hotel, the right airport."

"But you don't know who the fourth passenger was? What if that soul-freedom tweeter is right? That person could be the key."

"Really?" He felt the spike of heat that always came when he thought about what had been done to his dad, and how the truth was too little too late. "I understand more than you know."

She froze, then understanding and sympathy washed her face. "Your father."

"What else?" He scrubbed his face with his hands. "Look, I am more committed to truth than probably anyone else you'll meet. I understand what happens when it isn't a journalist's driving aim."

Savannah sighed. "You're right, and I'm sorry." Her fingers played with the edge of the blanket. "I just wish I knew if Dustin actually had evidence of his innocence. Even if he did, the words you published have a lasting impact. It will linger like a long shadow on a person's soul. That's a lesson I learned early in my legal career."

"It wasn't just me."

"What?"

"Everything in that article was run through the fact-checking department." He leaned forward again, trying to close what felt like a growing chasm between them. "Look, I won't retract words that are true. And until we find other evidence, mine is rock solid. Help me, and we can look for the fourth person together. See if we can figure out what Dustin meant. Frankly, he could have been high on painkillers and not known what he was saying."

She shook her head. "He seemed lucid to me."

"Let's find out."

She considered him, and he felt her positioning him on a scale. Did he measure up?

———

Savannah resisted the urge to fan her face. How could this man so easily turn her thoughts and emotions upside down? And the look on his face! It suggested he understood the power he wielded. She wanted to shake it from him, but that would only validate his influence over her.

The sun was starting to set and sent lengthening rays through her windows.

Did she want to work with Jett? He might help her figure out what had really happened to Dustin, because she didn't believe he'd committed suicide.

Would answers be worth the risks of being in close proximity to the man?

As she watched him, he pulled out his notes and studied them as if he'd find the Holy Grail somewhere in the pages. What did he expect to get out of their coalition? She wasn't willing to give him carte blanche to harm Addy and hurt her. And it wouldn't be possible to spend time with Jett without being impacted. She needed to walk away, yet she wanted to walk closer.

Was she playing with fire?

Probably, but she wanted to take the risk. For the first time in years, she felt the tug to see what this man was really made of. Was there integrity buried inside him that would rise to the occasion? There was only one way to find out. Give him the chance to climb behind her walls, even if he might hurt her deeply in the process.

On the other hand, she might experience the deep connection her heart longed for.

"You disappeared." His quiet words snapped her from her reverie.

"Just thinking." She took another minute. "I'll do it."

"Do what?" He looked slightly confused, though he shouldn't.

"Tomorrow I have to finish a project for my clients. Then I'll work with you on your article, but I'm not sure what you think I can contribute." She pushed her legs to the edge of the bed and then stood. She only swayed a moment before finding her balance.

The man had the audacity to smirk as he reached out to steady her.

She merely had to keep from being distracted by him. It might not be easy, but she'd do it to clear the fog that Jett's article had summoned around Dustin. She'd do it for Addy.

It would all be for her niece and for the truth.

That alone made the risk worth it.

He neared the home, slowed his car, and crawled down the road at ten miles an hour. The time was late, and the street was quiet. No one out walking a dog. No curtains pulled back by someone spying on the street.

All looked ready for him to make his move.

He continued down the road a block, and then parked on a side street. There was an alley between the small apartment buildings. Each looked to have six apartments. Three up, three down.

The man might think he had only traveled with the team.

But it wasn't true.

And now vengeance would be his. While his daughter was gone, he could prevent this man from partnering in harming anyone else. It was the call that had burned in him, building over time.

The article had outlined the evidence in stark black and white. No one could read it and not believe it. It was a roadmap of activities showing the way the men had plotted and planned their excursions that were little more than excuses to harm girls like his Grace. The young girls and young women might not be able to defend themselves. He might not be able to reach them. But he could ensure the men paid the ultimate price for the harm.

Some might argue he was distracted, focused on someone who didn't participate in the crimes, but he knew the truth.

So nice of the plane to take care of the leader.

He'd taken care of the pilot.

That left one more named man for him to punish.

Tonight he accepted the call. Then he'd turn to finding the fourth. With the resources at his fingertips, it would be an easy matter. He could find things the reporter couldn't.

He parked in the shadows at the outskirts of the parking lot. Better to let the darkness cloak him. Then he reached in the back seat and pulled a small bag from it.

He was ready.

CHAPTER
TWENTY-SEVEN

Savannah called a rideshare service and made it back to work in the morning despite Bella's argument that she should stay home. Emilie had called and walked her through everything she'd accomplished Thursday going through documents with John and Rochelle, but Savannah needed to see them for herself before signing off and forwarding everything to the FBI. That had her arriving at the office before the sun was fully up.

Fortunately whatever had caused her headache had cleared.

Her desk was bare except for two stacked folders. One was labeled *FBI*, the other bore her name.

She opened the top one and slowly flipped through the documents. They were neatly organized with the originals in chronological order, and a quick glance showed the other ordered the same. Savannah spent more time on the cover memo, which did a good job explaining the decisions Emilie had made in a way that even the agents should understand. Savannah signed the memo and then slid it back into the folder. Now she'd have to wait to see if the FBI agreed with their legal opinion. If the agency didn't, she'd still bought her clients time.

Her phone rang, and Savannah glanced at her clock. Nine o'clock?

She hadn't heard anyone come in for the day. The number was Rochelle's. Savannah frowned as she leaned back against her chair. "Savannah Daniels."

"Oh, thank goodness you're there. Men with government IDs are standing at my office door. They're telling me they want to interview me." Rochelle's voice shook, something unusual for the woman who had been so self-possessed the last two weeks. Was this her last straw?

Savannah closed her eyes and tried to imagine why anyone associated with the government wouldn't give her clients time to comply with the subpoena before harassing them. "Did they tell you why?"

"It was the classic 'you need to come with us, ma'am.'" Rochelle sighed. "John is sick and out of the office. The stress of the last weeks caught up with him. I can't handle this alone."

"You shouldn't. Get the agents' names and badge IDs. Tell them you will voluntarily come in later today, but only with your attorney. And try to find out why they want to talk to you." Savannah rubbed her temples.

"They say it's related to Flight 2840."

Savannah sat straighter. "But we're complying with the subpoena."

"I know."

"Hand one of them the phone."

"Okay."

There was a moment and then a male voice came on. "Agent James Martin. Who am I speaking with?"

"Savannah Daniels. Please identify your agency and the reason you're harassing my client."

"Not harassing, ma'am. Simply pursuing an investigation and all related leads."

"Your agency."

"FBI."

"Agent Martin, my client is complying with the subpoena. The documents will be delivered later today."

"The documents were due yesterday."

"We received an extension."

"Of a day?" He snorted. "You're late and now we'll be taking Ms. Lingonier in for questioning."

"I will bring her later today."

"Unacceptable."

"More acceptable than the lawsuit I will file this afternoon if you pursue this." She didn't have the energy to follow through on her threat. However, Hayden or Emilie did. "It would be a pleasure to sue the FBI for a violation of civil rights."

"One o'clock. Downtown. With the documents. Don't be late."

"Understood. Please return the phone to my client." A minute later Rochelle was back. "One o'clock. We have to be at the Hoover Building then."

"I heard. Meet you there at 12:45?"

"Let's meet around the corner." Savannah gave her the address, then hung up and leaned back in her chair. This was shaping up to be quite the day, and she felt the lingering aches from yesterday's accident. She'd probably feel the bruises from the seat belt for days.

Savannah called in Emilie and Hayden and created a quick plan of attack. "Any thoughts on why the FBI is doing this?"

Hayden shrugged as she twisted her engagement ring. "Your client hasn't told us everything."

"That's clear." Emilie crossed her arms over her stylish navy sheath. With a gold necklace and bangle bracelets, she looked ready to walk into any situation DC could throw her way, including an emergency hearing. "Rochelle didn't often make eye contact with me this week. Makes me wonder how much they aren't telling us. What other surprises might be waiting."

"Clients always make it harder when they lie." Hayden pushed to her feet. "I have a prospective client meeting in thirty minutes. Let me know if you need anything else."

As Savannah's phone rang again, she shook her head. "You two have been helpful. Thank you."

"That's why you brought us on." Hayden took a step away, but stopped. "Are you sure you're ready to handle the FBI after yesterday's accident?"

"Absolutely." What else could she do?

Emilie followed Hayden out as Savannah took the call. "Daniels."

"Savannah, this is Jett."

Just hearing his voice lowered her blood pressure—a reaction she didn't expect. "How can I help?"

"We're not that formal." There was a light tease in his tone, but also something else. Maybe a bit of pique.

"Sorry. It's already been a long day." Even though it was barely ten.

"I'll keep this short. Can you meet me at Dustin's apartment tonight?"

"Why?" Jett had no good reason to be there.

"Someone needs to look for his will and documents."

"Not you." She knew he couldn't do it without her.

"You can and should. While we're there maybe we'll find his evidence." He said the last word with a bit of inflection, as if he didn't believe anything existed. "Before I let you go. Are you sure you didn't know Evan Spencer?"

"Certain. Why?"

"He was killed last night. Police are calling it a burglary gone bad." Savannah covered her mouth with her hand. "That's awful."

"No one is left from my investigation, except the person I can't find."

"You didn't cause the plane crash."

"Or the burglary." But his voice didn't have the conviction of someone who believed his own words.

An hour and a half later, as she entered the King Street Metro Station for the trip into the city, she wondered why she had agreed to meet Jett when she had more pressing matters at hand. While traffic wouldn't be terrible over the lunch hour, parking could be tricky and was always expensive, so she'd walk the couple of blocks from the Archives yellow line Metro stop to the FBI headquarters. As the train pulled into the DC station, she texted Rochelle to remind her to meet at Red Velvet Cupcakery, and from there they would walk to the FBI building together. After all, the FBI building wasn't one you strolled into.

Rochelle was tense as she walked into the shop. The sweet aroma should have brought a smile to her face and had her reaching for her pocketbook. Instead she looked like she couldn't decide whether to bolt or stay rooted in place.

"Would you like anything?"

Rochelle placed a hand over her stomach. "I couldn't keep it down. I didn't expect to be this nervous. You'd think with my experience I'd seen it all. The last two weeks have disproved that notion."

"We'll sort this out together." Savannah forced a smile and finished her coffee. "All right, let's head over."

It wasn't a simple process getting into the building, but the agents had given Rochelle a letter, which helped cut a few steps. By the time they got through the security line and each had a visitor tag, sweat ran down Savannah's back. A stern-faced man in a dark suit strode toward her. "Ms. Daniels? Ms. Lingonier?"

"Yes, sir." Rochelle leaned nearer. "This is one of the two who came to the office."

"Ah." Savannah looked him over. Looked like standard government issue.

"Agent Martin. I'll escort you to the interview room." The agent was a bit older than she was and looked familiar. There was a haunted look about him that his ramrod posture couldn't cover.

She stepped into place next to him. "Have we met before?"

He gave her a sidelong glance. "I don't believe so, ma'am. Why?"

"You look familiar." She shrugged.

Rochelle nodded. "I had the same thought this morning."

He shrugged. "I get that a lot. It's this way to the conference room we'll use." While his expression was serious, it wasn't unkind. "Do you have the documents with you?"

She patted her oversized bag, which had been x-rayed and thoroughly searched. "Right here."

"Good." He stayed quiet as he led them through the bustling halls to the elevator bank. It had been a few months since she'd taken the FBI Experience tour, but this was a different part of the massive headquarters than the contained and sterilized public space.

After he ushered them to a small conference room, he left, and Savannah turned to Rochelle.

The woman's short hair stood up as if she'd been electrocuted, and her wrinkled khakis and polo suggested she'd slept in them. "What's the plan?" Her words quavered.

"Listen rather than talk. It's too early for them to have called you in." Savannah glanced at her watch. "I don't know what their game is, so we'll stay quiet." She took the seat next to Rochelle. "All you need to do is relax and be honest. I'll stop the interview if it takes an odd turn, but I don't anticipate that."

When Agent Martin walked in with a stack of files and a recorder, Rochelle straightened with a jerk while Savannah frowned.

"I thought you wanted to talk about the documents we brought." She opened her briefcase and slid out the bulging accordion file.

"We'll get there." He sat across the metal table from them, arranged his files just so, then pulled out a pen and opened the first file. "Thank you for coming in."

Rochelle sniffed, her gaze snapping as straight as her back. "I didn't have a choice."

"It's always good to cooperate." He flashed her a smile, but Savannah wasn't warmed by it. "We have a few questions."

Fifteen minutes later, Savannah decided this was the strangest interrogation she'd witnessed in a long time. It felt as awkward as the one from a mock trial class she'd had in law school.

Agent Martin leaned into the conversation in a way that struck her as overzealous, and Rochelle sat back with arms crossed and mouth closed. At least her client had remembered not to volunteer information.

The stack of files sat at Agent Martin's elbow. "Tell me again what your company had on that plane."

"Nothing." She glanced at Savannah, then continued. "We didn't put anything on the plane."

"What do you mean?"

"It's come to our attention that someone may have stolen our tech and put it on the plane, but we aren't sure."

"Interesting." He smirked at her, and Rochelle rolled her eyes, a gesture guaranteed to antagonize the man. "All right. Tell me about your relationship with Sahid Abdul."

Rochelle raised her hands in a what-are-you-talking-about gesture. "Who?"

"Your boyfriend." He slid a photo of a handsome, late-forties man across the table.

Rochelle's eyes narrowed, and Savannah hurried to speak before her client could. "Why does this man have anything to do with this?" She glanced at Rochelle as the woman's jaw hardened.

"He's a Saudi national."

"So?"

"He's on our watch list."

Rochelle stiffened even further. "That's ridiculous. I would have heard something."

His gaze narrowed. "Do you conduct background checks on your boyfriends?"

The color drained from Rochelle's cheeks. "Let's get back to the reason we're here."

The man stroked the top file. "Is Mnemosyne's code designed to spy on a plane or bring it down?"

Rochelle snorted. "What? Neither!"

Savannah placed a restraining hand on Rochelle arm. "What my client means is that without more she has nothing to say. This sounds like a fishing expedition. If my client knew anything that would help unravel the cause of the crash, she would divulge it. However, at this point, you don't even know what you're asking for."

The man leaned so far across the table, Savannah felt his breath on her face when he spoke. "We will nail the people behind this crash. If your client had anything to do with it, the only thing that will assist her is to cooperate now. If we find the information independently, there will be no leniency."

"It's a simple plane crash. While they are always tragedies, that doesn't make them national emergencies."

He slid a sheet of paper across the table to her. "Still think so?"

CHAPTER
TWENTY-EIGHT

Jett typed on his laptop at the *Source*'s offices, distracted with thoughts about his upcoming meeting with Savannah. The news that Evan Spencer had been killed rattled him. While Savannah was right that he didn't control the plane crash or a burglary gone bad, he couldn't shake the instinct that something deeper was happening.

If the first three team members had died, was the fourth targeted as well?

If so, he needed to find them now, and that made the trip to a dead man's apartment to find whatever evidence he could critical. His story about Donnelly and Tate was solid, but there was more at stake now. That's the only reason he was doing this.

Still, an unnamed doubt pestered him.

He recalled the time he refused to walk away from his suspicions about a company with a less-than-glowing reputation that was launching a college program for its employees. The CEO claimed he wanted to help advance his employees, when in reality he'd bought a large stake in the online college. It had taken diligent work to uncover the extent of that man's double-dipping and the fact that the degrees weren't worth the paper they were printed on.

That article had felt good to publish. Almost redeeming.

But then there was the time he pressed hard against a lobbyist who looked like she was colluding with enemies of the state, when in reality she was helping extricate adopted kids out of their African country. When Jett had gotten the call to join that mission, his laptop and cell phone were taken until they'd given him the chance to witness the whole truth. That story had been a pleasure to write too. Still, he wouldn't have received an invitation if he hadn't dug into the rumors and caused enough noise to get the lobbyist's attention.

One way or the other, Jett always got to the truth.

So why the whisper of doubt?

Wait a minute.

He'd gotten so distracted by Tate's death and his search for the fourth man he'd forgotten the man who'd called him claiming to know something. He pulled out his phone and dialed. The call rang repeatedly, but no answer and no voice mail. He frowned as he ended the call, then tried again. It still went nowhere. He plugged the number into a reverse number look-up search engine, but nothing. Then he went to Facebook and entered the number in the search bar. Sometimes that worked, but not this time.

He sent an email to the tech guy at the office to see if there was another way to back into the source of the number.

So many dead ends. Light Comes After Darkness. Bernard Julius. Jett shook his head.

His phone rang and he grabbed it. "Glover."

"You've been trying to find me." The voice was husky and low.

Jett took a quick look at his screen. Caller ID Blocked. "I'd begun to wonder if you were going to call."

"Life got . . . busy."

"How can I help you?"

"Check your mail. Then we'll talk again."

Savannah glanced over the paper, grateful for the speed-reading course her mom had required one summer. The page didn't mean a whole lot to her. It looked like scientific gobbledygook, but she noted the way Rochelle swayed momentarily.

"How did you get this?" The words were a reedy whisper, not Rochelle's normal commanding tones.

The door opened and another agent slipped into the room. He extended his hand toward Savannah. "Sorry I'm late."

She shook his hand. "I'm Savannah Daniels, Ms. Lingonier's attorney."

"Agent Owen Lawson." He sat in the vacant chair and gestured for Agent Martin to continue. Savannah studied him, trying to get a read on him. He wore a solid brown suit but no tie, and she noticed wear around the collar of his white shirt. He also had tired eyes, like he'd already lived a week today.

"Someone in maintenance for the airline came forward," Agent Martin said. "Told us this didn't belong on the flight. Talked to someone in design and engineering." He flipped open a file, glanced at something inside, then closed it. "Someone else at NTSB mentioned your little company. Didn't take long from there to sitting here with you. All you have to do is tell me how you got your program added to the flight computer."

"We didn't add anything." Rochelle found her fight and fire again. It was evident in every line of her body. "You should be looking for corporate espionage or something like that. We didn't authorize the program to be uploaded."

"But it was. You haven't denied you have the data." He tapped the stack of documents Savannah had given him. "I believe you said it's in here."

"Yes. We haven't figured out what happened, but whatever occurred was unauthorized. John and I were very clear about what the injunction meant."

"And your employees always do what you tell them?"

"Sure. They work for us."

Agent Lawson leaned forward. "How about your partner?"

"Of course."

The corner of the man's mouth tipped up as he stared at them. "You sure about that?"

Agent Martin turned toward his colleague with a frown but didn't interrupt.

"Yes." Rochelle sounded certain, but Savannah detected a tightening around the woman's blue eyes. Then she turned toward Savannah and put a hand over her mouth. "He wouldn't."

"Who wouldn't what?"

She shook her head. "I don't know. I need to think. Can we leave now?" She looked at Savannah. "I don't feel well."

Savannah glanced at the agents. Lawson arched an eyebrow in a way that mirrored her thoughts. Still she tapped the folder. "This has all the documents you subpoenaed. I've also included a legal memo explaining what is included and why."

Agent Martin nodded. "Let me take this to the requesting agent. Confirm there aren't further questions." He stood, took the folder, and left.

After watching them for a minute, Agent Lawson stood as well. "You need to think carefully about your partner."

Savannah met his gaze steadily. "Do you know something Rochelle needs to know?"

The man left without answering. Savannah immediately turned to Rochelle. "Keep your voice down, but start explaining."

"John didn't agree that we needed to keep waiting." She held up a hand as Savannah started to protest. "I know what he told you, but he's wrapped up not only his savings, but his grandparents' and other family members' money too. Some of them were applying pressure to get their investments back. John thought if we put the code into use, it would help our case in the lawsuit and get us to market that much faster. I told him the product wasn't ready." Rochelle's eyes were red-rimmed and her mouth tipped down. "What if he moved ahead and didn't tell me? What if it's not a corporate spy, but my partner?"

———

Four hours later that question still echoed through Savannah's mind. She'd danced as best she could around the question when Agent Martin returned to the room. Then she'd spent the balance of the afternoon with Rochelle searching for John. The man wasn't at his apartment or office. Savannah finally left Rochelle to find and confront him, because she needed to meet Jett at Dustin's apartment.

When she pulled into Dustin's slot, she parked and sat for a minute. Her hands trembled on the steering wheel as adrenaline flooded her. She was exhausted and probably should have stayed home.

What was she doing?

Someone knocked on the driver's window, and she jumped. She turned to find Jett looking at her. He opened the door, then stood to the side as she climbed out.

His gaze seemed to see through her. "You ready for this?"

She tried to suck in courage as she grabbed her purse and slid from the car. "Can you ever be? He was alive three days ago."

He touched her hand where it rested on the door. "You're not doing this alone. I'm walking into this with you. Together we'll look around, find his will and life insurance information. But whatever we find, it will be together."

His words wormed deep into her heart.

Could she reach out and accept what he offered?

She wanted to, but first he'd have to earn her trust. That would require her to tear down her walls. Maybe she couldn't knock them all down yet, but another brick crashed to the ground. She liked the sensation of freedom even as she knew she'd risk her heart.

This time it was worth the potential pain.

She let him take her hand. "Let's do this. Together."

They walked across the parking lot, her hand tucked in his, and she didn't try to tug free. Instead she sank into the protected feeling.

The apartment building looked different since the last time she'd been here.

Tuesday evening the strobes from the police and emergency lights had colored the scene with a blinding effect. Now the complex was transformed back to typical three-story brick apartment buildings with green space flowing between each one. They were only steps from Dustin's building.

The door opened as they approached, so Savannah waited until they climbed to the second floor to reach for her set of keys in her purse. For a moment she considered pretending she couldn't find the keys, but that would only delay the inevitable. She had to go in there, and she was surprised to realize she'd rather go in with Jett's presence and support.

When she pulled out the key, Jett gave her a sideways look. "Dustin give you that?"

"This one is Addy's." Savannah slotted the key in the lock and then hesitated. She felt Jett behind her before she twisted the knob. It didn't feel quite right having him join her, but she couldn't imagine a better way to show him Dustin wasn't the person he'd described.

She twisted the key in the lock, jiggling it a bit, and the door squeaked open.

CHAPTER
TWENTY-NINE

The apartment felt . . . empty.

Like the rooms knew the man who'd inhabited them wouldn't be back. The only thing that could make her enter was the idea that Addy Jo would be harmed by the lies spread about her father. And she needed the life insurance if it existed. The mama bear in Savannah couldn't stay away, even if the wounded twenty-six-year-old hiding inside wanted nothing more than to flee. She wasn't a runner. That had been Dustin's role.

"Dustin lived here alone?" Jett's voice caused her to jump.

"Yes." Her voice squeaked, so she swallowed and tried again. "Yes." That sounded better. "He was in and out erratically. Said it was too much to expect a roommate to put up with his schedule and he liked his privacy."

"You okay?" Jett's voice was quiet, concerned.

She wanted him to see her as strong and invincible. Not weak and cowering in the doorway. She forced herself through the door, pulling on all her courage. "Let's see what we can find. First order of business is his life insurance policy. I'm not sure who his carrier is but Stasi said he had one." As a pilot the profession was too dangerous not to have a strong policy. "We need to find his will too, if he has one."

"Any idea where he would keep it?"

"No." The practical question annoyed her. She lifted her chin and gazed down the corridor, then she entered.

It was stark.

White walls.

Nothing like the colors she'd painted her home.

The furniture was functional but looked like leftovers from a frat house trunk show. While her place wasn't immaculate or perfect, it had character in the lines of the vintage furniture mixed with newer pieces.

Jett stood in the small living room, and she wondered what he saw. Dustin hadn't taken much time to make the apartment more than a man cave. She was sure if she opened the fridge, she'd find yogurt and not much else. The cabinets would hold easy fare like Ramen noodles and cereal. Dustin had never enjoyed cooking, instead preferring takeout. There would also be four cups, four plates, and four bowls. The silverware would probably be plastic, the easier to clean or throw away. That minimalist vibe carried over to the living area, where he had a small table with two chairs, a pleather couch, and a coffee table that looked like he'd kicked his feet on top of it all the time. The TV was almost bigger than the wall, and his priorities were clear. When he was home, he'd watch a game or movie, maybe play on one of his gaming sets. That was it.

Jett stepped ahead of her, hands in his pockets as he strolled back to the kitchen. He opened the refrigerator door and let out a low whistle. "Guess he didn't believe in eating."

Savannah glanced around Jett at the jar of mayonnaise and wilted bag of spinach. Several containers of Greek yogurt lined the bottom shelf, but that was it. "Why buy groceries if you won't be home to eat them?" She frowned because the words didn't feel right. "He was going to be home." She stepped closer, nudging Jett to the side as she opened a couple cabinets. Boxes of macaroni and Ramen lined the shelf. "Some things never change."

Jett snorted. "You mean he didn't outgrow college."

"This was his idea of convenience food. Get hungry and eat ten minutes later." She shut the cupboard and turned to the living area. "At least there isn't much to clean out." The small folding table with two chairs looked like it hadn't been wiped off in weeks. "The police have been through everything, right?"

"Probably." Jett shrugged. "But if they were convinced it was suicide, there might not have been much of an investigation. Why?"

"Something isn't right." Savannah shoved her hands deeper into her pockets and took a moment to soak in the room's atmosphere. What was wrong? "It seems too neat. Where's the blood from his suicide?"

Savannah felt along the wall for the hall's light switch, since the sun had set and the apartment was dark. She toggled the switch up, but nothing happened. She frowned, then felt for the next switch. A small light illuminated the hall.

She looked at his bedroom door. Did she want to go in there? "I didn't hire a cleaning service, and I doubt the management company would have come without permission from the family." Wait. Stasi. She pulled out her phone and called her sister even as she wondered if the woman would have been listed as a contact on the lease. When her sister answered, she launched straight into her question. "Did you have someone clean Dustin's apartment?"

"Sure. When the management company called, I told them to do it. I didn't want to, and I can't imagine you did either."

"Okay." She paused. "How did you pay for it?"

"Told them to bill it to his account. That has to be paid from the estate, right?"

"Makes sense." In a Stasi kind of way. At least she hadn't asked for Savannah's credit card.

"Where are you?"

"At his apartment. We need to talk, but I'll call you later." She hung up, then sighed and strode toward his bedroom. She didn't want to go in there, but it had been cleaned and she needed to find Addy's things. If she wanted to find anything that indicated it hadn't been suicide, it would be in there. What could she locate that the professionals hadn't?

She stood in the hallway reluctant to enter. The bedroom looked sterile like a hotel room, only without the bland art on the wall. The bed hadn't been slept in, which made sense if a cleaning service had been in and out.

Behind her she heard Jett turn on the wall-sized TV.

Jett's silence worried her, and she turned to catch his expression. It wasn't vacant, more fascinated in a I'm-watching-a-train-wreck kind of way. "I should take photos to show my mom. She'd stop complaining about my lack of interior decorating skills after seeing this place. How much did he travel?"

"It was his job." Savannah shrugged, then turned back to the bedroom. "I got the sense from Addy he was in the air a lot. For some of the trips, he'd be gone a week or more."

"That matches what I found during my investigation."

An aroma held her at the door. It felt stifling, cloying, spicy, but unlike the cologne Dustin had favored. What was it? Cleaner? She sniffed but couldn't place it. With all that had happened in the apartment, she shouldn't be surprised that it smelled off. But she expected an industrial, hospital smell. The kind that seemed extra clean but felt dirty underneath. She steeled her will and then entered the bedroom.

A shadow shifted, and she froze.

Before she could do anything, a force pushed her against the wall with a jolt and the air rushed from her lungs. She felt a slice of pain along her upper arm.

Instinct rose and she kicked out. Flailed against the body.

Must be a man, based on size. He grunted, and she kicked out harder.

She was not prepared to grapple with someone as he pulled her farther into the room.

She tried to scream but couldn't as she flailed against him, all her energy focused on escape.

Where was Jett?

Why didn't he hear and come?

Her thoughts swam in a murky morass as she tried again to push the man off her. His weight pressed her against the bedroom wall, and she scratched with all her might. Then he yanked her hair, and she screamed.

She bit down on the arm pressed against her face, and the grip loosened.

She gasped. Stomped hard. Slid down the wall as he stumbled back.

With a desperate thrust she scrambled into the hallway and screamed again.

Jett was there. "What's going on?"

"There's a man in there." She trembled as she rushed toward the living room.

"Stay here." Jett slid around the door.

A gust of frigid air came through the room, and she sagged. The man must have escaped through the window. It would be a drop to the ground, but not too far.

She pulled her phone from her pocket and tapped it to life. Then she dialed Detective Jensen. "I'm at Dustin's apartment. A man was just in here, and we need help."

"On my way. You okay?"

"I don't know." She slid to the floor as the adrenaline seeped from her and wetness dripped down her arm.

CHAPTER
THIRTY

She looked so pale. Fragile.

Jett whipped out his phone but saw she already had hers out. "Who are you calling?"

"Detective Jensen. He's on the way." She grimaced, and he noticed red running down her arm.

"You're bleeding."

"I guess I am, Captain Obvious." She tried to smile, but it looked more like a pain-filled smirk.

"We need to get you checked out."

Her jaw squared. "Not until the detective arrives." She touched her arm as if assessing it. "I don't think I'll die today."

"While I'm glad, you still need to have it examined." He knelt beside her and turned on the flashlight on his phone so he could examine the wound. "Looks like he sliced you cleanly, but it'll need stitches."

"I'm not leaving until Detective Jensen gets here."

Jett didn't know whether to strangle her or go along. The cut was bleeding but if he could find some gauze to apply to it . . . no, that was crazy. She needed to have a professional check it out. "I'm calling an ambulance."

"No."

"Then I'm taking you."

"Not a chance." She moved as if to get up from the floor, then groaned. "Thanks to you I spent time yesterday at the hospital."

"You give me too much credit. I think the other driver was to blame."

"You called 911."

"After you called me."

"We're wasting time." This time the stubborn woman did make it to her feet, though she ignored his hand.

"I could have helped you up."

"No, you want to help me to the hospital. Let's find his office." She wobbled her way down the hall to the second bedroom. He ducked into the bathroom and grabbed a wet washcloth and rummaged around until he found Band-Aids.

The office was tiny, maybe ten by ten, typical of apartments in this area that cut separate living spaces out of cramped areas. A set of gliding doors covered a closet on the far wall. The room was barely big enough for the large wood desk. He found her leaning her hip against the desk.

He waved the Band-Aids and washcloth. "Before you poke around, we need to get this cleaned up. The moment it bleeds through the bandage, you're headed to the ER if I have to carry you."

She huffed but didn't stop him as he leaned closer to examine the cut. "We should cut your sweater sleeve off."

"What?" She frantically turned to look at it, as he grabbed a pair of scissors from a holder on top of the desk. "You can't do that. Do you know how much this cost?"

"It's already been sliced."

Her shoulders slumped. "Go ahead. Just hurry so we can look around before the detective gets here." Savannah's gaze shifted everywhere but her arm.

The moment he finished bandaging her as well as he could, she picked up the framed picture of Addy from the corner of the desk.

The woman's jaw clenched so tightly she could crack a tooth. Honestly, Jett was surprised it hadn't happened already. Savannah carried her tension internally, and as far as he could tell she didn't have a mechanism for releasing it.

"Let's see what's in here."

His words seemed to jar her from wherever her thoughts had taken her but didn't ease the tension locked in her jaw.

"All right." Her words were resigned rather than engaged. "I think the file cabinet is in the closet."

"I'll start there."

"Okay." Savannah eased onto the edge of the desk chair. She didn't want to be here. It was etched in the way her feet shifted and her gaze flitted about the room. He admired the way she squared her shoulders and went to work anyway. "Where did Addy stay when she was here?" She frowned. "I thought he had a bed for her."

Jett glanced around, then noted a twin Murphy bed up against the wall. "This must pull down somehow."

"Hmm. It'd be tight." She wore her discomfort like a coat. Her shoulders were uncharacteristically rolled forward, and she couldn't hold his gaze for more than a few seconds. Each told Jett more plainly than the words she couldn't find that this woman wanted to be anywhere but here . . . and with anyone but him. It hit him.

"You still loved him."

She startled and looked at him. "What? No!" But telltale red climbed her neck.

"The way you looked at him in the hospital. It makes sense now. He must have been your first love. No other reason you'd still be single otherwise."

"What? You're insane."

He shook his head. "You can deny it. But I was there and overheard him telling you he made a mistake. Must have fanned the flames."

"He left me fifteen years ago."

"Doesn't matter. You still love him. That's why you can't stand to be here now. Especially with me."

"Now I know you're crazy. If the article you wrote wasn't enough, this confirms it." She crossed her arms and leaned against the desk. "Is this how you write? Draw random conclusions from two unrelated data points?"

"Everything I write is well-researched, and—"

"I know, fact-checked. Well, if you want to stay, lay off the bologna that I was still in love with Dustin." She turned away from him and took a couple of deep breaths. She relaxed while he watched. "I suppose you'll say the fact I'm planning his memorial service for Addy is proof I love him. If I could, the man would not be remembered by my family. But I love Addy, so I'm planning a service on Monday for the man who left me. Addy's the one I love. Not him." She punctuated the words with a finger stab.

"Defensive much?" He regretted the words as they left his mouth. "Sorry. That was uncalled for."

She stared at him, then turned away. "I have documents to find. You know where the door is if you need it."

He went back to the four-drawer file cabinet crammed in the corner of the closet. It was an industrial-style unit, something that could have been a government reject from some Korean Conflict–era office. The battered gray showed years of wear. There were no labels above the handles, so he started with the top.

It held file folders stuffed with bills. There could be a treasure trove of information on each credit card statement if he examined them. The next drawer had a collection of correspondence and what looked to be invoices. He'd riffle through each of those folders just in case he found anything related to Thailand. The third drawer was mostly empty, which didn't make much sense considering the fourth drawer was filled with years' worth of tax records, and at the back of that drawer he hit pay dirt. One file labeled Will, and next to it, Life Insurance.

He pulled them out and opened the top one. He quickly scanned the thin document and then offered it to Savannah. "I found something."

"What's that?" She didn't bother to turn from the drawer of files in the desk that she was perusing.

"His will."

She spun around in the office chair. "Really?"

"I'm not sure you're going to like it."

"I don't want anything from him."

"Well, he wants something from you."

She shook her head. "I highly doubt that."

Jett handed her the file. "He named you his executor."

"No." The word's brevity punched.

"Yes."

He watched for the moment reality hit.

"No, no, no. I don't need this right now. There's no reason for me to be listed. He must have changed his will since our marriage."

Jett nodded. "He did. Look at the date at the bottom of the last page."

Her hand went to her throat as if that would protect her. "Six months ago."

She tipped back in the chair but kept reading. The will was all the proof he needed that there had still been something between them. She might claim the niece was their only connection, but she was wrong. Dustin at least still trusted Savannah.

He turned back to the file cabinet rather than watch her read. That was too much like watching grass grow when there was so much waiting right here.

A sniff pulled his attention from the files to the desk. Savannah's shoulders were tense, and her head angled away with her chin tipped down so her hair fell like a veil around her face. *Please don't cry.* He was all thumbs and awkwardness in those moments.

A knock at the door sounded. She squared her shoulders, then swiped under her eyes. "That must be Detective Jensen."

"I'll get it." As he passed her, he squeezed her noninjured shoulder.

Once he opened the door for the detective, he motioned for the man to wait. "I need to get her to urgent care or the ER. She's putting on a brave face but needs stitches."

"Need an ambulance?"

"I don't think so, and she's too stubborn to get in one. I'll be doing well to get her to let me drive."

"All right." The man pulled out his notebook. "Time to fill me in."

CHAPTER
THIRTY-ONE

The bright lights and sterility pressed against Savannah.

How was she in the emergency room for the second time in three days? She hated hospitals. She wanted to get up and force her way home, but she needed to stay long enough for stitches. Her assailant had sliced her arm, not deep enough to cause permanent harm but long enough for her upper arm to feel on fire.

Jett had been insistent, and Detective Jensen had gone along with it, letting Jett herd her to his vehicle. Then he drove to the hospital, back to Arlington and the facility where Dustin had recovered.

Jett sat in the chair to the side of the emergency room table. She'd wanted to argue she should have the chair and he could go home, but instead she'd laid down. Almost immediately she'd wanted to take a nap.

Now she had to deal with Detective Jensen and his questions. The man stood at the foot of the bed, arms crossed over his chest and frown dipping his mouth into a grimace. "Care to explain why you thought it was a good idea to break into the apartment?"

"No breaking involved. I have a spare key that my niece gave me." She tried to smile but it felt shaky.

Jett leaned forward but didn't launch from the chair. "Hey, we called you."

228

"Had to or I would have gotten a report from the hospital anyway."

"Not to you specifically."

"You might be surprised." The detective's grin was not friendly though it revealed the small gap between his front teeth. "I was getting ready to eat with my family for the first time in two weeks. You had to go and spoil it."

Savannah watched the interaction between the boys and failed to suppress the urge to get between them. "It wasn't like that. I needed the life insurance information on Dustin. We found the will that lists me as his executor." She looked at Jett, who gave her a quick nod.

"I've got it right here."

Savannah tried to thank him with her eyes. "Any idea who the intruder was?"

"I was hoping you could tell me." Detective Jensen glanced at his notes. "You didn't see much."

"There was barely enough light to note his bedroom was clean. I guess Stasi took care of that." Though Savannah still expected to get the bill.

"That's not who contacted us about cleaning."

"What?" Savannah's mind scrambled. "Who else would pay for something like that?" And there Stasi went taking credit for something she didn't do. How like her little sister.

The detective flipped back through his notes. "A woman named Hope Boonmee."

"Who?"

"Never met her. Said she was a friend of his."

"Dustin?"

"Yes."

"My sister said she ordered the cleaning service. When I walked into the bedroom, the man rushed me. I hadn't turned on the light yet so I didn't see much since I was fighting to escape before he killed me."

The detective turned to Jett. "And where were you during all this?"

He had the credibility to look sheepish as he answered. "In the kitchen and living areas. Did you learn anything about this Hope Boonmee, like how she knew Dustin?"

Detective Jensen shrugged. "No need. Did you see the man leave?"

Jett shook his head. "He was heading out the window."

At that moment a nurse breezed in with a tray of medical supplies. "Time to get you stitched up."

Savannah grimaced but kept her gaze on the detective. "I'll call if I remember anything."

He nodded, then exited the small room that had grown crowded. Jett stepped out to make a call. An hour later Jett drove her home and pulled into a vacant slot in front of her town house.

"Want me to come in?"

She studied him a moment. *So much it scares me.* "I'll be fine. Thank you for the ride." She started to get out, then turned to look at him. "Could I have the will and insurance information?"

"Sure." He patted his coat's inside pockets, then pulled out the documents. "Call if you need anything."

She nodded and took the papers, a lump welling in her throat at his care.

Savannah wobbled slightly as she climbed out of his car but waved him away. Jett drove away reluctantly but was soon preoccupied with a curiosity about the woman who had paid to clean Dustin's apartment. He called the research desk at the *Source* and asked the on-duty researcher, Tina, to work her magic and find Hope Boonmee.

"How do you spell it?"

"Not sure."

"Okay." She drew the word out and he could hear the click of a keyboard. "Anything else you can tell me about her?"

"She paid for Dustin Tate's apartment to be cleaned this week. After his death."

"Where did he live?"

Jett gave her the address, then hung up. An hour later she called back to say she had nothing but would keep looking.

"You're the best, Tina. If you can't find it, it doesn't exist."

He'd move to the next step, ask Savannah to let him ask Addy about the name and see how she reacted. Then he'd talk her into returning to Dustin's apartment. There had to be something more there, or they wouldn't have stumbled on an intruder.

SATURDAY, DECEMBER 19

Addy was still asleep when Savannah returned from getting her rental. She crawled into the attic space to get her Christmas decorations down. While it didn't seem worth it to decorate when it was just her, with Addy staying with her at least for a couple days and her parents possibly coming, it seemed like the year to make an attempt to decorate.

After she carried the boxes to the first floor, she made a bowl of oatmeal and pulled up a news app on her phone. She hadn't googled to see what had happened to Evan Spencer, and she needed to know what the papers were saying. Three men connected to one article dying in the span of a week was statistically improbable, even if one had died in a plane crash.

The *Washington Times* barely mentioned it on a back page of the Metro section. The *Post* didn't do much more. Even the *Source* seemed to overlook the death as one more petty crime gone bad.

Then she searched for Dustin's death. She's spent so much time living the aftermath that she hadn't considered how it was portrayed in the press. Barely more than the mention of police responding to a scene and in one case a statement that his death could be related to an article he'd been mentioned in earlier that month.

She slumped back against her chair. She wasn't sure what she'd hoped to find, but it was more than a few paragraphs.

The sound of movement overhead warned her that Addy was up and on her way to breakfast. Savannah prepared a second bowl of oatmeal and had it waiting on the table with a small plate of blueberries and strawberries when Addy made it down. Her hair was mussed and her eyes bleary as she sank onto a chair.

"Morning, Addy."

The girl picked up her spoon and plopped an elbow on the table and then propped her chin on her hand. "I'm glad you didn't say good."

"It's been a hard week."

"Horrible. That silly kid's book about horrible, terrible days has no idea what it's talking about. I do. And I never want another one like this." She spooned some blueberries on her oatmeal and then took a bite. "What were you thumping around for?"

"Thought we could decorate today."

"Why?"

"For Christmas. I've been slow in getting my decorations up. I decided I need your help and expertise."

"It won't make me feel better."

"It shouldn't make you feel worse. Anyway, I invited Grandma and Grandpa to come this way this year, so I'd better get a few decorations up. Make the place look festive."

"You don't have to babysit me."

"I know." And she did need to have a conversation with Stasi, but not yet. "I figured you'd stay here through the weekend, and then we'll see where things stand."

The girl looked up from her bowl, a frown marring her face.

Savannah reached across the table and squeezed Addy's arm. "I want to spend the time with you. We'll talk about the details for your dad's service and try to have some fun."

A knock at the door made them both startle.

Savannah pushed from the table. Who would be at her door on a Saturday morning?

She glanced through the window next to the door and saw Jett standing on the porch. "Addy, you okay if I let Jett Glover in?"

Her niece glanced up and then shrugged. "I guess it's okay. Just let me take this upstairs first."

The girl skittered around her and disappeared to her room. Savannah glanced outside again and then unlocked and opened the door.

Jett's hands were shoved in the pockets of a barn coat, a plaid scarf wrapped around his neck. She leaned against the doorframe, feeling the bite of the wind.

"Can I come in?"

He grinned at her, but it couldn't have its usual impact, not when he was more exhausted than rakish. He'd spent too much time searching for a thread that never materialized. That's why he was here on her doorstep at this time of the morning. He wasn't sure what she'd do with the unannounced visit, and listening to her conversation with her niece didn't give him assurance she'd let him in.

"You can." She stepped back, and he noted a surge of attraction as he moved by her.

"Thanks." The entryway was small in Savannah's townhome. Straight ahead was the coat closet, behind it the stairs. He waited for her to step into the living room so he could follow, but she seemed frozen in place, her gaze locked on him.

He leaned toward her, letting her feel the weight of his presence. Even if he wondered if a part of her still loved Dustin Tate, Jett was here now. He brushed a strand of hair from her cheek behind her ear, and noticed the shiver she tried to hide. He kept his grin in check but repeated the gesture on the other side. She didn't move as he tipped his head closer to hers, leaving his lips inches from hers, but far enough that he wouldn't accidentally brush his lips across hers when he talked. No, when he kissed her, there would be nothing unexpected or unplanned about it. "Do you have coffee?"

She startled and her lips moved but nothing escaped. Then she licked them and huffed. "In the kitchen."

She was skittish, so he'd be glacially slow if that's what it took. His thoughts turned back to why he'd come.

"Why are you here?" She tried to sidle around him to shut the door and winced.

"Bruised?"

She nodded gingerly. "Between the car accident and our adventure yesterday, I'll feel sore for a while. The stitches tug more than I expected."

He unbuttoned his coat but left it on as he stepped into the middle of her living space. "Had you heard of Hope Boonmee before yesterday?"

Savannah considered his words, then shook her head. "Not that I remember."

"Think Addy might have?"

"Why?"

"After Detective Jensen mentioned her name, I had a researcher at the paper look her up. Couldn't find her."

Savannah pulled out her phone and sank to the edge of her love seat. She started clicking away on the screen. "Not everyone is visible in white-page searches thanks to cells being primary phones."

"Yep, but the paper has access to multiple databases."

"What if she's not from here?"

"I wondered the same thing. Last night I checked and learned Boonmee is a Thai last name."

"What if she still lives in Thailand? Maybe she knows something?" Savannah set her phone to the side.

"Anything's possible." He undid his scarf and sat on a chair. "But how would she know about his death and pay for cleaning if she's not from the States? Have you published an obituary?"

"No." Savannah started tapping on her phone again. "I think we need to chase this."

"What do you mean?"

"Let's head back to Dustin's apartment. If she paid for the apartment to be cleaned, then he must have known her."

He tipped his head but thought there was another option. "Or she's connected to the killer and had it cleaned to get rid of evidence. And when we were there, we interrupted someone who was looking for something the killer left behind."

Savannah pressed a hand against her stomach as if to still the rolling waves that thought generated. "Maybe Dustin has some record of her. We didn't get very far in the search of the apartment."

"Even if we had, we didn't have her name."

"But now we do."

This was it. A thread to pull on. He had a good feeling about where it could lead.

———

The thought of going back didn't thrill Savannah. Neither did it cause her to hyperventilate. "Let me check on Addy first."

"She's here?"

"At least for the weekend."

"Will she be okay alone?"

Footsteps pounded overhead before a ball of energy flew down the stairs. "I'll be fine. Decorating for Christmas, right, Aunt Savvy?"

"I suppose." Savannah considered Addy, noting the dark bruising under her eyes. "Maybe you should focus on sleep today."

"Only if you do." Addy crossed her arms and jutted out her chin.

"Maybe later."

"Exactly." Addy edged closer to Savannah. "Just hurry back, okay?"

Savannah nudged Addy's chin until their gazes connected. "I will. Promise."

A bit later, she climbed into Jett's Jeep and tapped another search for Hope Boonmee into her phone. Still nothing. "Can you take us to the law firm before we head to Dustin's?"

He glanced at her quickly. "Why?"

"I think we need to use some of the online search engines I have access to there. Google isn't sufficient. If she owns property in the US, I should be able to find her."

"Only if Hope is her actual first name."

Savannah frowned as she tapped another tab. If she could just remember her password she could try to search on her phone, but the screen was too small to do it comfortably. "What?"

He beat against the steering wheel as if keeping pace with his thoughts. "Many Asians adopt an English first name when they come to the States to make it easier for us. What if that's what she did?"

"We won't know until we look."

"And I know the place to do that."

"What?"

"The *Source*. On my laptop I've got access to resources that are probably different from yours. We'll swing by my place, pick that up, and then go to the law firm if we still need to."

"All right." She added a quick note on her phone to look for a safe deposit box or similar account and key when she was back at Dustin's. It was possible any evidence he had might be stored offsite. "And while we're at the apartment, we should search for whatever Dustin had that told the real story of those trips."

"Agreed."

A few minutes of silence settled between them as Jett drove. Savannah's thoughts ran through their conversations. "Has anyone responded to your online requests for information?"

"No, but whether people readily volunteer information depends on the story. Some people love the idea of talking to the media. Others want nothing to do with us." He sighed as he followed the line of cars. "We haven't done ourselves favors by confusing people about what news is."

"What do you mean?"

"Anyone can be a journalist now, but so much of it is fabricated no one knows what to believe."

"Finding truth in a fake news world."

"Exactly." He stopped at a stop sign and glanced at her. "That'd be a great tagline for a news channel." He started driving again. "The reality is the market is so muddied by bad journalists that it's hard to discern who's good and who doesn't know how to ask the right questions." He tapped the steering wheel. "Eventually someone will talk to me or we'll find something."

She leaned against the window and stared at the trees they passed. "When Addy asks me who her dad really was, I won't know how to answer."

"You don't have to. She's a teenager."

"Who lost her father in a terrible, senseless way. And she found his body. I can't whitewash that."

"Maybe you don't need to."

She stifled a yawn. "Sorry." She rubbed the back of her neck and sighed. "Do you think we'll ever know the full story?"

He shrugged. "She'll be okay. She has you to help her. You okay?"

"I won't be until I know she is." She puffed out air, then tried to clear her worries from her mind. The drive to Jett's place was longer than going to Dustin's or the law firm. Jett drove through Old Town onto George Washington Parkway. Savannah had always enjoyed the drive with the park and trails along the Potomac River on one side and small neighborhoods on the other. The real estate was pricey with its great location and river views.

Still she was unprepared when he turned off the parkway and in a couple of minutes pulled in front of a split-level home. "This is where you live?"

"Yep."

"Reporters must make more than I thought."

"Or I found a creative house-sitting arrangement." He grinned at her shock. "Friends are on assignment overseas with the Secret Service. I'm helping them by staying here and maintaining the place, and they don't have to worry about renting to strangers."

After he climbed out, Jett hurried around to open Savannah's door. He seemed pleasantly surprised to see her waiting patiently. "I had you labeled as a woman who would insist on getting her own doors."

"No, sir." She swung her legs out and accepted his hand. "I like being pampered. When it happens, I choose to embrace the moment."

"I'll make sure you get more such moments." Then he walked beside her up the path to his door. He checked the mailbox and pulled out a few envelopes. He frowned as he flipped through them. "I guess my caller was lying."

"What?"

"I got a call yesterday that told me to check my mail. Nothing yesterday or today."

"Maybe it's still on the way."

"Maybe." He unlocked and opened the front door. "Furniture isn't mine for the most part. Neither are the doilies."

She tried to choke back a laugh but instead sputtered. "Doilies?"

"Beverly's mom lived with them for a year and crocheted doilies. They're still here even though she is in assisted living now. That's why I spend so much time in my workshop out back." He unlocked and opened the door, then held it for her with a hesitance she hadn't seen in any of their interactions. There was something charming in the dip of his chin, and as she brushed by, a woody scent wrapped around her, making her want to lean closer.

She felt his gaze and glanced up to find him focused on her, their faces inches apart. The tug to be closer about undid her.

Then he leaned closer.

Hesitated.

She drew nearer.

An intense action-movie theme song started blaring, and Savannah startled. Jett groaned as he pulled his phone out. "Stupid ringtone."

Savannah put her hand over her mouth and stepped into a home that looked like something out of Crate and Barrel, but with doilies on every surface. The explosion of delicate white mats uncorked her laughter and she turned deeper into the home so that it wouldn't disrupt Jett's call.

When he got off the call, he followed her inside. "I think we're getting somewhere."

"Who was that?"

"A source of mine at USCIS." His phone dinged and he glanced at it. "Pay dirt."

CHAPTER
THIRTY-TWO

The regret that his phone had interrupted what could have been an amazing moment lingered. But it had to take a back seat to Tina's information.

He studied the text for a moment, then grinned. "Hope Boonmee has traveled to the US three times in the last year. Each time for about a week. And each time to this area." He turned the phone toward Savannah so she could see the text. It wasn't much. Just a screenshot of travel dates and locations, but it was more than they had a few minutes ago.

"So she's traveled here. And you think that connects her to Dustin."

"She's connected somehow. But look at where she travels from." He waited as she looked at the phone again, and then saw the light of realization dawn.

"Each time she flew out of and back to Suvarnabhumi International Airport." She looked at him. "That's the airport Dustin used."

He nodded. "What if she's a point of contact in Thailand?"

"But you haven't found any record of her? Other than this?"

"Not yet. It means something that she's from Thailand."

"Then she probably doesn't own property here." Savannah took a screenshot that she forwarded to her number, then handed the phone back to him. "Why don't you show me everything else you have? Walk me through it."

240

"It started with a phone tip. Then I got a packet filled with receipts, which I confirmed."

An hour later the box of his research was open with files strewn across the top of the dining room table, and he'd given her the overview. She'd listened well and he could almost see her processing the data.

"No wonder you're convinced."

He started stacking the files. "There's too much evidence not to be."

She worried her lower lip and he tried not to fixate on it. "But Dustin insisted he was innocent."

"And I've got a random person who's called a couple times telling me I'm wrong. Same thing in tweets and email, but that's not unusual." He put the first stack back in the box. "It'd be more unusual if I didn't get people calling me crazy and a hack. Especially when someone of Donnelly's stature is involved." He pushed back from the table and leaned back in his chair, hands laced behind his head.

"So I need to find Dustin's evidence, whatever it was."

"If it exists, I'll look at it." He'd look, but it would take compelling evidence to change his mind.

———

Savannah glanced at her watch and stood. "I didn't realize it was so late. Can you take me home? I don't like that Addy's been alone so long."

Jett cocked his head and studied her, and she prayed he couldn't read her thoughts. She didn't need him to know how much his self-assurance made her determined to find whatever Dustin had meant to show her. She owed it to Addy and to the men to figure out whether there was more to the story than Jett had written.

"All right."

The ride back to her apartment was quiet and she ran through what he'd shown her. She glanced at him as he neared her neighborhood. "I just thought of something."

He smiled as he turned into Cherry Blossom Estates. "Shoot."

"Who gave you the initial information about the trips?"

"I don't know."

He pulled to a stop in front of her apartment, and she thanked him for the ride.

"I'll plan to go to Dustin's tomorrow," she told him. "I'll let you know when if you want to join me."

"You shouldn't go alone." His words fell heavy, but she ignored them as he came around the car and got her door.

"I'll call. Thanks for walking me through what you have."

He waited until she entered her town house before he pulled away. As soon as he did, she collapsed against the door. Her shoulder was hurting more than she'd let on. Though she wanted to go straight to Dustin's, rest was what she needed. First, she'd spend some time with Addy.

Soft Christmas carols played from somewhere and when she opened her eyes, Savannah saw her tabletop-sized Christmas tree sitting next to the TV, its limbs heavy with ornaments and lights. The aroma of something sweet and spicy like banana bread flavored the air. She let herself relax into the idea that Christmas was coming.

SUNDAY, DECEMBER 20

After attending the early service at her church, Savannah headed to Dustin's apartment. She wanted to see what she could find on her own, but she called Jett on her way as promised. "I'm heading back to Dustin's. Want to meet me there?"

"You caught me in the middle of something I have to finish. I can meet you there in about an hour."

"All right. Come on up when you arrive."

As she drove, she ran over the next day's memorial service. She'd barely had time to call a minister and send email notices to the few people she could think to alert, but the memorial was primarily for Addy. It was the best Savannah could do to help her niece process her grief until Dustin's body was returned to them.

Then her thoughts turned to what she hoped to accomplish at Dustin's apartment. Her first priority would be a careful search of Dustin's files for either his evidence or information on Hope Boonmee. And that would be easier to do without a reporter looking over her shoulder. Especially when said reporter possessed an uncanny ability to read her thoughts.

After she parked in a visitor spot, Savannah hitched her purse over her shoulder, fished out her keys, and held them at the ready. While she walked up to the building, she checked Dustin's second-floor apartment windows for . . . something. She might be paranoid, but it was justified.

She scanned the parking lot before hurrying to the entrance and finding it unlocked. Then she climbed the stairs and tested his door-knob before unlocking it.

As soon as she was inside, she closed and locked the door.

Her muscles thrummed with energy, ready to bolt at the first indication something was wrong. Maybe she shouldn't lock the door after all.

She squared her shoulders and flipped on every light as she proceeded down the hallway past the kitchen and living space to the office. Before she entered it, she checked Dustin's bedroom, then looked under his bed. She might be here alone, but she would not be surprised, not this time. Then she checked his closet. Stepped into his bathroom. Checked the shower.

Only after she'd confirmed she was alone did she feel the exhaustion of relief pressing against her.

She turned toward the office. She needed to get in there and check the files.

Instead, she felt a tug to his nightstand.

When they were married he'd kept a calendar that served as an early bullet journal to record anything memorable from the day. If he still kept a journal and she found it, it might answer some questions about his trips to Asia. But she didn't see one on that table or in its small drawer.

She sagged as she considered her next move.

There wouldn't be an easy answer. Not that she'd expected one, but it would have been nice to have Dustin's thoughts about his days since he couldn't defend himself anymore.

Time to move back to the office.

She closed the door to the bedroom on her way out and then turned on the office light. It looked as she'd left it, so she went to the desk and sat in the desk chair. The oversized chair leaned back beneath her weight, and she felt like a girl playing in her daddy's chair. How had he organized files when they were married? They'd barely had the money to buy each of them a desk, and she'd been so focused on her law-school studies that she hadn't paid much attention to his systems. She tugged open a drawer and riffled through folders of this year's bills. They were relatively disorganized. Utilities were shoved into one file, medical bills into another, rent and household in a third. Charitable giving crammed a fourth.

Wait.

When had Dustin begun caring about donations? She pulled the file out and set it to the side for a careful read. The next file had another copy of Dustin's will. She quickly read through it again. Dustin really had left her as his executor, something he should have changed years ago. Why had he listed her so recently?

She hadn't seen Dustin since a fund-raiser they'd both attended six months earlier. She'd been there at a client's request. He'd been there with the speaker, Logan Donnelly. Dustin had been relaxed, settled in a way that Savannah had never seen him. He'd looked good enough it made Savannah wish for a half minute that he'd settled down when he still had her. Then his gaze had slowly slid down her and back up, and she'd been ready to walk away and force herself to forget about him again.

Instead, she'd walked to the bar and collected a ginger ale.

When she turned around, he'd disappeared.

Dustin had had the ability to distract and capture her heart and soul from the time they met during the first week of sociology her sophomore year. The fund-raiser had proven that her heart would betray her and lean toward him even though her brain knew it was foolish.

Maybe Jett was right. Maybe a part of her was still in love with Dustin, but now Jett was here, and he seemed different in all the right ways.

Dustin was her past.

Jett was the opportunity for something new. That filled her with hope. And she decided that for once she would turn toward that feeling rather than away. It was her choice, and she was making it.

Savannah set the will aside with the donations file to take with her, then wondered where to look next.

Being his personal representative was a complication she didn't need. If only it were as simple as selling a few assets, filing a few pieces of paper with the courts, then sending checks to his heirs . . . namely, Addy Jo.

The files weren't looking through themselves, so Savannah turned to the next file and tried to ignore the fact that Christmas was Friday and she hadn't done any Christmas shopping.

Her phone buzzed. On the way.

Shoot. She needed to get through the files before Jett arrived.

It was Sunday and he should be relaxing.

The week had been demanding with the crash investigation and serving justice on those who preyed on innocence.

Now he was watching a dot on a screen. The position of the reporter's car. It had been too easy to slide the tracker under the man's bumper. He rubbed his hands over his face to fight the weariness that engulfed him. Then his vision settled on the last family picture that showed a complete family.

The one with Grace.

Before his wife left.

Before his son focused on career rather than on what truly mattered.

This was why he did what he did.

End the violence that destroyed families.

The thought froze him in place.

Who was he becoming?

His daughter would be an angel for the rest of time. She would never experience more pain, but her end had been ruthless. His stomach bottomed out again at the reality of how defenseless and alone she had been. He couldn't be her avenging warrior then, but he could now.

Was his drive for justice right?

Those who sinned must be punished.

The laws were clear. But the laws weren't always enough. He'd seen too many cases where the clearly guilty walked free to commit more evil.

God had taken care of Logan Donnelly.

He had taken care of Dustin Tate and Evan Spencer.

Now he'd let the reporter lead him to the fourth member of the team.

There was only one problem that he could foresee. Once he learned the fourth man's name, he'd have to kill Jett Glover too.

CHAPTER
THIRTY-THREE

The moment the sun glinted through his bedroom window, Jett had opened his laptop. He'd polished and submitted an article for Monday's paper before entering Agent Martin's name in a search engine. When Savannah had mentioned her encounter with him, his name had niggled something in his memory.

The man's daughter had disappeared two years earlier. Drove to meet friends and vanished.

Grace Martin.

He pulled up his notes on the Twitter accounts and saw @Gracie467. As he scanned through the content on that account, he noted it looked like a memorial account for a Gracie Martin, but he couldn't confirm it was Agent Martin's daughter. But now that account was being used to highlight his article on the junkets to Thailand.

As he scrolled through the account's feed, he noted several tweets also used the unique spelling of *trueth*. With retweets of other articles related to human trafficking, it could be an account focused on this tragedy, but he wasn't clear how it tied to remembering a Gracie Martin.

He shot a direct message to the account, and then checked for responses to his other messages. Nothing. He wrote another round of messages. He wished it was easier to reach the people behind the accounts.

He'd look into her family. Maybe one of them was using the account as an ongoing memorial to her and call to action to prevent future tragedies. Since no one using the account got back to him, maybe a friend who worked at Twitter might be able to help. He pulled up the woman's contact information and left a message for her.

As he drove to Dustin's apartment he wondered why that account would repost his article within an hour of its publication. The fact it had been retweeted thousands of times also stumped him, but once he learned more about who owned the account he'd piece it together. Maybe it was one of those things that would never be fully explained.

The sky was heavy with the threat of snow as he pulled into the apartment complex and parked next to her empty car. He didn't like that Savannah was in there alone, not after what happened Friday night.

He walked into the building as someone hurried out, then he hiked the stairs to the second floor. He texted Savannah to let her know he was at the door, and waited a few minutes for her to open it. He wiped his frown off as she greeted him.

Guess he wasn't fast enough.

She cocked her head and studied him. "You okay?"

"Yeah. Long day."

"Long couple weeks." She gave him a small smile, then led him to the office where she took a seat at the desk. "I've been collecting files to evaluate more thoroughly at home."

They worked in companionable silence. He sat on the floor going through the files after she did. He checked his phone for direct messages from the Twitter accounts every hour, but they were silent. He was beginning to think they were fake accounts. Then she turned to the desk drawers while he filled her in on his latest ideas about the tweets. While she didn't look overly interested, she was a good listener and it helped to talk through what he'd learned. He could see the article coming together in his mind as he wrapped up.

"So it's likely one person is behind the original tweets and then bots are picking them up and circulating them," he said.

"How will you learn the identity of the account owner?"

"I've sent them each direct messages. Since that hasn't worked, I'm reaching out to a contact at Twitter."

She looked skeptical as she opened another drawer. "I don't think they can do that. It would be a violation of privacy."

"Maybe. But I can ask."

"That doesn't address the why though."

"My guess is it ties back to how Gracie Martin died. This looks like someone's become obsessed with human trafficking and is using her account to keep the issue alive."

Savannah ran her fingers inside an empty drawer as she considered his words. "Maybe. I suppose it's possible that could happen."

"Possible and likely. It's just that tweets are more temporary than a Facebook memorial page."

Savannah pulled out a small key and examined it. "I think this is a key to a safe deposit box."

Jett leaned forward, itching to take it from her. "Which bank?"

She read the name off the key chain. "I'll go first thing in the morning."

"We'll go first thing in the morning." Savannah looked like she wanted to argue with him, but Jett didn't look away. He'd be there with her when they went through the box.

"Help me carry these files to my car?"

"Sure." He'd even make sure she got them in her town house. Just like he'd be with her in the morning.

———

Jett followed Savannah as she drove her rental home. She took comfort each time she looked in the rearview mirror and saw the familiar outline of his headlights. After she parked, he slid his car into the slot next to hers and then grabbed the file boxes from his trunk.

"I'll come back and get yours in a minute."

"You don't need to do that." As she unlocked her front door, she tried not to be miffed.

He shifted the boxes and his blue-gray gaze shot through her. "I know you're capable. But I'm going to make sure everything's okay inside anyway."

After he set down the boxes, she waited for him to start sliding through the space as if he had a gun and could clear it of any bad guys. She tried not to smile at the way he was acting all tough and defender-like, but she didn't want him to find someone. It was one thing to sense a threat. It was another to identify and clear it. She also didn't want to know someone had invaded her space.

When he came back, she tugged a box to the leather couch and opened it. "I'll start with these."

Jett's phone rang. "Huh. I may have to take this." He stepped onto her front porch and shut the door behind him.

She took a moment to check on Addy. The poor girl was already asleep, so Savannah went to work on the files. She pulled them out of the box a few at a time. When she opened one, she carefully flipped through the contents. This time she took the time to scan each page rather than assuming if the file said Bills, that's what she would find inside. She opened each envelope and pulled out the pages. After ten minutes of finding exactly what was marked on each folder, she wondered if she was wasting time.

No, someone had been in his apartment, and unless she wanted to assume the intruder had found whatever he'd been looking for before she and Jett arrived, she needed to keep digging.

She'd lost track of how many files she'd gone through when she came across an unmarked envelope. It wasn't in a file, so maybe it had been scooped up in a pile of folders she'd set on the desk.

The envelope was plain with nothing printed or written on the front. It looked like a standard #10 envelope that could be bought by the box at any store selling office supplies. It wasn't sealed, but the flap was tucked inside the back, so she pulled it out. A single sheet of typed paper was inside.

It read like a legal brief.

Wherefore the accused Dustin Tate was a key instigator of the plot to harm girls in Thailand.

Wherefore said Dustin Tate was a willing and knowing participant in the scheme,

Wherefore this man was an obstructionist to the trueth and

Wherefore said Dustin Tate must be held accountable for his many sins,

Therefore Dustin Tate has been found guilty and executed for his sins.

He will no longer harm young women nor participate in plans to harm them.

In addition his daughter will be forthwith protected from her father and any and all sins he would have committed with and to her. She will be forthwith protected from being drawn into his dark and nefarious schemes.

The trueth was determined and the trueth has set him free.

Savannah's hands trembled as she reread the page again.

Dustin had been executed.

Had it been left on the desk because the author expected it to be found? Or had it been moved by the cleaners? She might never know, but this seemed like proof that would change Dustin's death from a possible suicide to murder.

She picked up her phone and called Detective Jensen. Then she took a photo of the document and set it to the side after gingerly holding it by the edges.

CHAPTER
THIRTY-FOUR

Jett walked back into the town house and found Savannah curled into the side of the couch, phone on her lap, hands idle. The call hadn't seemed that long, but something had changed while he'd been on the porch. "What happened?"

"I found a letter." She pointed to the small wood coffee table. "I've called Detective Jensen."

Jett sat next to her on the couch and then leaned forward to read the document. "What is this?"

"The guilty verdict for Dustin."

He scanned the document. "Wait a minute."

"What?"

"Did you notice the way *truth* is spelled?"

She scooted closer and looked over his shoulder. "Yeah. Thought it was a typo."

"It's the same spelling used in the bot tweets. Nobody spells truth with an *e*. That has to be intentional."

"So the person who sent the tweets killed Dustin?"

"Maybe."

There was a knock at her door, and Jett got to his feet. "Let me check that for you."

Detective Jensen stood on the stoop. "This is becoming a bad habit."

Jett nodded as he shook the man's hand. "It is, but you'll want to see this."

The man slipped on latex gloves and then read the document. He pulled out a notepad and pen. "Where did you say you found this?"

"It was in this box of files we brought from Dustin's office." Savannah tried to sit forward, but seemed to collapse.

"Yes?" The detective pulled a chair from the dining room and sat on the other side of the coffee table.

Jett quickly filled him in on the tweets and what he'd learned. "I've been waiting for a contact from Twitter to get back to me so I can learn more about the account these tweets originated from."

"I can get a warrant for that information, especially now that it may be tied to a murder. Probably have it tomorrow late afternoon." The man jotted a couple notes.

Savannah swallowed but her voice was thin. "Do you think it was murder?"

"Yes. There were some anomalies in his tox screen that have us working on that assumption."

"Anomalies like what?"

"Similar to the ones in your tox screen."

Savannah straightened. "My tox screen?"

"Thursday when you were taken to the emergency room you had high levels of Midazolam in your system."

"Mida-what?"

"It's a sedative that eases anxiety. Here's what's interesting: it also causes mild amnesia."

"So that's why she doesn't remember much about the crash." Jett could feel the pieces clicking into place.

"Yes." The detective flipped to another page of his notebook. "When you mentioned that a man had given you water after the accident, I checked your vehicle. The bottle tested positive for traces of the drug. It was also a different brand from the others in your car, leading us to think it was the one the man who came to your aid gave you. Unfortunately none of the cameras in the parking lot got a good look at his license plate, because it was covered with something like mud."

———

Savannah had to remind her lungs to work. Inhale and exhale. "So whoever killed Dustin is after me too? Why?"

"I wouldn't jump to that conclusion yet." Detective Jensen rubbed the back of his neck. "Your case could still be a simple hit-and-run. I'll keep digging, especially now that a suspicious death has shifted to possible murder."

She nodded. "Yes. How old was the girl who was killed? The one whose Twitter account is being used?"

Jett pushed some buttons on his phone. "It's not entirely clear. I'd guess she was a teenager." He turned the phone so she could see the profile.

Savannah clicked a few buttons, then started scrolling backward in the profile's feed. "At some point she was the one sending the tweets. We could try to get back to that point to find out the date of her death."

"Or you could give me her name, and I can tell you." Detective Jensen cocked an eyebrow and waited with pen poised over the notepad.

"Gracie467."

"No, really what's her name?"

"That's her twitter handle." Savannah clicked around some, but the profile didn't have many details.

"I'm pretty sure her name is Grace Martin," Jett said. "I haven't confirmed it though."

"All right, show me her photo. If she was from around here, I might recognize her or someone else at the precinct could." Savannah handed

Jett's phone to the detective and he frowned as he squinted at the image. Then he pulled it closer. "Wait a minute." He looked at Jett. "You're sure this is the right account?"

"Yeah." Jett shrugged. "I could run you through the tech and analytics, but we're sure."

"I know her."

Savannah snatched the phone back. "You do?" She manipulated the image to make it bigger. "I don't."

"She disappeared two years ago. Went to meet friends at a local joint and never arrived. Three months later her body was found, and the FBI busted a suspected human trafficking ring. Her dad was one of the FBI agents who busted the case."

"So an FBI agent's daughter is nabbed and found months later in a raid." Jett ran his hands over his hair. "That had to mess with him."

"Yes, and the autopsy showed she'd died in the twenty-four hours before the raid. It destroyed her family. Particularly her dad. Everyone was upset with how it ended because he's one of us. Felt like a failure to everyone in law enforcement." Detective Jensen set his pad of paper down. "He disappeared for a couple months. Bereavement leave. Then came back divorced, a workaholic. Been working ever since. I'll see what I can make of this."

Savannah could too easily imagine the grief she would feel if something similar happened to Addy. "It must have shaken him to think he's supposed to catch evil, and instead it caught his family." She tried to dislodge the shadows of pain. "And now he's involved in the investigation into this crash."

Jett frowned as if bothered by something. "I'm overthinking this, but is there any way he'd be interested in my article?"

"That's unlikely." Detective Jensen stood, but Jett held up a hand as if to stop him.

"I don't think so. This account is the one that started the circulation of my article."

"Then he's just interested, allegedly, in informing others about situations similar to his daughter."

"Maybe." Jett dragged out the word, but stayed quiet after that.

"I'll get back to the office and see if a quick call can confirm whose account this is." He shook hands with Jett. "I can't guarantee anything."

"We understand." Savannah walked him to the door, and when she turned back, Jett was packing up. "You leaving?"

"I've got to get all of this organized in my head. There are connections and they are starting to come together." He stepped nearer and gave her a one-armed hug. "I'll come back tonight if they do."

Her home felt empty, even though Addy was resting upstairs.

Peace. She desperately needed some. She'd intentionally tried to make her home an oasis. While it wasn't perfect, the lavender-gray walls, the white furniture with gray accent pillows, the refinished hardwood floors, the gauzy white curtains, and the clean white trim were all designed to create a sense of peace.

Then why wouldn't it seep into her? Why did it feel like she couldn't shake the heaviness of quicksand?

Rhett walked with a curled tail around and between her feet. "It's too bad you can't join me for a walk, girl."

The sweet thing looked up and meowed. If felt like her cat would come if Savannah really wanted.

"I won't make you wear a leash. That would be ridiculous."

"Make who wear a leash?" Addy croaked as if she'd just woken up.

Savannah startled and turned toward her niece. "Feel better?"

"I'm not sure I ever will."

Savannah opened her arms and Addy walked into them. "I know." She gave her niece a hug. "I was just telling Rhett I wouldn't make her wear a leash, but maybe you'd like to go for a walk with me."

"Not really."

"A quick stroll around the neighborhood." It would do them both good to get outside and let the cold air clear their heads. Jett had been on to something, and the flurry of things she needed to do related to the memorial service and work would still be waiting when they got back.

"I think I'll wait." Addy covered a yawn. "Instead, I'll take some kitty therapy."

"All right. I'll be back in a few minutes." As Savannah bundled up, Addy settled on the love seat with Rhett and a blanket.

Savannah stepped outside, knowing she needed a minute to pause before she imploded from the weight of everything. Savannah Daniels did not implode. No, she was the one others relied on for help and steadiness.

This wilderness wouldn't have her. Instead she would press in even as she waited, somehow finding the holy tension in the balance. And that would start with a pair of tennis shoes, a bit of cold sunshine on her face, and words that whispered comfort to the angst in her heart. Maybe in the acknowledging she'd sense some release.

Calming her heart and directing her thoughts did not come easily. Instead it felt like every emotion inside fought for release. She paused on the sidewalk at the end of her block, closed her eyes, and lifted her face. It didn't matter if all of her neighbors saw the moment. Let them imagine she was enjoying the welcome sunshine that didn't really warm the air but still painted the day more brightly.

She raised her hands in front of her hips.

I surrender. I don't know what You're doing or what my response is supposed to be, so I surrender. Have Your way, Lord, and help me live with grace and reflect Your love in the moments of my days. Keep Addy safe, please. She's dear to me.

She stood there for a moment and let the words float toward heaven. If she didn't feel an immediate answering peace, that was okay.

God still heard, and He knew her heart. She'd trust Him to help her follow in His steps.

CHAPTER
THIRTY-FIVE

MONDAY, DECEMBER 21

Meet you at the bank when it opens? Trying to get there
before the service.

A minute later Savannah had Jett's reply.

Forty minutes?

Sure.

Addy had asked to go home to get ready for the service, and now
Savannah considered the small key that hung on a bank key chain.
Unlike in novels, Dustin had made it easy to know it was a safe deposit
box key, since he left it on a key chain emblazoned with the bank's name.

The question was why Dustin had one. When they were married he
had nothing of value. But that was a lifetime ago. His apartment didn't
indicate anything had really changed though.

Thirty minutes later she pushed through the bank's doors.

With a pasted smile and firm step, she approached the main counter
of the small branch.

A middle-aged woman looked up at her with interest. "May I help you?"

"I'm the executor of the estate of a man who had a safe deposit box here. I have the key and a copy of the will."

"I'll need to see that."

"Sure." Savannah reached in and pulled the copy of the will from her bag and slid it across the desk.

The woman picked it up and gave it a quick scan. "Everything seems in order. Do you have a copy of the death certificate?"

Savannah froze. "The death certificate?" Had one even been generated yet?

"Yes. Standard procedure."

"I'll have to call the detective for that."

"It usually comes from the Office of Vital Records in Richmond." The woman slid the papers back to her. "I'll be happy to help when you have it."

Savannah stepped back outside and hurried to her SUV as a cold wind cut through her coat. She called Detective Jensen. "Can you help? I don't even know if a death certificate has been issued yet."

"The autopsy was completed Saturday. I believe the medical examiner completed the form, but I'll confirm."

"Can you have him email it to me?"

"Now? What's the hurry?"

"A bank is requiring it to access his safe deposit box."

"Want a warrant?"

"No, thanks. There's no reason to think it has the fruit of criminal endeavors." She rubbed her forehead as the complication added to her morning.

The sound of rustling papers filtered over the call. "I just found a copy on my desk. I'll shoot it your way."

"Thanks." A moment later when her phone dinged, she pulled it up.

It was a bit blurry, but should be good enough for the bank's purposes, at least for today. She headed back inside and approached the receptionist. "I have the death certificate on my phone."

The woman reached for her phone. "Let me see it." A minute later the woman handed the phone back to her. "And the will?"

Savannah pulled it from her bag again.

The woman glanced at it, then gave a tight smile. "Let me get someone to show you to the safe deposit box center. Would you like water or coffee while you wait?"

"I'm fine. Thank you." Savannah stepped across to a small seating area and then sank onto a couch's pleather surface. What could Dustin have in that box? Based on Jett's article, she wondered if it would look something like the one in the first Jason Bourne movie. A collection of passports and cash?

That was so farfetched, she barely contained a snort. Her phone dinged and she glanced at the text.

Got held up. Not sure I'll make it.

Okay. In lobby waiting. Let me know if you get here.

She slipped the phone back in her purse. The bank was a basic branch. Sunlight pressed through heavy clouds to reach the front windows, and a steady flow of customers entered and flowed through the line to a teller, then left.

She glanced at her watch and sighed. Fifteen minutes with no traction. She didn't have time to wait with the memorial service later in the day, but didn't want to make the drive a second time. She stood and returned to the desk. "Do you know how much longer it will be?"

The receptionist looked at her with a blank expression as if she'd never seen her before. Then she startled as if poked with a pin. "Let me double-check." She picked up the phone and had a muffled conversation, and a minute later a middle-aged man strode toward her.

He held out his hand, revealing a Rolex watch. "Ms. Daniels, I believe."

"Yes." She shook his hand and noted it was damp. "You are?"

"Reginald Signs." He retrieved his hand. "I need to see your ID to confirm you match the will, and then we'll get you back to the box."

"All right." She tugged out her wallet and showed him her driver's license. Then she glanced around for Jett. Guess he'd been detained longer than he anticipated.

The man studied her license, dark hair not moving as he leaned forward. "Thank you. If you'll follow me."

Savannah frowned as she replaced her wallet. "Do you need a photocopy of my ID?"

"We should have it on file."

"I don't see how. You're the first person who's asked for it." She glanced around again. "I'm also waiting for a friend."

He stood at what looked like attention, his shoulders so square under his suit coat he could have a hanger holding him straight. "We wouldn't let you beyond this door if we hadn't confirmed your identity. Checking your license is merely a formality. I'm afraid we do not have time to wait for your friend."

That made little sense, but she followed him to a door that, after he swiped an employee badge, opened to a narrow hallway. The door looked thick enough to stop damage from an explosion.

"We were sorry to see that Mr. Tate died." Mr. Signs's voice held an insincere note. He'd probably never met Dustin.

"Yes."

"I will show you to a room and then bring the box to you. We will open it together."

He stopped at a door that held a keypad. After punching in a code, he opened the door and stepped aside for her to enter first.

The room was small with a harsh overhead light and petite table and two chairs. "If you'll wait here, I'll be back in a moment."

Before she could nod, the door closed behind her with a harsh click. Would it open if she tried the door? She pushed the crazy thought that she was trapped from her mind. Of course it would open. Who would want to keep her in a small room at the bank?

She was being ridiculous.

But Dustin had been killed. Someone had run her off the road. All of it conspired to make her a little crazy. Savannah hoped there would be something in the safe deposit box that helped her make sense of the last two weeks.

The door opened, and Savannah jerked back to a prim position. Mr. Signs strode in with a box clutched in his hands. It didn't seem very large as he set it on the table. "Your key?" He held out his hand, but she decided to hang on to it. A second key dangled from his other hand.

"It goes in there?" She slid her chair to the side so she had a better angle on the keyhole. At his nod, she smiled. "I'm ready."

Together they slotted their keys and then twisted them. She felt the lid release as they extracted their keys. "Thank you. Is there a time limit on using this room?"

"No."

"Wonderful." She maintained her smile as she waited for him to take the hint and leave. He spun on one polished heel and left her alone.

She studied the box.

No time like the present. She reached for the lid. While there was probably a camera watching her, she'd pretend she was alone. The lid stuck and she had to tug to get it to open.

When she did, she frowned. The contents didn't make much sense.

A couple small bars—were they gold?—were nestled at the bottom. She frowned. Dustin had never seemed the type to buy gold in anticipation of a rainy day. His investment activities had been riskier, bordering on day trading. Maybe the bars weren't really gold, but if not, he wouldn't put them in a bank box.

She carefully lifted the bars out. They felt solid and heavy as she set them on the table. Beneath them rested a passport and a small velvet bag. She frowned at the passport and opened it. Bernard Julius? The image was Dustin's but the name was crazy. All of the stamps seemed to fall in line with trips to and from Thailand. Would he have stored jewelry in the bag? She picked up the bag, which held a few loose gems. She'd need a professional to help her know for certain what they were. Then she noted the small box that had been beneath it. A jeweler's ring box.

Her breath hitched. Maybe he really had planned to ask Stasi to marry him.

She shook her head. She was being foolish to think it contained a ring or let it affect her. If he'd wanted to marry, that was his business. But a part of her heart still hiccupped at the idea.

She sank to the chair and stared at the small box. It was the kind that usually signified such joy. She reached back in and snatched it open. Her heart stilled as a small piece of folded paper fluttered from the black velvet that showcased her wedding ring. She'd given it back to him at the termination of their marriage, then assumed he'd sold it. Her fingers trembled as she set the box down and carefully unfolded the origami-folded paper.

His sloppy micro handwriting scrawled almost unintelligibly across it.

Addy, I've saved this for you. May you be the woman your aunt is. You make me proud.

Savannah collapsed against the chair's back and rubbed her hands over her eyes. She couldn't show the note to Addy. Not now.

Jett's smile floated into her mind, and she absorbed the image. He was her anchor to what could be. She needed to free herself from the past. She'd let too much time pass living with the certainty she was unworthy of love. But Jett seemed determined to show her the untruth of that.

She closed the ring box and returned it to the safe deposit box. It could wait here until Addy was ready for the gift, because that was what it was. A gift from a father to his daughter. It wasn't Savannah's any longer, hadn't been for a long time.

It was time to finally close the chapters that had dictated her story for too long.

All she had to do was release the past and face what might yet be.

She could reach out and grasp the future.

The future could be painted by hope if she'd let it.

First she had to get these items safely home and then prepare for the memorial service. After that she could focus on why Dustin had the gold and gems.

CHAPTER
THIRTY-SIX

As Savannah left the bank late Monday morning, the sky matched her mood with a covering of dense clouds. If she hadn't organized Dustin's memorial service for Addy, she'd wish for a way to gracefully skip it. At home, Savannah pulled on a pair of designer black pants and a matching tunic. It was an outfit she reserved for non-court days, and it was the armor she'd need to get through the afternoon.

When Rhett stood on her hind legs to be picked up, Savannah had to walk away so her clothes weren't covered in a fine coating of fur. She'd never been allergic a day in her life, but she blamed the cat's nearness for the catch in the back of her throat as she grabbed her keys and purse and hurried from the house.

The man had been the only man she'd allowed into her heart until the last weeks. The realization of the hope she felt for new love brought a slight smile on the hard day.

When Savannah reached Stasi's apartment building, Savannah had to sit in the car a minute and suck in deep breaths. Somehow she would find the fortitude to be the rock Addy required, while ignoring the fact that she and Stasi had yet to talk about Friday's school incident.

Who would be *her* rock?

I will.

The thought bounced around her mind and stabbed her. *Help me trust that You will.*

It wasn't seismic or loud, but she felt the beginnings of peace. A peace that would shelter her and flow from her if she let it. She wanted to let it, because if she didn't she would crack.

She inhaled peace for a minute, then closed her eyes and with one last exhale, pushed from her car.

A curtain fluttered at Addy's window. By the time Savannah hiked to the third-floor landing, Addy stood in the doorway.

"I'm not ready for this, Aunt Savvy." Her voice was small and fragile, and the circles under her eyes were as dark as her dress. Her niece had become a zombie, with her spark absent since the night she'd found Dustin's body. She would never unsee that trauma.

"I don't think we ever are." Savannah eased toward Addy and pulled her into a hug. She felt Addy's arms circle her waist and hold on tight. "We'll get through today, and then we'll figure out what we do next. I promise you will be okay."

"Isn't that sweet?" The sarcasm in Stasi's voice couldn't hide the hurt on her face. There was a hopelessness to the slope of her shoulders, and she looked like she'd lost even more weight to the point of emaciation.

"Hi, Stasi." Savannah reached to welcome her sister into the hug, and Stasi hesitantly stepped in. For too many years the sisters had lived on the opposite sides of Dustin. Today that could change, even if they had a lot to figure out. Addy relaxed, so Savannah cleared her throat, and the group hug ended. "Do you need to get anything before we leave?"

Addy glanced at her empty hands. "I don't think so."

"We have you." Stasi stepped back into the apartment's entryway. "You'll take care of us."

On the quiet drive to the church, Savannah mulled Stasi's words in her mind. It was true. She'd continue to be there for them, even when it hurt. It's what family did.

Before Savannah was really ready, they pulled into the parking lot of the church Dustin had attended when he'd been in town. The church was a small brick building with a parking lot that could hold around forty cars. If there hadn't been a cross illuminated on the brick, it would be easy to drive by and think it was another business. Today the lot was about half full, and as Savannah pulled in, she didn't notice any satellite trucks. That didn't mean there weren't reporters present though.

Addy sniffed from the back seat, and Stasi turned on her. "Stop that now. You will not let people think you are beat by this. He's not worth it."

"You thought he was," Addy said. The hint of defiance gave Savannah hope that Addy would be okay.

"Well, he's gone. No use wasting tears on a man who couldn't fully love." Her gaze shot to Savannah. "Any of us." She exited the car and walked up the sidewalk to the main doors of the church, then entered without waiting.

"Guess it's you and me, kiddo."

Addy nodded and leaned into Savannah's side as they walked together into the building and then the small sanctuary. There were about twenty pews on each side of the aisle. A small stage at the front held a piano, an undersized set of drums, and a podium.

"I think family sits up in the front row on the right."

Her sister smiled at a man walking down the aisle, and Savannah wanted to scream. When would Stasi grow up? When would she recognize that everything she thought she had to offer was washed up, drowned in a flood of alcohol and painkillers that had to be pickling her body from the inside out? If Addy wasn't enough to make her change, then the woman would flirt her way to an early grave.

Addy took a seat and leaned against Stasi's shoulder. A flawed mother was better than none. In this moment Addy wanted hers.

Savannah would step back and let them have this time. But when

Stasi failed again, and she would, Savannah would be there to protect Addy. Just like every other time.

———

Jett expected Dustin's family to slide into that row right before the memorial began. He'd arrived an hour early, wanting to see who would show for the service. It could be a great way to get a sense of the man, eavesdropping on unguarded comments. He'd gained salient details at other memorials and funerals.

But Savannah, Addy Jo, and an underweight woman were the only people who made their way to the front of the church. They slid into the second row, leaving the first open. Jett couldn't see what Dustin had seen in Stasi. Side by side, the better sister was evident. Where Stasi was all thinness and sharp edges, Savannah had a warmth and softness to her that she tried to mask but couldn't. A petite woman with Asian features walked up the outside aisle and settled in the row behind the trio. She kept her head bowed. The rest of the rows held a scattering of quiet people.

After an hour, Jett was ready to get off the uncomfortable pew and away from the slightly musty smell of the red carpet that was fading from overuse. A heavy floral aroma from the white lilies in a couple flower arrangements at the front of the stage cloyed in the space.

He remained where he was because he wanted to support Savannah, even from a distance. Something had shifted between them, and he hoped they were on the verge of becoming more. Much more.

She was here for Addy and her sister. Who was here for her?

The answer came in the next minutes as her friends and colleagues from the law firm made their way down the center aisle and sat shoulder to shoulder in the pew behind her, edging the other woman to the outside seat, where she stayed in the shadows. The solidarity in their expressions telegraphed their commitment to Savannah. These women would be her rock, and as the receptionist leaned forward to hug her from behind, Jett thought Savannah might not need him after all.

Then the memorial began. The eulogies were short. Addy stood to share a small story, constantly looking toward Savannah, who stood behind her, a hand on the young teen's back. After they returned to their pew, a couple of Dustin's flying buddies shared stories of a man who had been a bit of a *Top Gun* Maverick. A man who lived bigger than life until he met Savannah. From his seat a couple of rows behind and to the right, Jett could see the color flush up her neck.

Then the man had changed course again.

That was something Jett couldn't grasp. If a man captured the heart of a woman like Savannah, why let her go?

Sure there was something overwhelming and intimidating about the woman, but it wasn't because of what she did. It was who she was. She had more smarts in her pinky than many had in their entirety.

He turned his attention to the crowd, trying to see who might be there that didn't fit. He wasn't there because he knew Dustin, and maybe others were in the same position, only with more sinister reasons.

Was Agent Martin or whoever was involved in Dustin's death here? Those who committed crimes liked to see the fruits of them. Why? They got some kind of a thrill from it? He glanced around, but the photo of Agent Martin he'd found online didn't match any of the people at the service.

He surreptitiously glanced around during the rest of the service, then waited at the back for Savannah to step away from those who lingered to extend condolences. She looked exhausted, with Addy looking worse.

Savannah slowed when she neared him, and the women from the law firm fanned behind her. "Thank you for coming."

He nodded. "I wanted to make sure you weren't alone. Looks like you have lots of support." He turned to Addy. "You getting any sleep?"

She shook her head and sniffled. "I'm trying." She glanced at her aunt, then back at him. "It's hard."

"It will get easier someday. I promise. But it'll be hard for a while." He wished an adult had told him that truth when he was in her shoes. Instead, he'd had to learn the hard way. "Eventually you'll be okay again."

"I know." Addy studied him directly with a maturity someone her age shouldn't possess. "I have Aunt Savvy."

Her mother must have heard that last bit, because she stiffened and tried to grab Addy's hand. "We are going."

Addy leaned into Savannah even more. "I'm not ready and want to stay with her."

Before the tug-of-war could get going, the dark-haired woman he'd noticed stepped nearer. A look on her face suggested she'd made a mistake, yet her gaze seemed frozen on Addy.

"I think someone's waiting to talk with you, Savannah."

Savannah closed her eyes for a moment as if gathering strength, then opened them and turned with a smile to the woman. "Hello."

The woman glanced from Addy to Savannah. "You are Ms. Daniels?"

As she stepped out of the shadows, her quiet elegance became clear. From her simple black dress to carefully styled hair, even her makeup had an understated simplicity that enhanced her fine features. Her words had a lilting tone of someone who'd learned English after their tongue was set toward Asian languages.

"Yes." A guarded expression matched the stiffening of Savannah's posture. "Can I help you?"

"I would like to speak with Addy Jo if I may."

"I'm sorry, but who are you?"

"A friend." She stopped and swallowed hard. "A friend of Mr. Dustin's. I have something for her."

Savannah's arm tightened around Addy, and Jett braced himself to intervene. Savannah studied the woman. "You know my name, but what is yours?"

"You may call me Hope."

Jett leaned forward. "Hope Boonmee?"

CHAPTER
THIRTY-SEVEN

The woman startled at Jett's pronouncement of her name. She clutched her purse as her gaze darted about the sanctuary and she took a step back. "I must leave."

Savannah reached out with her free hand. "Please. We would very much like to talk with you."

Stasi was growing impatient. "Are you ready to go yet?"

Hope used that distraction to try to step into the shadows, so Jett cut off her path. "I bet you have time for coffee."

The woman's eyes and mouth rounded.

Stasi looked around the circle. "Who's she? What did I miss?"

Addy rolled her eyes. "Too much, Mom." She took a step away from Savannah and toward Hope. "I would like to hear what you remember about my dad."

The woman swallowed, still looking skittish, but nodded. "I will tell it all."

Stasi harrumphed. "If you're going to hang around, I'm out of here. Churches always make me nervous." She shuddered. "I don't know why we couldn't hold this at a funeral home."

Savannah dug through her purse and pulled out a twenty-dollar bill, then thought again. She put the money away. "I'll stay with Addy, so you can leave." She turned toward Hope and away from Stasi.

Stasi reached into Savannah's purse, but Savannah placed a protective hand around it. "How am I supposed to get home?"

"A taxi or carshare should work. You are a smart woman who can figure it out."

"Did you know my dad?" Addy asked Hope.

The woman gave her a solemn nod. "I did."

Addy looked at Savannah. "Where should we go?"

Savannah glanced around the sanctuary and then toward the exit. "I bet there's a Sunday school room we can use. Follow me."

They formed a snake winding down the hallways to the Sunday school rooms. Savannah felt a strong urge to look back and see if Stasi followed, but she needed to let her sister handle her own challenges. After all, grabbing a cab was a small piece of adulting. If Stasi couldn't manage that, Savannah had coddled her too much. She couldn't do that any longer.

The chairs in the Sunday school room were a rainbow of colors. They were small, designed for early elementary school kids. But the hall was quiet and the room empty of people, so she led the way inside. The four stood awkwardly until Savannah swept an arm to the chairs around the table. "We can sit there."

Jett looked from the chairs to her. "There's no way I'll fit in one of those."

"Then sit on the floor. I want to hear what Hope has to tell us."

The woman was of indeterminate age, but probably younger than Savannah. She sank onto a chair at the head of the table with a regal ease that suggested she could be at home anywhere. Then she gestured to the chairs on either side. "Come. I have much to share."

Savannah quirked an eyebrow at Jett, and he accepted the challenge. His knees were by his chin but he placed his elbows on top of them and grinned. "I feel like a giant."

Addy shook her head at his antics and sat on a chair across from Hope. "Why are you here?"

Savannah eased next to her niece and placed a hand on her shoulder. "Addy..."

"It is all right." Hope licked her lips, and then nodded. "Your father was a great man, Addy. He helped save girls like you."

———

A blend of curiosity and dread filled Jett. Where was this woman headed? "Can you explain?"

"Gladly." The woman opened the purse she'd clung to so tightly. She pulled out a photo and placed it on the table. Addy and Savannah leaned over it, and Jett not-so-patiently waited his turn to see. She looked at Jett. "I sent a copy of this photo to you."

"I haven't received anything like this."

"Then your postal service is glacially slow."

"That's my dad." Addy pointed at a dark-haired man on one end of a group of four people. Then she glanced up at Hope. "Is this you?"

Jett squinted to see who Addy pointed at.

"It is. The four of us were an advance team for Until All Are Free."

Jett's gut churned as he recognized the name. "That's a human trafficking organization."

"Yes. Are you familiar with Light Comes After Darkness?"

"What's that?" Savannah was looking between them as if she knew she was missing half of the conversation. She had no idea.

A knowing glint entered Hope's expression. "An organization I told him to look into." She lowered her voice, and its melodic quality was replaced by a sound he vaguely recognized. "Did you find Bernard Julius?"

"I did." Savannah's words didn't still the churn that filled his stomach. "Dustin's safe deposit box had a passport with that name on it."

What was left of his breakfast threatened to abandon him. He just hoped he could get out of the Smurf-sized chair in time. "You're my caller." Hope nodded, and he tried to right the world that had suddenly tilted. "Why?"

"Your story told only half of what happened in Thailand." She held up the photo so he couldn't miss the image. "Dustin told me he had called you once after your story was printed, but he didn't tell you his name. It was easy to do the same, but it has not helped. Did you even attempt to find them?"

"Yes." He thought of the internet searches and dead ends. "Had one of my associates help. Neither of us could locate either Bernard Julius or Light Comes After Darkness."

Savannah glanced between them. "Can one of you fill me in? I'm lost."

"Me too." Addy's voice was small, like she couldn't quite hope. "What does this have to do with my dad?"

Hope turned to the young woman, and a light shone in her eyes as she took Addy's hands. "Your father was a hero in my country. He and the two men worked to identify girls and women who had been trafficked and held in slavery." She turned to Savannah. "He would speak of you with a light in his eyes. About the crusading work you do." She returned her focus to Addy. "And you were his joy. He took these trips to help girls your age who were asked to do terrible things."

"They were bait." The words whispered from Savannah, and Jett's knees flopped apart.

"What are you saying? Give it to me."

Hope looked at him, and her light dimmed though it was not extinguished. "You saw the story they wanted those in Thailand to believe. But it was fiction. The truth was deeper."

Light Comes After Darkness.

Was that what it had all been about?

Bringing light into a dark place with the hope of helping some of the kids escape?

"The truth?" He choked on the word. Was this how Superman felt when Kryptonite was waved in front of him? Weak? Unable to think or defend himself? "I found the truth. It took months of research and two trips."

Her smile was sad as she nodded. "I know. I read the article."

"If I was wrong, why not tell me when I tried to interview them? I was clear about the purpose of the article. Why not hold a press conference and let the world know after the article was published?"

"Because they were in the middle of planning their next trip." A tear trickled down her cheek. "Now they cannot. Each of them has died in one week. I cannot save the girls because I cannot trick the pimps."

"Why are you here now?"

"Dustin asked me to come. Called when he was in the hospital." She looked at Addy. "He wanted to make sure you knew the truth, and I was the person to share it."

Savannah seemed to absorb the revelations with equanimity. "What's your role?"

"I am Thai, so as the police swoop in after the men have trapped the pimps in the act of selling, I assure the girls they are safe and will be cared for. I was once trapped as they are, but I use my experience to help guide them to freedom."

"Social work."

"Essentially."

Jett couldn't handle the easy back-and-forth of their questions and answers, not when there were more important facts to uncover. He lurched to his feet, propelled by the need to prove her wrong. "What proof do you have? How do I know you do what you say?"

She slowly rose to stand. "It brings me no joy to tell you these things. But it does make me filled with delight to share these photos with you."

She pulled out her phone and clicked a couple of buttons, then turned it toward him. Slowly her finger scrolled across the bottom. "These are the young women we have saved. The ones who have been removed from their captivity. We educate them and teach them how to support themselves in other ways. We reunite them with family when we can and it is safe. This is why the truth could not come forward. Our work had to be kept a secret, or the criminals would outsmart us." She touched Addy's cheek. "Your father would want you to know he was a good man doing a brave thing to help others."

Jett moved to the hallway. And then he walked away. Out the door. Past his car in the lot. He kept walking, even when his toes were frozen in his dress shoes, when he could no longer feel his fingers stuffed in his coat pockets. After his nose would fall off if someone touched it.

He walked.

Could he outwalk the words thrumming in his mind?

It was fiction. A story to protect and save the innocent. The truth was deeper.

This had to be a bad dream.

He was putting too much on this woman's words. What did she know?

Nothing!

He did the work and was a zealous advocate for truth.

How could what Hope had told them carry the ring of truth? Because it did.

And if he dwelled on that, it would wreck him, because that meant he was no better than the reporter who killed his dad. Only he'd killed Dustin Tate.

CHAPTER
THIRTY-EIGHT

Hope spent the next hour with Addy and Savannah sharing tales of the men's trips to Bangkok. Savannah appreciated how the woman sanitized them to make the stories age appropriate for Addy while still conveying the sense of how momentous the work was.

"These girls will have a chance at a good life thanks to men like your father."

"That's amazing." Addy's eyes were big as tears slid down her cheeks. "Why did he have to die?" The words were hollow as she looked at Savannah. *Help me understand* was the unspoken plea written on her face.

"There's more to the story." Savannah pulled out her phone and showed Hope the photos she'd taken of the contents in Dustin's safe deposit box. "Do you have any idea why he had these gems and gold?"

The Thai woman nodded slowly. "He told me he was doing this. It was his money to buy freedom for the girls they couldn't get the police to free. It is easier to carry than cash. Things have improved, but time is critical. He wanted to know he could do more when the need arose." She delicately ran her pointer fingers beneath her eyes. "He and Logan were on Flight 2840 to attend a meeting to raise additional support. Logan paid for the trips, but he had friends who helped with other expenses."

Addy looked at Hope with wonder. "Dad was doing something important."

"Very important to each young woman he helped." An alarm beeped on her phone, and Hope startled. "I must leave." She pulled a card from a pocket in her purse and handed it to Addy. "Here is my email. Feel free to write when you have more questions." She stood and extended her hand to Savannah. "I am sorry for your loss."

"Thank you. You and Dustin were close."

A flush of color warmed Hope's face. "Yes. You cannot do work like ours without a certain familiarity."

"I'm glad you found him." As she said the words, Savannah felt a release that surprised her. It was good that Dustin had found a cause to pour his energy into. And if this elfin woman had captured his attention like he had captured hers? That was something to celebrate . . . and mourn. She took Hope's hands. "And I am very sorry for your loss."

A tear leaked down the woman's cheek as she bobbed a thank-you over their intertwined hands.

Savannah motioned for Addy to stay, then followed Hope into the hallway. "Please be careful. Jett and I can't prove it yet, but we believe Dustin and Evan were killed because of Jett's article. If we're right, then you could be in danger too."

Hope gave her a small smile. "Everyone believes there was a fourth man on the trips. Thanks to your reporter, I will be safe here." Then the woman walked away, confidence etched in her form as she went.

Addy had pushed all the chairs against the table when Savannah reentered the room. "Ready to go back to my place, kiddo?"

"Could you take me home? I need to think and check on Mom."

"Are you sure?"

At Addy's nod, Savannah agreed since she had a lot to process too. When they arrived at the apartment, Stasi appeared to be deep in sleep. Savannah made sure Addy was settled. "Call me the moment you need anything."

Then she returned to her car and began the drive home. The memorial service hadn't quite released her from its grip. She'd felt every moment that Addy had tensed, sensed every tear the girl had cried. Savannah had tried to be strong for her niece, but she'd felt undone as each shift still reminded her of the bruises that were only now starting to fade from the car accident, and Friday night's stitches itched. It hadn't helped that the one time she deflected her gaze from the front, Jett had looked at her and in an instant she felt seen and understood.

The gravity of the service, followed by Hope's revelations, had Savannah feeling like she'd just experienced a crazy roller-coaster ride. She'd been shocked and then inspired by what Dustin and his friends did, but Jett had left and not returned.

All she wanted was to run to Espresso Yourself and pretend none of the last two weeks had happened.

Except Jett.

She very much wanted to keep him in her life.

His presence at the memorial service supported her in a way her colleagues' presence didn't, not that they weren't there for her. It just felt deeper with Jett, a man she barely knew.

Now it was her turn to be concerned about him. He'd left his Blazer in the church parking lot. On her way home from Addy's, she'd taken a circuitous route past the church and noted his vehicle sat in the same slot as when she left. He had to be somewhere nearby, but where? She drove in a slowly expanding route around the church but didn't see a place that made sense to stop and look for him.

She pulled into a restaurant parking lot and texted him. You okay?

While she waited for an answer, she ran through what was said prior to his exit. Something had caused his shoulders to brace and his chin to dip. As she replayed the revelations, the crescendo of them built in her mind. She thought about how they would have landed on Jett, a man who believed he was a purveyor of truth. His thorough research had been upended.

That had to be what had shaken him.

Every time they'd discussed the trips, he rolled out his files and copies. The truth he accepted. Now they were not what they seemed.

She headed back by the church. This time his car was gone. She knew where to go next. Her phone buzzed and she took the call through her car's Bluetooth. "Savannah."

"Are you done with your responsibilities with the memorial?" Bella's voice was apologetic.

"Yes, I've dropped Addy off and am headed home."

"I think you need to come in." Bella paused. "When I arrived back at the firm, John and Rochelle were waiting. Said they need to see you as soon as possible." She lowered her voice. "It looks serious."

She might be weary, but after the way things had been left on Friday, she needed to know what John had to say. "I'm on my way."

His friends' house wasn't big enough. Jett needed to get out and punch something . . . multiple times, because since leaving the church, all he had felt was the thrum of built-up tension.

Hope Boonmee was the fourth man.

No wonder Logan Donnelly's father got a funny look on his face when Jett had asked if he knew the fourth man. He'd never suspected it was a woman. Sincerity filled her words and raw emotion filled her face. Her photos had shown the foursome together and with different women and girls.

If she was right . . . and her evidence supported it . . . then he had been wrong.

But he couldn't be. The driving motivation for all he did was truth.

He knew the terrible consequences of not pursuing it diligently. It's why he had the profession he did. It wasn't a job but a calling.

Anything less than the truth drove against the very core of who he was.

The look in Savannah's eyes as she watched him absorb Hope's story slayed him. He saw a hint of accusation. Surely she knew that after he'd told her about his experience with his father he wouldn't lightly publish an article so potentially damaging.

It was hard to box a shadow.

And that's all Dustin was now. A shadow who could be perfect because he couldn't prove anyone wrong by screwing up. Someone had made sure of that, a reality that fell like a hundred-pound weight across Jett's shoulders. That was the shadow Jett had to identify. That's what the story required now, and he'd do it. He had no choice.

He pressed back against the darkness. After pacing the small length of his living room, he marched into the kitchen and grabbed a glass of water. He downed it in one long gulp, then filled it again.

He needed to verify what Hope had told him. Then he needed to draft a retraction.

He set the empty glass in the sink and moved back to the couch. He could solve what had happened in Asia. Savannah had sent him photos of the bank box. He pulled out his phone and studied the pictures. Passports. Gold bars. A ring box. He texted Savannah.

What was in the bag?

The next tab on his tablet included his notes on the tweets. Grace Martin. The slain daughter of Agent James Martin. The man had not handled her death well at the time. Could it still affect him? And was it pure chance he was part of the investigation into Savannah's clients? He rubbed a hand over his face.

His phone dinged with a reply from Savannah.

Thought I sent you that photo. Gems. Loose gems. Hope
said money to buy freedom when police couldn't raid where
girls were. Gotta run. Mnemosyne clients waiting for me at
firm.

Jett did a quick search of the *Source*'s archives. Grace had an older brother. John Martin. A nondescript name, but one that was familiar. Why? He plugged it into a search engine and started skimming links until one stopped him. He clicked through to the article.

John Martin was a founding partner in a tech company that wanted to take on black boxes. His company, Mnemosyne, was represented by Savannah in a lawsuit that had the possibility to kill the business.

———

It was four when she finally reached the firm. Traffic had been backed up on King from Seven Corners to 395 thanks to an accident that had closed part of 495. There was an open space in front, so she snagged it. Once inside she barely slowed as she walked past Bella's desk. "Where are John and Rochelle?"

"In their usual conference room with coffees."

After she dropped her briefcase in her office, Savannah grabbed a mug of fresh coffee and then headed to the small conference room. Once again the two were hunched over their phones, but this time they were on opposite sides and ends of the small conference table.

She closed the door behind her and took a seat at the end of the table. It put her closer to Rochelle, but she didn't think John would care. "Spill it."

Rochelle met Savannah's gaze. "I spent the weekend at Mnemosyne trying to figure out the way our software ended up on that plane. Do you want the good news or bad?"

Savannah adjusted the legal pad she'd grabbed and then took a sip of coffee. "I'm an attorney, so I'll go with bad news for $400."

Rochelle blinked, while John shook his head. "It's more serious than that."

"Sorry." Savannah rubbed the back of her neck. "What can you tell me?"

John looked up. "Is everything we say covered by attorney–client privilege?"

"Yes." She dragged out the word as she considered the possible implications of his question.

Rochelle pulled out a page of notes. Her hand trembled as she spread it out on the table. "There were four people in the company with the ability to release the code." She recited the names. "John, our tech guru, Alphonso in security, and me." She pinched the bridge of her nose. "I've confirmed John used his unique login on Wednesday, December 9. He's the one who put our software on that plane."

John snorted. "Like you have the tech skills to pull off that little bit of Nancy Drew."

"Don't forget I have a degree in computer science, John. It's one of the reasons you hired me. I was a woman, had a business background, and the tech degree. You called me the perfect package and then forgot what I brought to the company." She leaned into the table. "When you hired me you asked what I was willing to do. How far I would go to protect the company. This is how far. I can't let you get away with murder, because that's what it was when you released our tech on that plane against a court order and without my input. We were partners, John."

Savannah heard Rochelle's accusations with the certainty the woman had just confirmed the conclusion she'd reached Friday.

"John, did you do it? Did you put that tech on the plane and bring it down?"

"You don't know what you're talking about." John's lips turned up in a sneer. "I'm the one who developed the idea. I begged family members for investments. I brought you on so we could do great things to protect people, and instead we got stalled by a lawsuit. And you wanted to let the system handle it. Well, for two years, we've lingered in a holding pattern thanks to not attacking the lawsuit."

"John." Savannah leaned into the table and waited until he met her gaze. "How did you do it?"

He crossed his arms like a petulant toddler and clamped his lips together.

Rochelle's eyes filled with tears. "I'm not sure the company can recover from this, but John needs you to negotiate with the government on his behalf."

"No, I don't." He cracked his knuckles. "Drop it. I don't need another mother."

"True. You need a Jiminy Cricket." She looked at Savannah. "What do we do?"

John pushed back from the table, and in a smooth motion pulled a gun from the small of his back. "I told you to be quiet."

CHAPTER
THIRTY-NINE

Savannah looked at the small revolver and then at the man holding it. "John, calm down. Put that away, so we can talk."

"My *partner*"—he sneered the word—"can't leave well enough alone. She believes in my ability even less than my father did. All she does is dig, dig, dig to catch me doing something she doesn't like."

She glanced from John to Rochelle and read the shock on Rochelle's face in her slack jaw and wide eyes.

"Together you've built an amazing company with the potential to do powerful things."

"Only if we win the lawsuit. Do you know what it's like to build a company from scratch? To ask your grandma for money? To tell your dad that you've got companies like Boeing interested, only to have him ignore you because he's fixated on your dead sister?" He slammed a hand on the table and Rochelle jumped.

"John, breathe." Savannah's mind raced as she tried to think how to get him to surrender the gun. "What do you want?"

"I want her to quit questioning me. I'm the one who has to tell Grandma she can't have her money back. Not Rochelle. Not you. Me. It's always on me." He sighted down the gun at Rochelle. "I told you to quit looking into the accident. It has nothing to do with my company. Maybe it was cosmic justice, perfect retribution for the sake of truth."

"Our company." She met his gaze defiantly. "And if that's the case, prove it. You were the only one to log in on Wednesday, December 9. You uploaded the software. Violated the injunction. You did that."

"You have no idea what I did." He turned his attention to Savannah and jabbed his finger at her. "You just never stopped. Always more questions. Always wanting to know the truth of what happened. Like you think the truth will set us free. The distraction worked until Rochelle started nosing around again."

The distraction? Savannah's mind raced through what he'd said. "You hit my car."

"Never saw that coming, did ya? You couldn't make the lawsuit go away. Instead you were failing at every turn, but we *have* to win. Then I heard that attorney talking with his client. His client's even more broke than we are, and he's plotted to keep things going as long as possible and bankrupt us. They know they can't win. But they can destroy us by delaying. And you couldn't even see that."

"So you rammed my car to get my attention?" She shook her head as she made eye contact with Rochelle. "No. To distract me from focusing on you. Why?"

His breath was hot on her face. "You were getting close. Asking all the wrong questions." She had to find a way to alert the others.

"Rochelle didn't get interviewed by the FBI until the next day."

"True, yet every question you asked as we prepared for the subpoena showed you were getting close. Wondering if I'd done something. It should have been a mystery that never got solved."

"How could you use our code for a personal vendetta?" Rochelle asked.

He rolled his eyes. "I had a buyer for the company. If I could prove it worked, I would finally be free of the pressure of trying to keep

Mnemosyne afloat. First the buyer wanted to see it in action. I could pay my family back for their investments, get my dad off my back, and go anywhere I wanted. Freedom."

Savannah glanced at Rochelle. Her mouth was gaping like a fish as she listened to her partner spin his tale. Then she snapped out of her fog. "Why use it on a full flight?"

John shrugged. "It fit. But then the plane crashed and the buyer disappeared."

"Why would you risk putting it on the plane?" Savannah watched the gun that didn't budge as he pointed it at her.

"What do you mean?"

"You were violating the court's order, but there was the concern about the software causing a power surge."

Rochelle nodded. "That's why we planned to halt the tests before the injunction."

"And that kind of power surge could bring down a plane."

John frowned. "That's wrong. I didn't cause the crash. It was just a terrible accident. That's what you've insinuated for days." There was a thin crack in his tough veneer as the gun wavered for a moment.

Rochelle reached toward him. "You're right. Until you pulled the gun, you just needed legal help for loading the software in violation of the injunction. I waited to tell Savannah until it was clear we didn't cause the crash." She ran through a technical explanation of how she knew the software didn't cause the crash. "This is one of those tragic times where a series of events cascaded to the crash. Because our software was on that plane, I know it. You didn't cause it." She reached toward him. "Put the gun down. It wasn't your fault."

"But Mnemosyne is done. The lawsuit is going to fail."

"I can't help you with that piece. But I can tell you with certainty that the captain became distracted by a false positive alert on the deicing system. Then the lead flight steward asked a question, and the flight didn't get deiced at the gate a second time. It was that simple, and that complex. Like so many other accidents, this one was a combination of pilot distraction and system error. Because of the weather and the fact it's National, it would have been almost impossible to get the plane up." There was compassion in her eyes as she looked at her partner. "Sometimes history does repeat itself."

Savannah's mind spun for a solution to get John to put the gun down, while the words John had spoken earlier were sticking to her mind like Teflon to a frying pan. "John, please put the gun down."

He stiffened. "No."

"Perfect retribution for the sake of truth?" Savannah tried the words on her tongue. "Sounds like Shakespeare. Does your dad often talk like that?"

"Did you know that Logan dying in the crash was a sign?" As Savannah shook her head, his face collapsed and the gun wavered again. "Neither did I, but good ol' Pop did. Said it was the perfect retribution for the sake of truth. Who talks like that?" His fists were clenched on the table, and he almost vibrated in his seat. "I hate the man who killed my sister because he destroyed my family."

Rochelle frowned. "Your sister?"

"Little Gracie Martin. The perfect daughter. Her death was like a nuclear bomb destroying my family. Then this stupid lawsuit is going to kill my company? I don't think so." His gaze hardened. "But you couldn't do your job. So I tried to help motivate you to be careful and think, but it didn't work." His finger quivered on the trigger.

Time was running out.

She had to keep him talking.

"You're not making sense." But even as she said the words, Savannah felt the pieces click together. "Your father is Agent James Martin."

"So?"

"Did he kill Dustin Tate? Evan Spencer?"

"You'll have to ask him someday." He sighted down the gun. "I'm done talking and will walk out of here. But you won't."

Time was up.

Savannah knew that if the police hadn't arrived by now, then none of the gals understood what was happening in this conference room. She had to stop him herself because she was not going to let him harm anyone. She lunged across the table but he remained in place, gun extended but frozen.

Savannah karate chopped his arm and grabbed at the gun as she yelled, "Someone call 911. We need the police." He might not have pulled the trigger yet, but his fingers seemed frozen around the barrel. She needed help to end this nightmare.

Rochelle squeezed his wrist while Savannah continued to wrestle for the gun. The door crashed open and a uniformed officer hurried into the room. He drew his gun. "Everyone, hands where I can see them."

CHAPTER
FORTY

Jett stood in his woodshed, but not even the tools his grandpa had used could settle his racing thoughts.

He had become just like the reporter who carelessly wrote the story that led to his father's suicide. His article had led to Dustin's death. While it wasn't suicide, the man had still died because Jett had framed him as being involved in human trafficking.

He leaned heavily on the wood that someday would become a table.

How had this happened? He'd been so careful. Everything had been confirmed by the fact-checkers at the *Source*, and he'd still been horribly wrong.

He'd painted the group as deviants instead of as heroes.

He picked up the plane and threw it across the shed. It clattered against the wall as he fell to his knees. "God, what have I done? How can I make this right?"

The image of Addy's tear-stained face was seared in his mind. A sound behind him barely registered.

Then something cold and metal was pressed against his neck.

Savannah's mind spun with the implications that John Martin had intentionally put the software on a plane in violation of the court's injunction. Even more, she tried to grasp the implications that he was Agent Martin's son. Had the man understood his son was the one behind the software being on Flight 2840 or had he guessed well? Savannah needed to head home and soak in a bath with soft music playing in the candlelight. Anything to ease the tension of the longest day.

She had new clarity about the crash and Dustin's death, but she wanted to talk to Detective Jensen about a growing certainty Agent Martin was involved in Dustin's and Evan's deaths. She'd left a message to update him on John Martin's role in her hit-and-run and the revelation he was Agent Martin's son, but the detective hadn't responded yet.

After she locked up the law firm she sat in her car for a minute. Jett hadn't responded to her earlier texts. Maybe she should swing by his home first. Make sure he was okay.

All his efforts had been laid bare as built on a foundation of illusion, and three men had died as a result.

It had to be devastating.

She tried calling him, but he didn't answer. A drive-by then.

She pulled into a drive-through for a couple of sub sandwiches. He probably hadn't eaten and if his fridge looked anything like Dustin's, he'd need food. It also gave her something to carry as she walked to the front door.

At his home she rang the doorbell and then waited, shivering as she waited.

Christmas was definitely in the air with the cold temperatures, but the snow from the storm that had brought down Flight 2840 had long since disappeared, leaving the world gray and dead.

Jett didn't come to the door, but she heard a noise behind the house and headed that direction. He'd mentioned he had a workshop of some sort back there.

She froze as she heard voices.

Maybe coming unannounced had been a bad idea.

She stood at the side of the house, uncertain whether to go forward or back to her car.

———

Jett stiffened, but didn't say anything.

"Figured it out, did you?" The man's voice was unfamiliar to him.

"What?"

"Who the fourth man is."

"I don't know what you mean."

The man snorted, but the metal dug deeper into his neck. "You're a liar. Usually that wouldn't be a big revelation. We expect that of our journalists."

Jett tensed and fought the urge to launch to his feet. He didn't know who was behind him or what he'd do with his weapon. "I'm telling the truth."

"Well, you did write an exposé on the ugly underside of the rich and famous."

Jett tried to shift, but the man shoved the gun a little further. "I wouldn't do that if I were you."

He froze. "Who are you?"

"You can call me an avenger. Going after those who harm the innocent."

"I don't harm the innocent."

The man gave a short laugh. "I didn't think so, so you'll tell me who the fourth person of that little band is." The metal—a gun?—pressed deeper into his neck.

Jett's watch buzzed, alerting him to a text. Good thing notifications were silenced, so whoever was behind him didn't notice. But he couldn't chance moving to read the scrolling message. He needed to keep the man talking and distracted.

Since the man wouldn't freely give his identity, Jett took a stab at it. "I'm sorry about your daughter."

The man shifted behind him. "You know nothing."

"I understand what it's like to lose someone you love."

"You have no idea." He pulled the gun away, then pushed it into Jett's back. "To your feet, hands over your head. I want you to see my face as I complete this task."

Jett slowly stood, then pivoted. Saw the gun aimed center mass with steadiness. His gaze traveled to the man's face. "Agent Martin."

The man gave a slight bow of his head.

"You used Grace's account, and language from the tweets matched the letter left at Dustin's."

"Maybe you should have been the agent since no one else has figured that out."

Jett bit back the words that it wasn't true. No, he'd protect Savannah from Agent Martin even if it meant he had to die to keep the man from knowing the extent of what she understood.

"Does your crusade end here? With me?"

He cocked his head and considered. "It should. But there's one more person from the merry band to kill before they hurt anyone else."

That didn't sound promising.

"What if I had proof Dustin and Logan were doing good things in Thailand? That they were on a mission to help girls like your daughter."

"Not possible. Logan Donnelly"—the man spit out the name— "received his judgment. So did Dustin Tate. Both were held accountable."

"What about Evan Spencer?"

"A pawn. Logan did the planning, and Dustin got them there. Still, the man received his due." The gun wavered, just a moment, but long enough to give hope the agent was tiring. "Now I need the name of the fourth man. Your article was silent on that." He cocked an eyebrow. "Ironic, isn't it. The story ran incomplete."

The man had no idea. "Dustin had gold and jewels in his safe deposit box."

"So? That means nothing. I want a name."

"But it does." Jett knew that changed everything. "They were buying freedom for those that couldn't be rescued any other way." He swallowed hard against the bile that wanted to erupt. "They were heroes in every sense of the word."

———

Savannah edged closer and then froze when she recognized Agent Martin. The man's back was to her, but he had Jett on his feet, hands up. She stepped back around the corner of the house and placed a 911 call, then hesitated. She should go back to her car and wait. That was the safe thing to do. But she couldn't. Not while Jett was in there. Somehow she had to help Jett.

But what could she do that would help Jett without becoming Agent Martin's second target?

She edged around the house, using it to shield her while a plan came to her.

She hurried to the front door of the house and went inside. Then she dialed the number on the card Martin had given her Friday and asked to be patched through to the agent.

The woman who answered hesitated. "He's in the field right now."

"This is really important and related to his case. He asked me to reach him this way if he didn't answer his direct number." She bit her lower lip as she waited for the woman's response.

"Can you tell me the nature of your emergency?"

"Just that it relates to him and it's life and death." As she looked through the sliding glass doors toward the shed, she wanted to scream. This wasn't working.

"Ma'am, you need to explain yourself."

"There isn't time."

The woman hesitated. "All right. I'll patch you through."

This was taking too long!

Didn't the woman understand a man's life was at risk? While Savannah waited, she scrambled for another option. There had to be something she could do.

The sliding glass door. If she opened the curtains and turned on all the lights, would that be enough to distract Agent Martin and give Jett a chance?

She had to try.

———

Jett thought he should feel angry or terrified. Instead he felt a weight of sadness.

"I am sorry."

Agent Martin startled. "Sorry?"

"I unintentionally added to your pain with my investigation and article." His hands felt heavy from being up in the air so long. "If I could unpublish it, I would. But that won't bring back Dustin, Ethan, or your daughter." He inhaled. "I was wrong."

"What do you mean?" Confusion flickered across his face, and the gun wavered. It must be getting heavy.

He couldn't believe he was saying this, but it was right. "The truth is those men were on a mission to save trafficked girls. They created a false trail that I followed, that made it look like they were solicitors. Instead, they were the bait in traps." He swallowed and shifted his feet slightly. "They were heroes. If I could change the article, I would. But I can alter what people know moving forward."

A movement caught his attention.

———

Savannah's mind raced. She crept toward the light switch and first flicked off the lights. Then she moved to the curtains and eased the first panel to the side. This wouldn't work if Agent Martin saw the movement before she was ready. She paused between the first and second curtains. Glanced outside. His attention hadn't shifted from Jett, but she saw Jett glance her direction.

No, no, no.

Don't lead him to look this way.

Jett shifted his stance. She squinted. Was he shifting his weight forward? She couldn't wait.

She eased the final panel to the side. Then she scuttled to the light switches and flipped all the switches. She jumped at a whirring, grinding noise. Then she put her hand over her heart. She'd turned on the garbage disposal along with the lights. She flipped it off, then glanced outside.

Agent Martin hadn't moved.

What else could she do to distract him?

She started flipping the switches in a Morse code pattern. He had to see that.

———

"I had it all wrong." Jett kept his face toward Agent Martin as he tried to catch what Savannah was up to out of the corner of his eye. Why was the crazy woman here? Had she called the police? If so, he'd keep talking as long as it took for help to arrive. "My research was good, but it only caught the side of the trips they wanted the world to see."

The agent looked at him blankly. It was as if part of him had slipped away and all that was left was a vindictive shell that didn't really understand what he was doing.

"Logan and Dustin weren't there to abuse the girls." He shook his head and laughed. Now who sounded deranged? "They were there to save them."

"You have no proof. And the article was clear."

"Yes, the article was clear because that's what the men wanted everyone to think. To do their work, to bring girls from darkness to light, they had to find them. That meant looking like rich Americans who wanted a good time with the girls." He'd piece it together in a way the agent could hear. It wouldn't change the fact he'd executed judgment on Dustin and Evan, but it might stop what he planned now. "Why kill Dustin? You could have joined me in bringing him to justice."

"People don't understand the great harm this evil does. My daughter isn't the only one who's disappeared or been harmed by the monsters who only care about their debased needs." Agent Martin's arm wavered and then he firmed his grip on the gun. "You haven't seen the things I have. Our country is filled with men intent on evil. That's why you have to give me the fourth man's name. Then I can exact justice on him, and rest. For a while."

His words made Jett wonder how long Agent Martin would rest before he found someone else to exact justice on. "I can't give you that."

"Wrong answer." His finger twitched on the trigger. "You have one more chance. What. Is. His. Name?"

A voice startled them both as Savannah stepped into view. "Don't." She took a shuddering breath as if realizing she'd just placed herself squarely in harm's way. "The world is filled with people trying to do good. Imperfectly, but they're trying. That's what Jett does. It's what you did before."

"Savannah." Jett groaned at the way Agent Martin seemed to snap out of his reverie and look at her like fresh prey.

"Ms. Daniels, you are a fool to come out here."

"No, I'm trying to keep you from compounding a wrong. Did you know your son is the reason the software was on Flight 2840? You were talking to the wrong partner Friday."

"You're wrong."

Savannah shook her head. "No, you are. We all have been. But it's time to push through to truth. You need to talk with our new friend. She'll help you understand the good that's being done."

Jett needed to get the focus back on him. He made a small waving motion toward Savannah and mouthed *get back*. "You've robbed Dustin of that opportunity to continue his good works. But you get to choose what you're going to do here. Will you continue or allow us to leave?"

The man snarled at him. "You two haven't proven anything other than you are a well-trained, fast-talking reporter with a sidekick attorney."

Savannah firmed her stance instead of leaving. "How did you do it?"

Agent Martin quirked an eyebrow and tipped his head to the side. "Do what?"

"Kill Dustin. Addy was in the next room."

"She wasn't supposed to be. I never wanted her near." Then his expression cleared. "It was easy to slip into his room and trade out his medicine with a sedative. Just enough to make him compliant. Then I slipped back inside and talked him into slitting his wrists. May have helped him a bit." He shrugged. "I left the letter, but no one found it."

"I did."

"You've read it."

"Yes."

"Then you understand. I had to help him."

—

Savannah was rethinking her decision to come outside. It had seemed brave and smart while she was inside. Now she didn't want to be killed when he decided to pull the trigger.

"Police!" The yell was followed an instant later by some kind of explosion. Then what felt like a flood of police appeared.

The next instant she was led to the side by two officers. She looked over her shoulder to see another placing cuffs on Agent Martin even as he yelled he was with the FBI. Jett was taken in a different direction.

She couldn't stop shivering. It felt like the cold had crept deep into her bones and she'd never be warm again. She answered questions again and again, until it felt like she was in a crazy time loop.

Finally, the police were done questioning her.

She scanned the throng of police and emergency crews, but felt herself relax when she spotted Jett in the middle of it looking for her.

A minute later he ran to her and pulled her into a hug. And finally Savannah felt safe.

CHAPTER
FORTY-ONE

Jett had stayed up all night writing a new article.

It was a hard one. One where he had to admit he hadn't gotten the whole truth in the first. Savannah had given him Hope's number, and he'd interviewed her. Then he and Chase had spent the night making calls to confirm the new information. The middle of the night in DC had meant morning in Bangkok, expediting matters.

Then first thing that morning he'd placed a follow-up call to Albert Donnelly, Logan's dad.

He'd been asking the wrong question all along.

Instead of asking what Donnelly had done in Bangkok, he should have asked why. Why would the upstanding ballplayer change so drastically in that place alone?

Albert had the answer.

One of Logan's high school friends had been trafficked. Unlike Agent Martin, though, he'd turned that pain into a fight to make right. He'd seen an article about another professional player working with local police in a country to help locate trafficked girls. He'd taken that on as his off-season mission and brought Dustin into it, since he could fly them there. Evan had helped provide muscle, and

Hope had provided the security the rescued women needed to go with them.

They'd helped the local police in Thailand break up several small cells. Ironically, they'd been successful enough they were known on the streets, so they'd been talking about assisting a different country.

Now it was time to face the music with his boss.

"Glover."

At Ted's booming call, Jett hurried to the editor-in-chief's office. "Thank you for seeing me, sir."

"What's this about your article being bunk?" Ted wanted quick answers. One didn't keep the man waiting when he used that kind of clipped speech, not if one wanted to stay employed.

Jett opened his tablet and hit send on the draft email that contained the retraction.

"Have a seat." Ted took the chair at the head of the small table.

Jett sat on one of the uncomfortable wooden chairs that always made him think he was being sent to the principal's office. The chair forced him into a posture that felt unnatural and stiff. He leaned forward and met Ted's glance. "I made a mistake with the Logan Donnelly story, Ted. I just sent you a follow-up article."

"Give me the highlights."

Jett gathered his thoughts, then walked Ted through them. "So while the men acted like they were there for the parties, those were a tool to aid local police with rescuing young men and women."

"So you really needed the extra time you asked me for?"

Jett had spent time thinking about that in the dark hours of the night while he was waiting for calls to be returned. "No, sir. While I'd like to think that would have made a difference, the reality is that everything I had uncovered to date pointed to what I wrote. I was right . . . but lacked the rest of the story." He ran his fingers through his hair, then met the editor's gaze. "At the hospital Dustin Tate said he had evidence, but he couldn't give it to us before he talked to Logan, who was already dead. A few days later, Dustin was murdered."

"Is that what police think?"

"Yes, his ex found a letter that was tied to Agent Martin. The man was on a mission to avenge the loss of his daughter." He fought a yawn as the weariness pressed against him. "Chase helped me do the research that's in the article you have in your in-box. The kid did a great job and is ready for the next level."

"That level is currently full."

"Not after this morning. You'll also find my letter of resignation attached to the email. I've let you and the paper down."

Ted leaned forward on his desk. "Glover, you've made the truth this massive taskmaster. As journalists our goal is always to report the truth, but never forget we live in a complicated world with shifting standards. This story had multiple lenses. You found what they wanted you to find." He cocked his head with a shrug. "Way I remember it, I'm the one who gave the ultimatum to print or cut bait."

"I should have done better."

"Maybe, but anyone who's lived has those moments. I'll read the article. If it's as good and well researched as I expect, that will be the end of this." He paused. "On second thought, I want an editorial that addresses this tension with truth. It's important for our readers to understand how highly we value it and how elusive it can be. If after that you still want to resign, we'll talk. Now get out of here and let me read this work of art."

Jett sat for a minute, stunned by his pronouncement. "You aren't accepting my resignation?"

"Not unless you insist, but I'd like you to take at least a week and think about whether that's really what you want."

Jett nodded and stood. "Let me know about the article."

"I will. Now get to writing that editorial."

Jett left the office, stopped by his desk to get his briefcase and keys, and then kept walking. Out the door. To the garage. And to his car.

He didn't know where he was going until he arrived.

Savannah's.

And then he sat. He wanted to thank her for calling the cops last night and see how she was doing, but he was frozen in the car. This was stupid. He needed to get out of the car, climb the steps, and knock on that door. What was the worst that could happen? She'd slam the door in his face?

Nope, that had happened numerous times before, a natural consequence of his job.

The worst thing that could happen is that she could stand inside her town house and ignore him. That was far worse, because it would indicate indifference, and that wasn't what he felt.

No, he wanted her to open the door so he could update her and make sure she was okay. Then he'd have an excuse to spend more time in her presence. That's what he wanted.

———

He was sitting in his car, staring at her house, and Savannah didn't know what to do. No, that wasn't true. She wanted to race out the door and into the car. She needed to feel the safety of having him near, but she couldn't invite him in. Not while Addy slept on the couch, the soft light of the Christmas tree illuminating her face.

Her niece was back with her at least for a while. That was good and it was okay. Savannah would make sure the girl was okay.

The reality of what her heart wanted and what her head knew her niece needed collided.

She felt the reverberation like she'd felt the impact of John's car rear-ending her.

What would Addy do when she saw Jett next?

Could the young woman see him as anything but the enemy? Addy desperately needed one place that she could feel completely safe. For the foreseeable future that was right here. Stasi needed time to get her life sorted, so Addy had to come first.

If she wasn't sure he could come in, then she would go to him.

Savannah grabbed her coat and slipped out the front door. Snow had started flurrying and only took a moment to dot her coat. A moment later she tapped his passenger window. He unlocked the door, and she slid inside. She swiped a hand down her face, then turned to watch him. "Were you planning to sit here all afternoon?"

"I wasn't sure you were home."

"Most people would call or knock." She smiled at him. "You look terrible. Did you get any sleep last night?"

"No. I had massive amounts of research to do halfway around the world. So I was up all night researching and writing an article." He looked at her with eyes so burdened she thought her heart would break. "I am so sorry, Savannah."

"For what?"

"For losing sight of the truth. I set events in motion that led to Dustin's death."

Wow. She hadn't seen him going there. "That's not true, Jett. That burden lies at the feet of the man who kidnapped and murdered Grace Martin. It lies at the feet of James Martin. Those are the men who killed Dustin, not you."

"If I hadn't written the article, Martin wouldn't have fixated on him."

"True, but most of us don't read an article and start plotting to kill someone." She paused as an idea began to form in her mind. "Jett, did you think that any of the information contained in the article was false or untrue?"

"No." His answer was quick and adamant. "It was all rock solid."

"Did you intend to knowingly spread lies?"

"Of course not. I'm offended you'd ask."

"Then the law won't find fault with what you wrote. It's not defamation. Your heart is heavy, and that's good. But you can't carry this forever. Learn from it. Name what you could have or should have done differently. Then let it go."

They were silent for a moment as she studied him. His face had taken on lines in the couple of weeks she'd known him. "You'll make it through this."

"I tried to resign this morning."

"I take it your editor didn't agree."

"Not yet. I'm supposed to write an editorial about truth."

She wanted to reach over and smooth the lines from his face, the pain from his heart. "No one better than a champion of truth to write that."

"You sound like you're okay with everything." He inhaled as if to push words out. "With me."

"I am." She nodded toward the house. "Addy will be too. And eventually you will. I think that's what you told her yesterday."

"Truth doesn't have an expiration date." He reached over and took her hand. "I'm glad we found it."

"So what's next?"

"Write and pray. Figure out if I can stay at the paper, and then I want to forget everything about the last couple of weeks except meeting you. There's a press holiday dinner Saturday. Would you come with me?"

"That sounds like you're asking me on a date." Warmth flooded over her at the thought of dressing up for a night with him.

"That's because I am."

She allowed a smile to cross her face. "Then I would love to." She glanced toward the front door. "I'd better get back inside."

As she walked back inside she paused to take in the sight of Addy curled into the corner of the couch, a zebra-stripe blanket pulled over her shoulders.

Rhett had curled into the girl's side and both dozed in a pool of sunlight. Addy stirred and then stopped when she noticed the cat. Rhett shifted and nosed the girl's cheek. Tears began to stream down Addy's cheeks, and the cat licked one and then another. Addy scooped her up and held her as she cried.

Savannah settled next to her niece on the couch. She laid her head next to Addy's and wrapped an arm over her as Rhett licked Savannah's fingers. They sat there without words.

Savannah silently prayed over her, but Addy must have sensed the direction of her concern.

She twisted to look up at Savannah. "I'll be okay, Aunt Savvy."

"Absolutely." *If I have anything to do with it.* "I promise."

CHAPTER
FORTY-TWO

SATURDAY, DECEMBER 26

Savannah had insisted on meeting Jett at the dinner, and now that she stood outside the hotel with the taxi driving away, she wanted to call it back and go home. The jewel-toned ruby color of her dress felt like too much now that she was here. In the store it had made her feel confident and strong. Now the dress seemed to scream *look at me*.

The room was filled with people she didn't know, though she spotted Tom Brokaw and George Stephanopoulos. What was she doing here?

This was not her crowd, and she was out of her league.

That thought stopped her cold. When had she accepted the idea that she was less than anyone?

She used to walk into any space as if she belonged. She was an interesting person, one others enjoyed getting to know. But now she felt like she should crawl back to her town house and settle in with a good movie or book.

No, she would not retreat. Not tonight. She would stay and hope Jett found her soon, especially as the latest blonde bombshell who co-anchored a FOX network show walked by. The woman's understated mint gown emphasized her classiness.

Would Jett take one glance and realize he'd made a bad decision asking her to be his date? The man could have anyone he wanted on his arm with his understated good looks and suave charm.

Another woman walked by in a simple black dress that hugged every curve. Savannah looked from the chic elegance to her vibrant gown and groaned. She had tried too hard tonight. From her styled hair to her gelled fingernails, she had gotten the details wrong.

She should have followed her gut, kept her walls high, and stayed home with Rhett and Addy. She was safe there. Her heart was safe there.

All she had to do was turn and head home.

So why wouldn't her feet move?

———

The volume of swirling voices increased with each moment. Everyone vied to be heard over one another, and the movement and energy vibrated around Jett.

Savannah hadn't allowed him to escort her to the dinner, but she'd agreed to come. So where was she? Should he have insisted? Maybe, but he'd seen the hesitant longing in her eyes. And when he'd asked her to come, he'd sensed a wall come down.

It was time she stepped into the freedom that was hers.

While he wanted that freedom to include him, he most wanted her to understand how much she could be loved as she was, an amazing woman who served others wholeheartedly and fought for those she loved. She should understand her worth.

No strings or expectations attached.

As he watched the powerful people of his industry mix and mingle, her absence was a disappointment.

And then there she was. A pop of breathtaking red in a sea of muted tones.

She stepped through a doorway at the top of a staircase, and it felt like the room shifted from black and white to color.

Her hesitation to venture deeper into the space was evident in the stiff lines of her form. He wanted to drink in the vision. She was beautiful from her wonderfully visible shoulders to her classy red heels. The dress skimmed her waist and cascaded over her hips into a waterfall of fabric that swayed around her calves.

She stole his heart.

Her uncertainty rested on her like a cloak.

That was not who she was, so he pushed off the wall and headed her direction. Every woman wanted a Cinderella moment, and he would give her one that didn't end at midnight with a pumpkin instead of a prince.

A flash of relief crossed her face when she spotted him as he wound through the crowd. He liked that. Her spine straightened and she walked down the steps to meet him with the elegance of a beauty queen. A light floral fragrance wafted around her and a shy smile tipped her lips, tinted a rich red to match her gown.

"You look stunning."

"Thank you." She swayed, and he wondered if it was an unconscious movement the dress summoned as it swirled around her knees. "I'm sorry I'm late. Caroline insisted on helping me get ready."

"Well, it was worth every moment. You're the most beautiful woman here."

Her gaze assessed him as if looking for any tone of untruthfulness or overstatement.

"All you have to do is say thank you." He gave her a half smile. "And then let me introduce you to the people you'll want to meet."

"Thank you, but you really don't need to take me around."

"Of course I do. You're my date for the evening." He watched the sparkle ignite in her eyes and hoped being his date would become her routine. "You'll enjoy yourself, I promise. There are a lot of interesting people in this room. They'll be fascinated by you. Someone who doesn't work in government or the nonprofit world."

"Don't forget the high-tech industry."

"Yep. You're what we call ordinary." That elicited a chuckle that warmed him. "Ready to mingle?"

She straightened and morphed in front of him into a strong, vibrant woman. "Yes."

This was who she really was. And she was free to be herself with him.

The speaker that evening was an improvement over the often-off-color comedians of the past, a biographer who wrote sweeping histories of tycoons and leaders. Jett enjoyed watching Savannah lean in and absorb the keynote just as she'd expressed intelligent interest in all the people he'd introduced her to. She'd refrained from fan-girling, but he could almost hear her inner squeal when Katie Couric stopped to say hello.

But the magic happened when she let him take her home.

He walked her to the door.

She hesitated under the pool of light from her porch. Her hand slipped into her small bag to collect her keys, but she didn't move to enter the town house, instead looking at him with an unfathomable expression.

Was it a polite hesitation?

He felt the weight of the moment. The importance of getting it right. Letting her know she was beautiful and desirable, yet affirming she was a treasure trove of value not to be underestimated.

Her breath seemed to catch. Definitely an invitation.

One he would accept.

So he leaned in. Brushed her lips with the lightest of touches. And felt the jolt to the corners of his soul.

Was this what the prince felt when he rediscovered Cinderella? The connection that cascaded from his deepest heart and threatened to flood his very being? If so, Cinderella had been a drug, and he would make Savannah his. He wanted to lean in and promise her forever, yet he held back. It was too soon, too quick, but that didn't mean he couldn't hint at what was being unleashed inside him.

She was what he'd imagined and so much more as he leaned in and deepened the kiss. Then she followed, and the invitation was sealed with an answering yes.

———

The world shifted and morphed, disjointed pieces sliding into place, all within the parameters of a kiss that felt like a homecoming for her weary heart. Could she believe the gift Jett offered? It felt like much more than a kiss. An invitation to trust and explore what could be with him.

Her soul wanted to scream yes, but her mind warned that he was dangerous.

Jett was the one who had written the article about Dustin.

He'd gotten it wrong.

Would he wake up and realize he was wrong about her too?

Jett reached over and brushed her lip. "You're doing it again."

"Doing what?" She could barely form a thought as electricity zinged through her at his touch.

"You're thinking too hard. Want to talk about it?"

"No." But then her lips betrayed her. "What happens when you realize you were wrong about me too?"

He stepped back like she'd slapped him. "What? Where did that come from?"

"You were wrong about why Dustin and his team were in Thailand. One day you'll wake up and realize you were wrong about me too."

He shook his head, and a bit of hair flopped into his eyes. Her fingers itched to brush it back in place, but then she'd be lost in wanting forever with him.

"You are one thing I am absolutely certain of."

"I'm not sure I can recover if you change your mind."

"I won't."

She eased back and he leaned his forehead against hers, as she kept her gaze fixed on his chest and fiddled with a button on his shirt. Then she realized what she was doing and dropped her hand. With her other hand she unlocked the door.

"Thank you for a nice evening."

His clouded gaze cleared at her words. "Nice?"

"You were right. I had a good time."

"Good time?"

"Is there an echo?"

He gave his head a small shake and then stepped back. "I'll be in touch."

"Yes." She gave him a small smile, and then slipped inside.

She closed the door and leaned against it, willing herself not to part the curtains to see if his world had been jolted as much as hers. What was she supposed to do with what had just happened? It was more than a kiss.

She had felt its earthquake in her soul.

She wanted to believe it was real.

Could he love her well and understand what that meant? She'd given her heart to one man who hadn't protected it.

She wanted to risk. She longed to believe it was possible. But she was also a realist. Could she push beyond that to trust that more was possible?

She wasn't sure.

She opened the door ready to race as fast as her heels would let her after his Blazer. Instead he was standing there, a slow grin spreading across his face and accenting his dimple. And she was gone. Lost in the circle of his arms and resting in his love. She tipped her face toward him and her heart toward the light of love that was worth every risk.

ACKNOWLEDGMENTS

Writing a book is a work that can feel very solitary, yet at the same time is done in community. *Flight Risk* was no exception.

Many thanks to Bernie Wulle and Julius Keller for sharing their expertise on how to bring a plane down. Thanks for the people around us at the Chipotle on Purdue's campus who didn't call the police to alert them to three folks around a table discussing plane crashes. It was during a conversation in our IMPACT class that Bernie planted the what-if that got twisted and turned in this mind of mine to become Savannah's story. Thanks also for making the IMPACT experience so fun. ☺

It was a THRILL—and terrifying—to work with Erin Healy on this novel. She is well-known in Christian fiction as the queen of editing suspense, and this was my first time to work with her. Erin, you did an amazing job of identifying exactly what wasn't working in the first draft while honoring the heart of Savannah's story. Rewrites were WORK, but so very worth it. I'm delighted with the way Savannah and Jett's story turned out.

To the entire HarperCollins Christian Publishing fiction team including Amanda Bostic, Jocelyn Bailey, Becky Monds, Paul Fisher, Matt Bray, Allison Carter, Laura Wheeler, and the rest of the amazing team. It was a long-time dream to write for this publisher, and the experience has been everything I hoped for.

Karen Solem is my agent and the woman who challenges me to dig deeper and do more with each book. Her rock-solid support and encouragement have been key to my career. Thank you for always believing I could write these types of books.

Colleen Coble, Robin Caroll, Rachel Hauck, and Denise Hunter have always been quick to brainstorm when I need it. They have helped me add the layers that keep the tension moving across the page. I love you, ladies!

And thank you for reading this book. When I started out, Savannah was the mentor character, but after reading the draft of *Beyond Justice* Amanda told me Savannah needed her own story. It wasn't until I was writing *Flight Risk* that I realized as much as Savannah had appeared in other books, who she was at the core was a mystery. I knew she had a story and that I wanted to crash a plane into the 14th Street bridge. The rest evolved as I tried to imagine what would keep you engaged with so many other books pulling for your attention. Every time you read one of my books, I am grateful. The gift of your time is the greatest gift, because until you read this story about these characters, it's not a living, breathing book. Thank you!

DISCUSSION QUESTIONS

1. Savannah's past is still affecting her present as the pain overshadows her. If you were her friend, what steps would you suggest she take to fully overcome the past and step into freedom today?

2. Jett believes the truth is what ultimately matters and that belief is core to who he is because of what happened when he was a boy. How have events in your past affected you to this day?

3. Jett says there are "some sins soap doesn't touch." Do you agree? What can touch and clean those sins?

4. Family relationships can often be complicated in today's world. What advice would you give Savannah as she tries to navigate the space between Addy, Stasi, and Dustin?

5. How would you counsel Savannah to work with her sister Stasi? Is she too accommodating or do you think she's struck the best balance she can in a difficult situation?

6. Truth is a theme that runs through this book. How do you find truth in a fake-news world where so many platforms are dominated by everything but truth?

7. Toward the end of the book Jett has to wrestle hard with how he's going to respond to what he learns is truth. What would you encourage him to do?

8. Savannah has a hard time letting people behind her walls. While she's a great mentor and aunt, she only lets people in so far before she walls her heart off. Is love worth the risk? Why or why not?

9. Rochelle is faced with a situation where her business may fall apart and collapse if she exposes the truth. If you were in her shoes, what would you do?

10. Jett makes the statement that every woman wants a Cinderella moment. Do you agree?

Don't miss any of the books in the thrilling Hidden Justice series!

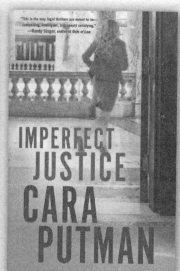

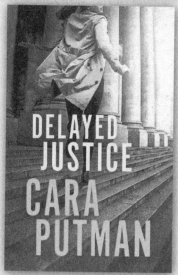

When Caroline takes a job with a promising
medical start-up, she believes she's on the side
of angels . . . until she's asked to go too far.

LETHAL

INTENT

COMING JANUARY 2021

Available in print, e-book, and audio

THOMAS NELSON

Since 1798

ABOUT THE AUTHOR

Cara Putman is the author of more than thirty legal thrillers, historical romances, and romantic suspense novels. She has won or been a finalist for honors including the ACFW Book of the Year, Christian Retailing's Best Award, the Holt Medallion, and INSPY Short List in Mystery/Thriller/Suspense. Cara graduated high school at sixteen, college at twenty, received her law degree at twenty-seven, and her MBA in 2015. She is a practicing attorney and teaches undergraduate and graduate law courses at a Big Ten business school. She lives with her husband and children in Indiana.

Visit her website at CaraPutman.com

Facebook: Cara.Putman

Twitter: @Cara_Putman

To stay up-to-date on all her writing news, be sure to join her enewsletter at caraputman.com/contact